SAPPHIRES AT WAR

(2nd title in *The Sapphires of Yogo* series)

Additional titles by Roland Cheek

Nonfiction

Learning To Talk Bear
Learn About Elk
Dance On the Wild Side
My Best Work Is Done At the Office
Chocolate Legs
(about the life of a single Glacier Park grizzly bear)
Montana's Bob Marshall Wilderness
(coffee table book about an American wilderness)

Fiction

(six titles from the "Valediction For Revenge" series)
Echoes of Vengeance
Bloody Merchants War
Lincoln County Crucible
Gunnar's Mine
Crisis On the Stinkingwater
The Silver Yoke

The Dogged and the Damned
(World War II New Guinea and the effects of PTSD)

For Love of Sapphires
(first title in the "Sapphires of Yogto" series)

Published in e-book version 2014

For information about permission to reproduce selections from this book, write: To Permissions, Skyline Publishing, P.O. Box 1118, Columbia Falls, MT 59912

Publisher's Cataloging in Publication

Cheek, Roland, 1935---
Sapphires At War

1. USA—England—Fiction. 2. Johnson, Walker, and Tolhurst, Ltd.
--Fiction. 3. World's foremost jewelry firm. 4. Sapphires, gemstone faceting and marketing.
I. Title

ISBN: 0-918981-18-2

Skyline Publishing, P.O. Box 1118, Columbia Falls, MT 59912
http://www.rolandcheek.com
email: roland@rolandcheek.com

Acknowledgments

Sadly, I've many readers who've waited much too long to see the "Sapphires of Yogo" series in actual print-on-paper book form. Most of those followers haven't moved into electronic readers, or have tried it and decided they prefer more traditional book form.

"When are you going to put your Sapphire books in print, Roland?" has been an oft-stated question. That I've finally decided to do so, readers can thank my wife (and best friend) Jane, who pushed and prodded and at last used a metaphorical stick of dynamite to blow me away from placing all my faith in e-books.

I thank her, too.

Chapter One

They made a striking couple as they emerged from the stage amid the swirling dust of a windy day during Easter Week, year of our Lord, 1903. Only moments before there'd been clattering hoofs on the hard-packed road, and the bounce and jounce of the swaying coach. Then sawing reins and a shouted "WHOA!" from the driver brought the horses to a sudden halt in front of a long log cabin with a sign above its single door: "Utica Hotel".

"She's near 'bout the sweetest thing," Pete Weatherwax told saloonkeeper Hanley Duncan, who sagely nodded. Pete added, "Better lookin' than a bowl full o' turnips after a long winter." The cadaverous man stepped outside the batwings for a better look, then ambled back inside. Both men had gone to the swinging doors to view the town's single predictable social occasion: arrival of the thrice-weekly stage.

"Reckon it's the new mine manager?" Weatherwax asked after he dumped two fingers of whiskey in both the saloon man's glass and his own.

Duncan shrugged. The barman picked up Pete's whiskey bottle and swabbed with an almost clean rag at an imaginary spot beneath. "Prob'ly. Don't the fella look like the one what left last fall?"

Weatherwax patiently waited for the whiskey bottle to be repositioned so he could reach it should any emergency arise. "Beats me," he muttered. "Lobsterbacks been comin' and goin' out at the Yogo so thick I can't keep track." When all Duncan said or did was shake out his rag, Weatherwax picked up his glass and said, "Here's to you!"

Hanley Duncan return-saluted his lone customer.

1

Out in the single Utica street—actually the main road up the Judith Valley—the young man assisted the elegantly dressed lady onto the hotel's board sidewalk, then returned to the coach's rear luggage compartment to help the driver struggle with two large trunks bearing shipping tags from the transoceanic "White Star Line."

A lounger who'd been whittling while perched on the plank walk stood, dusted himself off, tipped his hat to the lady, folded the knife, and then helped haul one trunk inside the hotel.

A second man, greasy and bald and wearing the leather apron of a blacksmith, hurried across the street to help.

As the second trunk was carried inside, a buxom gray-haired lady of indeterminate age came from the kitchen, dusting flour from her hands. "I declare, is this Mr. Gadsden? It surely is! Where is she?"

The man's smile was broad and winsome. "Good afternoon, Mrs. Waite," he said with a clipped British accent. "I shall bring her inside in a moment." He threw arms around the shoulders of the two Utica gentlemen who'd helped with the trunks and, as all three men passed back outside, said, "You, sirs, are scholars and judges of fine whiskey, which, if you'll step next door, I shall buy."

In a few moments, the handsome Charles T. Gadsden returned to introduce his recent bride to the hotel proprietress. "This Madam Waite, is Maud Margaret Gadsden, recent resident of Birkenhead, County of Cheshire, England, and a threatened old maid until rescued by a" ... grinning, he avoided a kick in the shin ... "shining white night from across the broad water."

Mrs. Waite said, "Old maid, hmph! She hardly looks out of her teens." The elder woman grasped Maud Margaret by both hands, then murmured, "My, you are the lovely one, aren't you?"

The Britishers were indeed a handsome couple. Hers was an unblemished heart-shaped face, in the current popular style that permitted no sun ever to burnish the image. The face was inset with a Celtic button nose and wide, saucy blue eyes. Rich blonde curls framed the cheeks, falling well below her shoulders. The lips were unpainted pink. She was clad in a close fitting plum-colored habit with extravagant lapels and buttons of pearl down the front. A high-necked white silk blouse squeezed through the habit's lapels, and brown leather riding boots peeked from beneath the habit's skirt.

For his part, Charles Gadsden seemed tall enough, though close inspection disclosed his presence to be more commanding than overwhelming. His was an open face, angular, browned from exposure and possibly from a "black-Irish" heredity. The eyes were as drops of chocolate, hair thick and dark and wavy, nose straight, lips—what one could see beneath a drooping shoe-brush moustache—were full and curving upward. Beyond the moustache, dimples winked either side. The man's attire was of forest-green corduroy. His trousers were pulled over the tops of coal-black boots that were shined to brilliance. He, too, wore a white silk shirt beneath an unbuttoned jacket. The shirt was open at the throat.

Charles Gadsden held out his hand to the Hotel proprietress. "Then am I to suppose, Mrs. Waite, that you approve of my choice of a foot-warmer for cold wintry evenings?"

The elderly lady perused the young bride; saw only good-humored pride for a husband she obviously adored. "Well," Mrs. Waite murmured, "if I were you, Mr. Gadsden, I don't think I'd wait for winter."

* * *

Charles Gadsden had originally arrived at the Yogo from

England during the summer of 1899, in the company of two school chums. The three young men accompanied English mining engineers Lansing McWilliams and Reginald Kensington and were to comprise the labor battalion as the New Mine Sapphire Syndicate prepared to re-open the dormant Yogo Sapphire Mine.

Owned primarily—now that Matthew Dunn had been squeezed out—by the London gem firm of Johnson, Walker, and Tolhurst, Ltd. who adjudged their market sufficiently prepared to absorb a modest increase in world sapphire production. Though the lone holdout shareholder—discoverer Jake Hoover's grubstake partner, Simeon Hobson—still retained his twenty-five percent block of stock, negotiations were under way to obtain that last vestige of American ownership.

"We'll want to set the mine up to weather the companion rock for three years," Lansing McWilliams told his employers in 1898. "If we begin mining operations next year, it'll be at least 1901 and probably '02 before we can get production into full swing."

"Good!" Brownstone Tolhurst exclaimed. "Two or three more years of but a few pounds return will lay our Mr. Hobson by the heels sufficiently well to transfer that bloody Yogo millstone to our account, what?"

It was mid-July before the English team arrived at the Yogo mine. The first order of business was for the two engineers to survey and mark out a series of additional holding pads for ore storage, one after the other, stairstepping down the hill toward the Middle Fork of the Judith.

McWilliams hired a lead carpenter and obtained several wagonloads of tongue-and-groove "car decking" for pad construction. Then leaving Kensington, the junior engineer, to design both tramway system and water pipes to each individual pad, McWilliams spent the remainder of that season's mild weather mapping the extent of the sapphire-bearing dike and estimating the number of shoring timbers needed for a full season's work.

The first full-scale winter blizzard blew in during October and blew out Jeremy Waterston, who had little stomach for below-zero Montana when the balmy south of England beckoned. With the pads and trams not yet completed, the remaining carpenter crew shoveled snow and marked time until the second blizzard struck on New Year's Day. Melvyn Lexington jumped the Yogo for England after that second blizzard, and Lansing McWilliams decided to lay off Dolph Galla, the lead carpenter, until Easter.

Reginald Kensington was next to leave, returning to England, so he said, for a fortnight's holiday. When one fortnight stretched into two, three, four, and eight, McWilliams elevated his sole remaining English comrade, twenty year-old Charles Gadsden to the Yogo's second in command—an elevation without any real portfolio when only the two Englishmen and a watchman constituted the Yogo's full winter's crew.

But the following spring ushered in momentous change. First of all, Dolph Galla returned to complete the series of storage pads and tram systems, bringing with him his own crew. Meanwhile, Lansing McWilliams and Charles Gadsden devoted most of their attention to getting the Yogo into mining condition.

Gadsden, displaying a remarkable and previously unknown mechanical wizardry, busied tuning up the mining equipment while McWilliams devoted his efforts to obtaining a crew of experienced miners. Gadsden also provided oversight for Galla's construction, as well as welcoming two teamsters and a blacksmith to the crew.

Before April turned into May, one shift of miners began work—two four-man crews, digging both ways along the sapphire-bearing dike at the three hundred-foot level. Ore spilled onto the original leaching pads Jake Hoover had designed and cleared and Galla's carpentry crew went to twelve-hour days to extend the tramway scaffolding as needed.

Lansing McWilliams returned at the end of May with a second-shift mine crew and a second blacksmith. Charles Gadsden was assigned the duty of overseeing that shift.

By the end of June, thirty-one men toiled in the New Mine Sapphire Syndicate's Yogo operation, spilling ore-trucks filled with crumbling gray-green host rock onto a stepping-stone series of washing pads. By the end of June, Dolph Galla's carpenters had finished all trestle scaffolding and the two blacksmiths toiled to lay tracks and switches and hand brakes and metal-plated spillways along the tramways.

Both teamsters were kept busy hauling sheet iron and dimension lumber and loads of coal to fire boilers and cooking and heating stoves. Barrels of flour and beans and sowbelly and beef were wagon freighted to the hungry mine crew, where feeding the mass was more than two cooks could handle during a twenty-hour operating day. So two helpers and a third cook were thrown into the cookhouse mix.

The now thirty-four-member crew, of course, was so large that armed guards were employed to bring the payroll from the railhead. Meanwhile, cowboys and ranchers and a single banker from Lewistown rode out to watch the beehive of daylight-to-dark activity.

Throughout 1900 and 1901 great heaps of ore was piled on the Yogo's weathering pads to be repeatedly soaked and exposed to the elements. But none of the deteriorating ore was washed through the sluices. And when the year 1902 rolled around with additional stockpiling going on while it was still all financial outgo and no income at the Yogo, Simeon S. Hobson threw in the towel and sold his twenty-five percent interest in the mine to Johnson, Walker, and Tolhurst, Ltd. for one hundred and fifty thousand dollars (less the eighty-seven thousand, four hundred and twenty-two dollars he had already borrowed against his hundred thousand letter-of-credit with the English firm).

As soon as the transfer was consummated, a cable to Lansing McWilliams crossed the Atlantic with only two words: BEGIN WASHING.

When the sluicing began, it was carried out by McWilliams and Gadsden, supervisors who could be trusted not to high-grade rough stones of gem quality. But it soon became apparent that the scale of the job was too much for the British supervisors alone. So Pete Weatherwax, who already had previous sapphire washing experience back in Jake Hoover's time, was hired. In addition, Pete vouched for Lawless Laulis's integrity, and the second aging Yogo Gulch placer miner was hired to help direct water and crumbling ore into the sluices. Meanwhile Charles Gadsden kept the tramway machinery running and the sluice traps emptied while Lansing McWilliams maintained oversight.

Sluicing and its consequent recovery of raw gemstones stopped with the onslaught of winter weather, but mining and stockpiling the crumbling gray-green dike rock continued full apace.

Then Charles Gadsden was ordered to accompany the latest shipment of Yogo gemstones to London, with a directive to report to the owners upon arrival.

* * *

Until ushered into the display lounge of Johnson, Walker,

and Tolhurst, Ltd., Charles Gadsden had never seen such opulent surroundings. The chair to which he was directed was of Roman design, with velour upholstery and richly carved mahogany legs and armrests. The floors were carpeted in deep Persian wool. Silver chimes tinkled at the double doors and sunlight was multi-color refracted through stained-glass inserts in high cathedral windows.

Gadsden had paused in New York sufficiently long enough to purchase a suit of top quality wool cheviot cloth; dark brown (with the occasional twist of gray thread) in round cut sack style. Grinning at the recollection, he'd taken it at face value when the clerk told him his new suit "will stand wear, hold its color, and retain its shape."

The suit, coupled with his MacHurdle full dress shirt with changeable collar and silver cuff links (three for $4.85), along with the shiny new satin calf dress shoes, made him feel ridiculously elegant. "But," he whispered to himself as he flicked at an imaginary speck of dust on the Trebor hat perched on his lap, "at least I'm in keeping with the tenor."

Across the lounge, two clerks hovered around an elegantly dressed elderly couple the young Yogo mine foreman took to be Continentals; but what nationality, he couldn't guess. One of the clerks hurried away with what looked to be a golden tiara perched on a satin pillow, then returned moments later with a glass-fronted display case, probably holding an assortment of faceted gemstones.

"Mr. Gadsden?"

His head snapped around. "Yes."

"Would you be so ever kind as to follow me, sir?"

He knew he was being ushered into the august presence of Brownstone Tolhurst—the name etched into the frosted glass of the end-of-the-hall double doors told him so. The usher opened both doors at once, paused, and said, "Mr. Gadsden, sir."

The man who leaned back in an upholstered swivel chair was huge. And corpulent. Gadsden wondered if the gold watch chain spanning the opening in his coat and vest actually held a watch, or whether it was anchored on each side to hold together the man's straining middle? The man in question pushed ponderously to his feet, took the half-chewed cigar from his mouth, and waved his young arrival from America nearer. When Gadsden stood across the desk, Tolhurst leaned forward to extend a hand. "You're Gadsden, right? I'm Brownstone Tolhurst."

Tolhurst nodded toward the servant. "Kind enough of you Weystruth. Would you do me the privilege of conveying the news of Mr. Gadsden's arrival to Mr. Walker."?

"Right away, sir." The doors clicked quietly together as Weystruth retreated.

Tolhurst gestured to a plush chair. "Um, yes. Do have a seat."

The young man had no more than taken the proffered chair when he again leaped to his feet as the firm's second partner, a white-haired, tall, thin, older gentleman tottered into the room from a previously hidden door that swung a section of bookcase aside as it opened. After introductions were made and Charles Gadsden and Brownstone Tolhurst had again taken their seats while Ernest Walker leaned at the window, gazing disinterestedly outside, Tolhurst said, "We wish for your report on the New Mine Sapphire Syndicate's operation in America." He let his words settle for a few seconds, then added, "Tell us what marvelous things we might learn from your experienced observation."

Charles Gadsden twisted uncomfortably, wondering if he was expected to criticize Mr. McWilliams' management?

"Lansing McWilliams is a splendid manager, sirs, if that's what you mean. He's impeccable in both his work and personal habits, and his performance is outstanding. Besides that, he's ..."

"That's not what we mean, young man," Tolhurst growled. "Our confidence in McWilliams knows no bounds. It's you in whom we're interested."

Charles' heart leaped. "May I ask in what way, sir?"

"How do you find America?"

"How do I find...." The young man eyed Mr. Walker, but he responded to Mr. Tolhurst's question. "I like it. It's wild, but it's free. It's raw and its people are rough, but there's a certain peace there, too."

"What do you know of the mine's prospects?"

Charles gazed down at his new hat while choosing his words. Then he gazed up at Brownstone Tolhurst's porcine face. "What I *know* and what I *think* may differ, sir. What I know is that we've moved roughly four thousand tons of gemstone-bearing rock from the mine; that we've recovered eighteen hundred tons from which we've taken approximately seven hundred and fifty thousand carats of uncut gemstones, seventeen percent of which is of a size for cutting. What I think is that ..."

Brownstone Tolhurst interrupted. "Mr. Walker and I are given to believe you've brought one stone of nine carats in the last shipment."

"And another of eight carats and three more of seven."

"And what do you think?"

"The mine is absolutely unlimited. Mr. McWilliams and I both concur that we should start a vertical shaft down into the bowels of the discovery with twin purposes, to better examine its dimensions, and to see if there's a chance of extracting larger stones from the discovery's depths."

Ernest Walker turned from the window and tottered over

10

to perch on the edge of Tolhurst's desk, but he continued to avoid looking at the young miner.

Gadsden took a deep breath. "Of course, if you gentlemen wish increased production, a vertical shaft as well as two horizontal ones can employ a much enlarged crew of miners." When neither of the two Yogo owners commented, he added, "I think."

Tolhurst's eyes met those of Walker. Then he said, "What of your compensation? Are you satisfied?"

Charles nodded. "I feel I've earned both opportunity and its financial reward, sir. I've received both."

"If you were in charge of the Yogo mine, Mr. … ah …" The big man fumbled for a sheet of paper on his desk and the young man wanted to help Tolhurst by reminding him that his name was Charles Gadsden, but he hesitated. Meanwhile his heart was beating a staccato tattoo on his ribcage. "… Yes, here it is—Mr. Gadsden—could you follow the policies of your predecessor while taking direction from the owners? Give guidance to a crew? Maintain desired production levels?"

"Yes! Absolutely, sir!" Then the young man's face colored. "But, sir, I'm not a mining engineer."

Brownstone Tolhurst swiveled his chair to glare at light streaming through the window, then swept back, noting Ernest Walker's brief nod as he did. "Lansing McWilliams wishes to return to England. He recommends you as his successor."

There was a gasp, then silence. At last, Charles Gadsden murmured, "I'm quite young, sir, only twenty-three."

"McWilliams has nothing but praise for your talent, industry, and commitment to the work. I will hazard with some confidence that age has nothing at all to do with those attributes."

Charles again studied his hat. When he looked up, he said, "This will require a dedication to America, won't it sirs?

You must be tiring of Englishmen without tenacity, who flee back home at the slightest reverse."

Brownstone Tolhurst murmured, "I trust you're not talking of Lansing McWilliams."

Charles cursed to himself, blurting, "Oh no, sir!"

Both owners were peering at him now. He said, "I would be happy to accept, sirs, with one condition—that I'm permitted to take ship from Liverpool and that I'm accorded sufficient leave to visit Birkenhead—which is just across the bight—and take a wife."

Ernest Walker's face appeared as sorrowful as that of a bored bloodhound. For the first time, he spoke to their new mine manager: "An insistence on celibacy is not a requirement for a position at Johnson, Walker and Tolhurst, young man."

Chapter Two

It was Easter Sunday, 1903 when Maud Margaret Gadsden first laid eyes on what had recently been dubbed by its neighbors "Yogo Village": the bunkhouse, mess hall, office, blacksmith shop, barn, and storage sheds composing the sprawl of buildings at the Yogo Sapphire Mine. "It's beautiful, Charles," she murmured, gripping her husband's arm with both hands.

He turned a sardonic smile to her; saw she'd passed over the ugly jumble of mine-mouth buildings to the mountains round about. "Aye, 'tis that, Maud Margaret. 'Tis that."

Their buckboard was borrowed from the Utica Hotel, as was the single horse laboring up the rough mine road from the Middle Fork of the Judith River. Their steamer trunks rattled in the buckboard's cargo sweep, along with several cartons of groceries Maud Margaret had purchased at the Utica Mercantile.

Dr. Wyzczek Poska, newly arrived from Hungary, dangled his legs out the rear. As chance had it, the Yogo mine's replacement doctor had arrived in Utica only the day before the new mine manager and his recent bride, and was awaiting transportation to Yogo Village.

"I can live here," Maud Margaret murmured. Then noting her husband's amused expression, added, "As long as you are here, of course."

He chuckled. "Know what I think, love?" When she squeezed his arm, he said, "I think you'd soon learn to *live* no matter where you happened to surface."

She smiled, reached to tuck a wisp of hair beneath her bonnet, then smoothed her suede traveling skirt and matching jacked. "Can that be my creed?"

"I hope so."

13

"Why is the horse, she stop?" Dr. Poska called from the rear.

Charles Gadsden, flushing from the neck up, shook the reins and the Utica plug plodded on.

Yogo mine manager Lansing McWilliams waited outside the office. "Heard you were coming." He shook Gadsden's and Poska's hands, bowed to the lady, then directed a nearby lounger to help the people with their trunks and bags. "I've cleared my things from the rooms over the office; that'll be your's and your missus' quarters." He shrugged. "It's the best we got, unless you two want to take up wedded bliss in the bunkhouse."

Maud Margaret blushed, Charles chuckled. "I'm sure quarters over the office will do fine, Lansing."

Later, Gadsden, noting the gleaming desk in McWilliams' office said, "My word, Lansing, I've never seen that desk without it piled with undone work."

"I'm ready to leave, young man," McWilliams murmured. "I've been ready to leave since long before you journeyed to London to be offered the position as my replacement. All knots are tied, machinery greased, my escape route clear. I will hazard with some confidence that as soon as you're up enough to give it a go at running this place, that I'll take myself off to a much needed South-of-France holiday."

"And may you have a rattling good time at it." Gadsden sought in vain for the right words, shrugged and said, "I will ... ah ... always be grateful for the recommendation you accorded me."

The older man waved Gadsden's gratitude aside, strode to a file cabinet and took out a ledger. "Take a chair, Charles. I want to start going over your 'to-do' list as soon as possible." His smile was tight. "All the sooner the South-of-France."

14

* * *

Gadsden's cram sessions began with roster, job assignments, work directives, pay scales. Then it turned to maintenance schedules, trackage, emergency repairs, accident prevention and the unfinished medical room design. From there, McWilliams briefed his replacement on present and planned drifts and tunnels, stopes, shafts, crosscuts and winzes within the mine itself. Diagrams and maps were unrolled and studied, questions asked and replies provided. Before they'd finished, the evening meal whistle sounded.

McWilliams turned down the lamp and invited Charles and Maud Margaret to accompany him to the mess hall.

The smiling, diminutive blonde proved an immediate hit. Not that she struck like dynamite heaved into the miners' midst; word of her arrival had already flared like wildfire through a windburned hayfield. Few of the men had actually glimpsed her, but when the old manager and his replacement arrived at the hall with the beautiful lady in tow, the boisterous dining room fell so silent a teamster's shuffling boots sounded like thunder's distant roll. Every eye was on her, every mouth open, every motion suspended. Maud Margaret's cheeks flushed, but she bravely smiled, curtsied to the group, gripped her husband's arm and walked smartly with him to the serving line. Later, when she was introduced to the men, she curtsied again and told them how proud she was to join them in such a grand adventure. She captivated them. And they captured her heart.

That night, lying in her husband's arms, she said, "They blushed didn't they? It was a group blush. They're just bashful, Aren't they?" When he only said, "Mmm," she asked, "Am I the first woman in this camp?"

"Here, perhaps. But over in Yogo Gulch, it is said there are women there."

15

* * *

The next day, Lansing McWilliams and Charles Gadsden moved to actual gem recovery: the spreading of the ore on weathering pads, the washing process, sluicing, riffle and trap cleanup, grading and sorting of the gems, security storage, shipping.

"We've had some theft problems, Charles," the older man said. "Some gem high-grading, one attempted payroll robbery. I'm afraid you'll have to elevate security to a more prominent level. But I'm at a loss as to what to do, or how to implement it."

Again and again, McWilliams went over various reports to be sent to London. "They want to know everything, Charles. Tons of host rock excavated, gems recovered, their number of carats, grades, percentages of various qualities. They want to know your numbers of miners employed, support workmen, your total wage package including benefits where applicable, such as Christmas and their Fourth of July Independence Day."

When his trainee nodded, McWilliams said, "It's the bottom line that interests them, of course. They want to know what dividends you can produce for their investment. And if you want to make any improvements—and I'm sure you'll want to do so—that's the only means through which it can be done: selling it to them as a way to produce more revenue."

Gadsden cleared his throat. "You mean if we want to double our shaft levels and add more miners, including additional facilities to handle the expansion of men and livestock and equipment, then we'll first have to work up a report that will show them its cost, but also how much the increased production can mean to their dividend return?"

"Exactly. Except it won't be 'we' who must propose expansion and marshal the support for it in a proper report, it'll

16

be 'you'. I'm going to the South-of-France."

Gadsden smiled. "How much more do we have to go over today?"

"We're about finished. I'd like you to understand the ages of our livestock: horses, mules, milch cows. We buy our beef and hogs locally. Some of the coarse flour comes from the mill in Lewistown, the rest from Great Falls. Our hay is furnished by farms along the Judith. We buy local vegetables when available." Expecting the new manager's thoughtful nod, McWilliams added, "It's painful to have to deal with every farmer who wants to sell his produce, but sometimes one must take on duties not within his realm."

"I presume it's good diplomacy."

"Yes. Sometimes simply being English is a mountainous hurdle to overcome with many of these Americans."

Three days later, Lansing McWilliams was gone.

* * *

Maud Margaret quickly set up housekeeping in the office building's upstairs apartment, turning one room of the three, with Charles' help, into a kitchenette. She also planted a vegetable garden in a plot behind the office, and flowers and shrubs around several of the buildings—too early as she discovered in mid-May when a killing frost settled into the little swale where Yogo Village nestled. So she smiled wistfully and began anew. It was with such industry that first one workman, then another would pause on their rounds to share advice. Some even assisted her in her project during their off-duty hours.

Charles Gadsden ordered a barrel of white paint, carefully drawing up a cost-benefit analysis to prove the long-term positive of painting the buildings would eventually offset repair and maintenance costs.

George Wells, the English remittance man and present-

17

day Utica rancher who'd been instrumental in bringing the Yogo sapphires under Johnson, Walker, and Tolhurst control (elevated to President of the New Mine Sapphire Syndicate for his efforts) had sufficient authority to approve the paint. But when the new manager submitted a report that justified extending his miner's work day (at an increased daily wage), and thereby adding to the Yogo's gem production, George had to pass the request along to London (with his signature of approval). In addition to the miners' added wages, Gadsden also won a proposal to add Thanksgiving and New Years Day to Christmas and the Fourth of July as miners' holidays. The men loved him from the outset. Now they worked harder for the new boss.

Gadsden began washing and sluicing operations on the first day of May, turning giant hoses filled with ditch water onto the weathering ore, slicing off portions to send the weathered muck and mud down the sluices. He also instituted a policy of retrieving the trapped gems by cleaning the riffles of yesterday's stones in the morning, before a new day's work began. But that policy was abruptly terminated as soon as it was found some unknown thief had beaten them to the cleanup during the night.

It was the sinister-appearing Pete Weatherwax who made the suggestion that they should simply sluice all night. "All we're doing is running mud over the riffles anyway, Mr. Gadsden. Ain't gonna lose no more sapphires during the dark than during the day. And ain't nobody cleaning out no riffles while the mud's a-runnin'." Weatherwax, who'd been seasonally employed during the skeletal sluicing for several years, clenched the idea by volunteering to oversee the nightime work crew.

* * *

Naseby Ringgold whispered, "Ma, there's somebody comin'."

18

She paused in shoveling gravel to her rocker and said, "Naseby, I've about told you enough that it's 'mother', not 'ma', and not to drop your 'g's. It's 'coming', not 'comin'.'"

The little nine-year-old hopped excitedly about. Since his buddy Pete Weatherwax had left a month before to work on sapphire sluicing, he and his mother had seen no other soul in Yogo Gulch.

"Say it!" she commanded, eyeing first her son, then the oncoming rider.

"Someone is coming, mother!"

"That's better." Then, eyeing the newcomer, she said, "Howdy stranger. You look like you've been rode hard lately."

"That I have ma'am. That I have." The bay horse he straddled was thin and rawboned—gaunt even, with protruding hipbones and sorrowful eyes. The saddle appeared to have been recently pulled from a fence rail after having weathered there through a long winter. The man's hair hung to his shoulders and was unkempt. In addition, it'd been at least a month since his shaggy beard had been combed, let alone washed. His clothes were ragged. Eyeing her like a cottontail tiptoeing through a dog kennel, he suddenly blurted, "I need food. My horse, too; we both are hurtin'."

Millie leaned on her shovel handle, peering up at the newcomer, appraising him. "Ain't got no gun," he said, apparently on the verge of tears. "No money neither. But"—he reached into his ragged trousers' watch pocket and held out a hand—"I got these." Three raw, uncut sapphires rolled around in his palm.

She handed Naseby her shovel and slapped sand from her palms. "Best get down, mister, before you or the horse falls down. I got some oats for the horse and can get some vittles for you."

Though the man was so gaunt he couldn't have weighed much, the feeble horse still staggered sideways as the rider swung down. He staggered himself, but said, "I'd be obliged if you could see to my horse first." When Millie nodded, he pointed to the creek and said, "I'll do what I can to make myself more presentable."

As they walked away leading his horse, Naseby blurted, "How come you let him get away with saying 'ain't', mother? And he dropped his 'g' on 'hurting'." She never replied.

The man stayed for two days. When he left, Millie Ringgold added six uncut sapphires to the collection given her by Jake Hoover. It was three days after the man disappeared when the bright little Naseby figured out that those sapphires were stolen. When he asked his mother about it she sighed and picked him up, plopping him on the kitchen table while she bent to peer into his eyes.

"Yes, Naseby. Those sapphires were stolen—though if anybody asks, we know nothing about that; all our sapphires were given to us by your father, okay?"

The boy nodded, but it was obvious he didn't really understand.

"What I do know, is they were stolen from the people who first stole them from your father. And for that reason, I say those sapphires have as much right here as in any thief's hands, no matter first or last." She blinked back tears as her son stared wide-eyed at a mother he'd never before seen. She sighed again. "I guess you're man enough now for me to tell you that story: how those bastards stole your inheritance...."

* * *

The night and day sluicing at the Yogo not only stopped the looters cold, but it led to the year's cleanup being completed in early August instead of late September. Thus a proposal was

20

soon under way to Gadsden's London superiors proposing, since cleanup could be handled so much more profitably by going around the clock, that he be allowed to add additional weathering pads and consider adding additional shafts at differing depths in the mine, permitting more men to dig more ore.

Gadsden received approval for the additional weathering pads, but was told to hold off on increasing mine production until Johnson, Walker, and Tolhurst completed a market analysis—in short, whether their markets could absorb a significant increase in sapphire production.

Chapter Three

"Pete! Pete!"

The floppy-hatted cadaverous rider leaned down and swept up the onrushing boy to perch ahead of him in the saddle. "How you doin' whippersnapper?" he murmured, tickling the boy's neck with his great handlebar moustache in their long-standing game.

The boy giggled and twisted to peer up and pout, "Why you been gone so long?"

"Hell, boy, I was here just yesterday."

"Was not."

"Well, last week?"

"Ma says it's been a month of Sundays."

Reining the palomino horse to a halt in front of the flashing-toothed woman who raised her shovel like a bar, the sinister-appearing rider dropped the boy to the ground and swung down himself. "'Lo Millie."

"I'm surprised to see you out to the Gulch, Pete. They can't be through with the wash-up already."

Weatherwax pulled off his big black hat to run long, boney fingers through hair that had once been dark as coal, but now peppered with flecks of gray. "Naw, we ain't done yet, Millie. But the ditch had a blowout somewheres t'other side of Etienne's, so I got a day or two off. Thought I'd see how things're goin' up here."

"Well, that's *white* of you, Pete." She saw he'd caught her double entendre by his quick, gone-as-fast grin and added, "You'll have supper with Naseby and me won't you?"

"Only reason I rode this far."

The boy touched his sleeve. "I'll take your horse, Pete. You go ahead and visit with ma ... mother."

They stood side by side, the tall hollow-cheeked man and the woman who neared his height, but outweighed him by twenty pounds. He watched the undersized boy lead his palomino to the lean-to stable. "He's fetchin' up, Millie. Purty soon he'll be swingin' some gal in a cotillion."

Millie Ringgold bit her lip as she watched her little man with the big horse, but she only murmured, "He turned ten last April Fool's Day."

Later that evening, Pete spooned up a second helping of mashed potatoes and stewed rabbit, asking, "Need anything, Millie? I mean from outside?"

She studied Naseby, then nodded to the fierce-appearing man who paused with a biscuit halfway to his plate. "Yes, Naseby needs books. I've already got a list made out to a Boston bookseller. Could you help us out?"

The biscuit plopped into Weatherwax's plate of stew. "Sure. You mean you want me to mail it, don't you?"

"More than that, Pete. All I've got is some money Jake left for us. But it don't seem right to send cash money when a money order would be better."

"So you want me to get a money order at the post office in Utica to send with your order."

"Utica, Lewistown, Great Falls, wherever you go next. Then I'll want the books sent to you so I'll know they're in good hands. After that, we'll see about getting them from the mine to the Gulch."

The man's handlebar moustache wriggled and one eye sank to half-mast as he offered his best—and most sinister-appearing—smile. "Consider it done." If she hadn't known Pete Weatherwax to be her, and Naseby's most loyal friend in all the

23

world, she would've shivered in spite of herself.

* * *

They came just as the office's big grandfather clock began bonging its first of twelve. They wore no shoes, clad only in tight-fitting black underwear to avoid the risk of accidentally snagging something in the darkness. By the clocks third bong, the first man had opened the closet door with a skeleton key, and by the fifth bong, the second man had twice spun the safe's combination dial to clear it. Meanwhile the first man quietly closed the closet door and lit a candle.

The first tumbler clicked during the eighth bong, the second on the tenth bong, and the last when the clock bonged twelve. The first man smiled and patted the second's shoulder, so pleased was he with their planning, rehearsal training, and successful penetration.

The safe's heavy door swung open with only the softest shudder and the men quietly loaded the safe's boxed contents into gunny sacks. Then they closed the safe, blew out their candle, and eased open the closet door. In only moments they'd pulled the outside office door softly closed and slipped into the nights' shadows.

When they reached the far corner of the blacksmith shop, Pete Weatherwax said, "Find what you wanted, boys?" The question was accompanied by twin clicks of Pete's sawed-off double-barreled shotgun. More or less to keep the one-sided conversation going Pete said, "Just for your information, this is the same sawed-off gun Jake Hoover used to cut Ben Munger into little pieces when the last bastard tried to steal sapphires from this mine."

Both loaded sacks tumbled to the ground while Pete ambled into the moonlight. Kyle Davis and Robespierre Hurlman shivered in spite of themselves. "Aw go ahead and

24

pick up the sacks, boys. Somebody has to help get 'em back to the office, and you all are right handy."

* * *

"Don't you reckon they're about the most pitiful lookin' jackasses you ever did see?" Weatherwax drawled as Charles Gadsden stumbled downstairs carrying a Harrington & Richardson Automatic Bayonet Revolver in .38 caliber. Pete blinked when he saw the revolver fully cocked, it's two and a half-inch bayonet extended. It was the first bayonet on a handgun the cadaverous night watchman had ever seen.

"Charles!" a voice called from upstairs. "Do be careful. You've never fired that thing, you know."

Weatherwax grinned and called up the stairs, "Never you mind, Mrs. Gadsden, I know how to shoot this 'Hoover Special'. And these two packrats know that to be the truth."

Hurlman and Davis stood against the inside wall, three feet to one side of the entry door, hands clasped behind their heads. A knee was out of Hurlman's black wool longhandles.

Gadsden strode over and threw the door's deadbolt, then returned to jerk on the locked closet door to the mine safe. He ran back upstairs for the key, returned and unlocked the door. The safe looked secure. But for a lingering smell of candle wax in the closet, nothing seemed amiss—except for the lumps thrusting up in two gunnysacks perched in the middle of the office floor.

"What happened?" he asked at last.

"Took 'em about four or five minutes by my reckoning," the security guard said. "Had it timed pretty good, they did."

Davis unclasped his hands and started to drop them to his side when a sharp crack rang out and a hole appeared in the wall by his head. The hands jerked back in place.

Mrs. Gadsden tumbled down the stairs and burst into the

25

room wearing a terry cloth bathrobe. Her hair was mussed, eyes wide, and a fist jammed against her mouth. "Get back upstairs, Maud Margaret," Charles ordered. When she hesitated, her husband thundered, "Dammit, woman, I said get back upstairs!"

After his wife disappeared, Gadsden pulled a box from a sack and pried the lid open. A thousand points of lamplight flickered back from its contents. "You fools!" he said, shaking his head in wonder. "You bloody, idiotic fools! What were you planning to do with a hundred pounds of sapphires if you escaped with them? These are uncut. Don't you know there are only a few places in the entire world to sell quantities of uncut sapphires? Even if you got away from here, you'd never get away with trying to sell this many uncut sapphires!"

Gadsden returned to the safe and tried its handle. When he returned he said in a level voice, "All right, which one of you is the safecracker?" Neither man answered. Charles tilted up Kyle Davis's chin with the Harrington & Richardson' bayonet. "You, I know. You're a teamster, right? You're the inside man. You're the chap who did the scouting, timed our patrols, probably planned the getaway route."

He turned to a malevolently grinning Weatherwax. "Where are their horses?"

Weatherwax shrugged. "They'll show up come daylight, Mr. Gadsden. But I doubt the horses had a damned thing to do with crackin' your safe."

The manager returned to his desk, laid down the revolver, and pulled out his swivel chair. Both Hurlman and Davis began to drop their hands, eyeing the sinister Pete Weatherwax as they did. Gadsden picked up the handgun and pointed it at Hurlman. Both thieves' hands jerked back into place. Still pointing the uncocked revolver at Hurlman, Gadsden's black eyes turned sad as he said, "That makes you the safecracker. Did Davis bring you in? Or did you recruit him to be your inside agent for this attempt?"

When neither thief stirred, Charles said softly, "Why, gentlemen, why?"

Davis blurted, "You goddamned English bastards got no right to steal our gemstones!"

"But you do?"

"At least I'm American!"

"You're American. And I'm English. So that gives you every right to steal from me?"

"Not from you!" Davis cried. "You've been a good enough boss. But from them as hires you. And Weatherwax, too." He glanced at the grinning guard. "Pete, you'd ought to be ashamed of yourself, a-workin' for them lobsterback bastards!"

The manager sighed. "Look here, there's no need to make a song and dance of it. Just convey the basic facts and be done with it. Simple approach, that's my advice." When neither man offered more, Gadsden prompted: "You say you engaged in this robbery because you hate the English, right?"

Again, neither answered. Again Charles Gadsden sighed. "You may as well answer my questions, gentlemen. You see you are in my possession for at least the three or four days it will take the sheriff to get here from Lewistown."

"Stanford, Mr. Gadsden," Weatherwax murmured. "They put us in that new Judith Basin County t'other day."

"They got a telegraph line into Utica," Davis said hopefully. "That'll bring the sheriff quicker."

"And we'll have one up here by the end of the summer," Charles murmured. "Who knows? I may choose to hold you until then." He stood back from his desk, pondered the two thieves, then strode to the door, throwing the deadbolt open. As he stepped outside, the manager said to Weatherwax, "If they move, shoot them."

Within minutes, sluicing operations had been halted and the four men of the night crew followed Charles Gadsden into the office. The manager said to his security man, "I see everything went well."

Weatherwax grinned. "They offered to cut me in."

Gadsden's smile was humorless as he unlocked a gun cabinet and handed out a lever action rifle and a pump shotgun to two of the night crew. The other two night crewmen were directed to lash the thieves hands behind their backs and tie ropes around their necks. Then he had them led to the barn where he hung a lantern and had their hands tied around different ones of the big runway support posts.

The manager then told the four night shift men to return to their work. After they disappeared into the night, Charles used his pistol bayonet to slit the back of each man's long underwear from neck to waist, jerking the remnants aside. Finally he strode to a sidewall and lifted down a bullwhip from a nail.

"You may go, too, Mr. Weatherwax."

Weatherwax murmured, "I ain't in favor of this, Mr. Gadsden."

"Nor I. But I *will* have some answers, one way or another."

"The sheriff...."

"Davis only said what most people think. This is an *English* mine. Therefore it is alright to steal from it. If that sentiment is true—and you and I both know it is—do you really think the Judith Basin County Sheriff is going to come up with sufficient answers?"

Pete Weatherwax shrugged and said, "Then I'll take your offer and leave."

"Lean the shotgun against the barn door on your way out."

"It's cocked."

"Then be kind enough to lock the hammers to 'safe', Mr. Weatherwax."

* * *

Judith Basin County Sheriff William Teat held his pencil over the open notebook. "So they've pulled this before?"

"They admitted so. I've given you the list. And I'll testify to what I heard."

The sheriff wagged his head. "May be hard to get a conviction on any of these; not with their backs striped up the way they are."

The Yogo manager smiled. "No matter. That's all background information anyway. What I'm really interested in is whether there's a conviction on the robbery attempt at the Yogo."

"Well, that might be hard, too...."

"You will get that conviction, Sheriff. Or else we'll handle our own justice out here."

The sheriff folded his notebook and raised his eyebrows. "That sounds suspiciously like a threat, Mr. Gadsden."

Charles stepped closer to murmur with dark eyes snapping, "It is, Sheriff. I have no intention of letting a robbery at the Yogo go unpunished." Then he stepped back and said, "Let me know when you want my crew to testify for the trial."

* * *

They were just a week beyond washing the stockpiled ore and collecting the last of the year's sapphire production when a particularly virulent influenza epidemic struck Montana from the Pacific Coast. Charles Gadsden and George Wells had recently left for London and a conference with the New Mine

29

Sapphire Syndicate's directors. The influenza was in Lewistown before they learned of it at Yogo Village. It struck Utica two days later, then the first miner at the Yogo fell ill. Within a week, half the crew was bedridden. A week later, the other half was down and the first half seemed little better. Unfortunately, Dr. Wyzczek Poska had been felled with the first group. Eventually, miners not sickened by the runamuck disease fled. And it was only Maud Margaret left who worked tirelessly to ease her miners' illness. Then, miraculously, as exhaustion threatened the little blonde, Millie Ringgold appeared.

"Pete told me you need help. He's staying with my boy."

The weary Maud Margaret seemed puzzled. "But Pete left before the epidemic began; how could he know we're in trouble?"

Millie shrugged. "Pete Weatherwax keeps his ears to the ground. I think my Jake taught him that."

"You are indeed an angel of mercy, Mrs. Ringgold."

One miner died. Then another. Millie paused by an infirmary cot and said, "You can't be much of a doctor if you can't even keep yourself well enough to help them that are really sick."

When the dark woman left, Doctor Wyzczek Poska sat up in bed and asked another patient, "That woman, who she?"

Slowly the epidemic ran its course. Dr. Poska rose from the almost-dead, and others began to respond to Maud Margaret's soups and Millie Ringgold's demands that they get their lazy asses out of bed so she could change their linens.

Then, as mysteriously as she appeared, Millie Ringgold, without even so much as a by-your-leave, disappeared.

* * *

"Millie?" the villainous-looking Pete Weatherwax said upon his return. "She lives up Yogo Gulch with her son."

To Maud Margaret's following question, he replied, "Oh about ten, fifteen years, more or less. I disremember."

Mine production was just getting up to normal after the disastrous flu epidemic and Charles Gadsden's assistant, Preston Douglas, was pleased to have Weatherwax back on security detail. That's why he was so dismayed when Maud Margaret told him she was taking Pete away to guide her into Yogo Gulch for a few days.

"Oh I can't allow that, ma'am," he said. "Why your husband would skin me alive if he came back and we didn't have our security at full strength. Besides, you running around up Yogo Creek with Pete—why them things just ain't done, ma'am."

Maud Margaret stamped her foot. "Perhaps you misunderstood me, Mr. Douglas. I'm not asking you, I'm telling you what Mr. Weatherwax is going to do. That woman came to help us in dire need. Why she even ministered to you! She came without being asked, without us even knowing of her. She should be properly thanked and I'm the proper one to do so. As it happens, Mr. Weatherwax knows where she dwells and how to get there. Mr. Weatherwax will lead me there."

Preston Douglas nearly wept. "Mrs. Gadsden, our payroll comes in on Thursday. Because we never turned a wheel for two weeks, probably half of it will not be paid out. That means we'll have to store a bunch of money in the safe. I've got to have Pete here to watch over it. I've just got to!"

"Find someone else, Mr. Douglas."

"How about I find someone else to take you up Yogo Gulch?"

"I want Pete Weatherwax, Mr. Douglas. And I shall have Pete Weatherwax."

* * *

As a last resort, Preston Douglas called Weatherwax into the office in an attempt to enlist the cadaverous appearing villain in his support. The villain turned a half-lidded eye on the assistant mine manager and said, "Sorry, Press, but I'm going up Yogo Gulch anyway, with or without Mrs. Gadsden. You see, I've got a bunch of books to deliver and if I have to quit to do it, I will."

"You're joking!"

Weatherwax shook his head. "You're a good man, Press. So is Charles Gadsden. But Millie Ringgold is a better woman than either of you are a man. And Millie Ringgold had a better man than any of us will ever be."

"I don't understand ..."

"No, I guess you wouldn't. But she needs to know what happened to him."

"I still don't understand."

"She will."

Preston Douglas, still confused, said, "Well, what about Mrs. Gadsden. Will you insist on taking her?"

Weatherwax pondered for a period, then said, "If I had my druthers, I'd druther not. But under the circumstances, Maud Margaret Gadsden might be just the thing that Millie Ringgold needs. And Lord knows, both Millie Ringgold and Maud Margaret Gadsden had what this camp needed when they needed 'em."

Chapter Four

"Ma! Ma! Pete's comin' again! And there's a woman with him!"

Millie Ringgold grabbed her son by the ear and marched him to the washbasin. "I told you I'd wash your mouth out with soap, and I'll do it!" But curiosity got the better of her, and she turned the boy loose as Weatherwax and her friend Maud Margaret Gadsden, riding sidesaddle, turned onto the trail to her isolated lodging house.

The two women embraced as Pete swung the boy up to his saddle and said, "Hold on a minute, boy, and I'll mount Miz Gadsden's hoss sidesaddle and we'll have us a race."

As it turned out, Weatherwax won the race out to the main Yogo Creek Trail and back because both spectators and the other rider were laughing so hard, first at his ridiculous ascent to the sidesaddle, then at the ludicrous efforts of the side-perching scarecrow to urge the horse onto something besides a choppy trot.

Later, while Pete and Naseby put away Pete's and Maud Margaret's horses, Mrs. Gadsden, still holding Millie Ringgold's hands, said, "There was no need for you to leave so abruptly, Millie. Every man—and the one woman there—wished to thank you for all you'd done."

The dark lady blushed and tried to withdraw her hands. Failing, she gripped her friend's fingers more tightly and said, "Black people, especially women black people, can only serve, Mrs. Gadsden. They got to know their place."

"That's utter nonsense! I thought you New World people fought a war over that sort of thing a half-century ago!"

"They did, but I didn't. And I'm not ready to fight one now, either." She stared at the corner of her deteriorating log shed where her son and Pete had disappeared with the horses. "I'm half-nigger, Mrs. Gadsden. It's not my fault, but it's the truth. I'm gone and done with, but I got hopes for little Naseby; he's only a quarter black and someday down the trail he might just pass for white."

Maud Margaret squeezed Millie's fingers in return and gazing up at the taller woman said, "You're talking nonsense. What is this useless talk of 'color'? You are a fine, giving woman, and I want to be your friend."

Millie Ringgold's teeth flashed. "You are my friend, little lady. You have courage and stamina and ... when you rode out here today ... you have perseverance ... and a fine sense of indebtedness. I'll be mighty proud to have you as my friend."

Pete Weatherwax and Naseby Ringgold returned. Maud Margaret said, "And this is your son, Naseby is it?" She held out both hands to the small boy.

"Yes'm," he replied, blushing pink.

Maud Margaret held Naseby's hands and couldn't help wondering if Weatherwax was the father (though there was little resemblance). Then she realized her thoughts must be plain to Millie and Pete simply by her pausing glances at each of them. So she quickly knelt until her eyes were on the same level as Naseby's and said, "You know, someday I'd like to have a little boy exactly like you."

"Really?"

"Really!"

"I must be pretty good, huh?"

The three adults laughed.

* * *

At supper that evening—again rabbit stew and mashed

potatoes—Millie said, "I heard while I was at the mine that you had a bungled robbery a couple of months ago."

Though Millie Ringgold addressed Pete, Maud Margaret answered, "I should've thought Mr. Weatherwax would've told you already. He played a prominent part in catching the thieves, you know."

Millie's smile was fleeting. "Pete don't talk about what goes on at the mine, even the once in a while when he stops by."

"What'd they steal?" Naseby asked. "If it was sapphires, we already know about one guy who stole some."

Millie and Pete locked eyes, then Millie said, "Naseby, why don't you go out and look in on the horses?"

"But ma!" the boy protested.

"Mother," she said.

"Mother. Me and Pete just checked them before supper."

"Go check them again, Naseby. Please."

The boy said, "Aw, mother!" as he slipped from his stool.

Fortunately Maud Margaret had heard nothing alarming and Pete broke eye contact to say, "They got into the safe. Stole a whole month of clean up. One of 'em was a professional safecracker, the other one was his inside man, a teamster."

"I heard they were whipped," Millie said.

Pete glanced at Maud Margaret and gave Millie a quick shake of his head.

"The horses are all right," Naseby said, rushing in to take his place on the stool.

Later, Pete said, "Well, I'll be making my way down to my cabin." He tousled Naseby's head and said, "But before I do, Shaver, I got some books for you in my saddlebags. Should I hold 'em for tomorrow, or give 'em to you now?"

"Now! Now!" Naseby shouted, jumping up and down.

When the two males disappeared to bring in Pete's

saddlebags, Millie softly said, "No, Pete's not the boy's father."

"Oh my goodness!" Maud Margaret said, turning crimson. "I didn't think ..."

Millie murmured, "Yes you did. But it makes no difference to me. What Jake and I had—and hopefully will have again—is as great as any love could be."

Maud Margaret wisely remained silent.

* * *

Pete Weatherwax sopped up the last of Millie Ringgold's syrup with her last hotcake, then pushed his plate to the side. He eyed both women for a few moments, clearly wanting to say something, but at a loss as to how to begin. Finally he eyed Maud Margaret. While staring at her, he said, "Naseby, why don't you take Mrs. Gadsden down and show her yours and my secret grotto?"

"Aw, I want to stay with you."

Millie said, "I'll bet Maud Margaret would love to see your grotto, Naseby."

Maud Margaret picked up on their need by clapping her hands and saying, "Oh! I love grottos. And to be able to see one with such a handsome young man as you would be a delightful treat, indeed!"

After the grotto appraisers were gone, Millie said, "Did you have to whip them, Pete."

He hung his head. "I didn't have nothin' to do with that, Millie. You know that. But Mrs. Gadsden's husband is a tough man. Fair, but tough."

"As fair and tough as Jake?"

He steeled himself. "Fair and tough, all right. But not as tough as Jake was."

A tiny alfalfa beetle fell from Millie's ceiling to the puncheon floor; the little bug's collision sounded thunderous in the sudden silence. "Was?" she said, her voice little more than a squeak.

He sighed and dropped his eyes to the tabletop. "Word came in on the same mail shipment as your books. They think it was diphtheria. Anyway they found him dead in his cabin. Buried him on his claim on Klondike Creek. Word has it the boys shoveled up a layer of placer gold when they dug him in. But I'd discount that." He paused, raised eyes to hers.

She regarded him levelly, lips a fine line, face taut. "And you believe it—about him being gone?"

"There was a package of his belongings with it," Weatherwax said, "including these." He poured the contents of an envelope on the table: a dozen facetable sapphires. "You know and I know that Jake would never let these get out of his hands. So, Millie, he's gone. He's gone, and it was honest men who buried him."

Neither moved, nor said a word until they heard Naseby and Maud Margaret returning. Then Millie murmured, "Well, that makes the books you brought doubly important, don't it? If Jake won't be coming back, Naseby will have to prepare somehow to make his way in the world."

* * *

Two weeks to the day, after Pete Weatherwax and Maud Margaret Gadsden returned to Yogo Village, a rider pulling two packhorses stopped in front of Millie's lodging house in Yogo Gulch. One packhorse was loaded with sides of veal, the other with succulent hams. "Miz Gadsden said to tell you this is compliments of a grateful bunch of miners at the sapphire mine."

Charles Gadsden and George Wells returned from London on the same day the packstring returned from Yogo Gulch. The mine manager brought with him approval to increase Yogo production by hiring more miners, as well as adding the necessary shafts and winzes to accommodate them in the mine itself. Instrumental in getting his go-ahead for more investment at the Yogo was the just released United States Geological Bulletin No. 983, excerpted below:

> The Yogo sapphire deposit is the most important gem locality in the United States. Cut sapphires of excellent quality, valued possibly at as much as $1,000,000 to $2,000,000 have been produced from the deposit, and reserves of sapphire-bearing material are probably adequate to supply several times the quantity mined....

Included within the bulletin were figures of rough (uncut) stones from the early years of British involvement through 1905.

1898 129,914cts. Gems / 296,862 cts. ind. $55,000
1899 (no figures available)
1900 (no figures available)
1901 150,000cts. Gems / 5,000oz. industrial $90,000
1902 200,000cts. (gems?) $115,000
1903   40,000 cts. Gems / 1,000,000cts. ind. $100,000
1904   38,529cts. gems / 808,404cts. ind. $100,000
1905 (no figures available) $125,000

With time critically short before winter's onslaught, Charles Gadsden ordered wagonloads of lumber and bricks and cement. He hired carpenters and bricklayers and cabinetmakers that worked from daylight to dark, seven days per week. A second bunkhouse was the first building framed, then an addition to the mess hall and a second barn went up.

It was by the grace of God that the first winter blizzard blew in on Christmas Day. By then all new buildings were roofed and the sides sheathed so work could continue inside. First completed was the added bunkhouse, then the mess hall extension. By then, also, additional mine crews began drilling new winzes and drifts, then stockpiling ore from new tunnels.

It took but eight months for Charles Gadsden to have the Yogo Sapphire Mine spitting at enviable production and he felt on top of his world. Or so he thought until word came that Raphael Etienne discovered the sapphire-bearing dike continuing across Yogo Creek, near his cabin.

"Can this rumor be true?" the Yogo manager asked his resident expert on the history of Yogo sapphires, Pete Weatherwax.

"Oh, I reckon it's possible, Mr. Gadsden. Jake Hoover himself once told me he stopped looking for the dike after he got to the busted-up canyon of Yogo Creek. Later he told me he figured the dike might show up again across the canyon, but by then the outfit was having trouble selling what they took out of what they had. So I guess he just didn't care no more."

Gadsden mopped his brow—it was a warm summer day. Then he saddled and rode first to Etienne's place, then to report what he'd learned to George Wells. "So Raphael Etienne says, he and two others—men named Sweeney and Burke—have filed on a cross-canyon extension of the sapphire dike. Etienne says they'll sell to us if the price is right. But Weatherwax says Jake Hoover told him earlier management decided to digest what they already had, rather than trying to discover any more lode."

The Syndicate President nodded. "What Weatherwax says is quite true. There was absolutely no sense in kicking against the bloody prick. And we were extended. Much too far extended."

"And how are we now, sir?"

Wells laid the two month-old London newspaper he'd been reading across his lap to better study his mining manager. Finally he said, "I wonder if I may draw your attention to the fact that our employers have recently authorized considerable expenditures for increased sapphire production. Surely you cannot think it wise to approach them about measures for even more production."

Charles Gadsden shuffled his feet; he'd not yet been asked to sit. "No sir, I wasn't thinking so much about further increasing our production as much as limiting possible competition."

Wells lifted his paper. "Did Etienne mention a price?"

"Fifty thousand dollars was suggested, sir."

The paper scattered to the floor as Wells spluttered, "Fifty thousand! Do you mean dollars? Are you both insane?"

Gadsden turned for the door. But before he stepped outside, he said, "I fully understand, sir, that I'm not to investigate additional sapphire properties in the district."

Wells, who busied himself picking up his scattered newspaper, growled, "I should think that would be a proper understanding between the mine manager and his superior."

"Still, I feel obligated to mention Etienne's approach in my mid-summer report."

A red-faced Wells glanced at his manager and said, "Do what you feel you must. And I will do what I feel proper—which is that it will go forward without my recommendation."

The door clicked as it was closed.

Chapter Five

Books delivered to the Ringgolds in Yogo Gulch included a *McGuffey Reader; Tattered Tom* by Horatio Alger; two Mark Twains, *Huckleberry Finn* and *A Connecticut Yankee in King Arthur's Court*; *Call of the Wild* by Jack London; Owen Wister's *The Virginian*; and *Rebecca of Sunnybrook Farm* by Kate Douglas.

It wasn't that the eleven-year-old Naseby Ringgold could not read. Since his earliest recollection, his mother had read to him from such sources as was available: scraps of old newspapers brought into the Gulch as packing paper for packstring loads carrying food and mining equipment, the occasional prized book of a neighboring miner, even printed labels on cans and boxes and flour sacks. Millie, of course, was the proud possessor of a bible, ostensibly given her by a former employer (President Rutherford Birchard Hayes, she claimed).

Because Naseby was an unusually bright child, he was soon reading along with his mother, first following with his finger, then sounding out the words as she read them, and finally reading the words on his own.

No, it wasn't that Naseby couldn't read, it was that he never understood what he read in a context beyond the narrow gulch in which he lived; no concept of a world beyond, where millions teemed; no buildings scratching at the sky; no cobblestone streets; no great cathedrals; no vast ports where huge steamships called. Yes, he'd seen three pictures of ships: woodcuts, each a two-master with sails spread wide, heeled over in a swelling sea. But steamships were beyond his ken, even though his mother told him of them. And railroads? Huh-uh; how could he?

41

It was the *Reader*, and Twain, Wister, Alger, London, Douglas that Millie Ringgold hoped would suffice for her son's intermediate education.

And it worked. Boy howdy, did it work! From the day Pete Weatherwax and Maud Margaret Gadsden rode from the Gulch to return to their world, the boy immersed himself in the books. From daylight to dark, seven days a week the boy disappeared into the misty nether world of make believe. He followed Tattered Tom on the boy's serendipitous rise from street waif to wealth, Huck's and Jim's picaresque journey down the Mississippi, the Yankee's tumultuous time with King Arthur and his Knights of the Roundtable.

For a boy familiar with horsemen appearing on distant horizons (or, in his case, around bends of the creek) one could easily enough grapple with Wister's hero. But until *The Virginian*, Naseby had no idea they could be so heroic, so capable, so brave, even so honorable.

Seeing what he read, sometimes reading along with him, Millie gave the boy to understand that his father and the Virginian were interchangeable. When the wide-eyed boy asked if Jake Hoover had *really* been brave, his mother, with tears in her eyes, told everything she knew of the real Jake. "Tough? Naseby, he'd make Pete Weatherwax look like a drugstore Indian."

"What's a drugstore Indian, Mother?"

So she explained drugstore Indians. And when the boy asked, "What's a drugstore?" she explained that, too. When he wanted to know what other kinds of stores existed in cities and towns, she told of haberdasheries, general mercantiles, blacksmith shops, millineries, feed stores. She explained hotels and newspaper offices and bookstores where hundreds of books sat patiently waiting on shelves for boys just like him to wander by and take them down.

To the skinny, wide-eyed, impressionable lad it all seemed an impossible dream. But there it was, saying so in *Tattered Tom* and *Rebecca of Sunnybrook Farm*.

But it was *Call of the Wild* that had the greatest effect on both Ringgolds. "Your father died in the Klondike, Naseby." And the boy was diverted from the actions of the heroic dog to his heroic father. "They drove him to it," she said, dabbing at her eyes with a dishtowel. "They stole his mine and drove him away to try to find another fortune in another place."

When tears came to his own eyes, she continued, "He was driven to provide for you and me, honey. He was in a young man's game, but he never would admit it because he was the toughest, bravest, most true man who ever lived. And when they took by chicanery what was his by right, he shrugged, gave us enough to live on while he was gone, then disappeared into the Arctic."

"What's chicanery?" Naseby asked.

So she pulled down a tattered copy of Webster's Dictionary—the only other book besides the Bible in the house until Pete Weatherwax's delivery—and read: "A tricky and deceitful maneuver."

He stared at her for the longest time, then asked, "What's a maneuver?"

So she shoved the dictionary across the table, showed him how to spell maneuver, then how to thumb through the wordy volume. Thus Naseby Ringgold learned the power of words and how to spell them. But he still wanted to know about the trick the British played on his father to steal his fortune.

And that was a thing his mother was not in the least loathe to tell the impressionable young boy, perhaps even embellishing the chicane tale along the way.

Raphael Etienne, Honus Sweeney, and Josiah Burke eventually filed on eight lode and placer claims across the broken canyon of Yogo Creek from the English Mine to the east.

Etienne, not caring for the sweat and danger of hardrock mining, soon sold his three claims to Burke and Sweeney for the same five thousand dollar amount Jake Hoover received for his share of the original Yogo Sapphire Mine. And, as happened with Hoover, Burke and Sweeney sold their combined holdings for fifty thousand dollars to a syndicate headed by the still embittered Matthew Dunn of Great Falls. Dunn renamed his acquisition the American Sapphire Syndicate, blasted out a road down into the Gulch, and brought in the kinds of stamps, crushers, acid vats, and other standard mining equipment he'd always believed essential to successful high-volume sapphire production. Then, after already investing over two hundred thousand dollars in the American Mine venture, he engineered their capitalization for an additional one hundred thousand, then set out to drive the English out of the sapphire business.

* * *

"Mother, I want more books."

She turned from the stove. "Good. You got any way to pay for them?" When he shook his head, she said, "Books cost money, boy. And we got to watch what we spend because we're not taking in enough to get by these days."

"I could set up another rocker and shovel up my own gold." When she continued stirring her porridge, Naseby said, "There's a rocker down at my father's claim on Skunk Creek. I could work that. If he's really my father, it's mine by right."

She nodded and turned from her stove. "I'd say you got every right, son. If you want to earn money for books, that might be your best way to do it."

Edward Keller's arrival was unexpected. One day the hatchet-faced London barrister appeared without warning at George Wells' ranch. He rode in an extended-top cabriolet, with a driver. "Hell, I didn't know they had such a buggy in Lewistown," Wells said, scratching his head. Within the hour, a messenger rode to Yogo Village summoning Charles Gadsden to conference.

"The principals of the New Mine Sapphire Syndicate sent me," the lanky barrister said, "on discovery relative to this so-called 'American' sapphire mine."

In contrast to the impeccably dressed Keller and the freshly scrubbed and hastily changed Wells, Gadsden wore the soiled work clothes he was in when Wells' summons arrived. The mine manager's direct supervisor avoided eye contact.

"Well?" Keller growled.

George Wells cleared his throat. "Actually we know very little, Edward. Charles advised me of Etienne's discovery earlier last year and I believe he advised the principals of that fact in a mid-summer report." Wells gestured at Gadsden (who nodded), for confirmation.

Keller actually sneered. "And you did not know Matthew Dunn now has control of the American Sapphire Syndicate?"

"Ah, well, I'd heard as much," Wells admitted.

"Did not you think—just possibly think—that the man might hold vindictive thoughts toward us?"

Wells flushed pink, averted his eyes. Keller glared at Gadsden. "Are you both idiots? Don't either of you have one scintilla of brains? How could you let this happen?"

Gadsden decided it was the man's eyes. They were as pale as clear water in a white dish, bright, but empty as a clear marble and as cold as an ice cube. They were set in an unhealthy pale, hatchet face, and they stared through an opponent with a blind hollowness that left a pit in the middle of one's stomach. Still, the Yogo manager was incensed.

George Wells shifted in his chair and said, "The fault is mine, not one of Charles's making. He came to me early, as soon as he heard of Etienne's discovery. I'm the one who told him our syndicate wouldn't be interested. In fact, I believe his report advised you of the discovery. It may also have included the fact that Etienne offered the discovery to us. But I can't remember for how much. Can you help me there, Charles?"

"Fifty thou ..."

"Oh dear me," the barrister sneered again, "we're well aware of that." He pulled a neatly folded handkerchief from his lapel pocket. "Please don't cry, either of you. Here's a hanky. It's almost clean, only blew my nose on it once this morning. Have a go, mates."

George Wells recoiled from the extended handkerchief, flushing scarlet. But Charles Gadsden stood firm, black eyes flashing. "I have no intention of staying here to be abused, Mr. Keller. If you have nothing of importance for me, I'll take my leave."

The icy stare; combatants locked in clash. Finally Keller said, "Do sit back down. I'm almost over with admonitions."

"Then let me advise you that you are already past any with me."

There appeared the slightest smile on the hatchet face. "Sit down. Please."

After Gadsden had again taken his seat, Edward Keller told them the American Sapphire Syndicate had just dumped a great quantity of rough gems into the world market. "We suspect they have shortages of operating capital. But we can't overrule the fact that Matthew Dunn might be out to take revenge on us."

Gadsden said, "Have you investigated the quality of their stones?"

Keller nodded. "We have. Few large gems, though it appears there might have been some that were damaged in their crushing and extraction. Poorly sorted."

"Then they can't hurt us much," Wells murmured.

"And you're the President of our New Mine Sapphire Syndicate?" Keller sneered. "Don't you understand that by their dumping on the world market, they will soften ours?"

Wells, taking heart from the mine manager's defiance, said, "Get to the point, Keller. You weren't sent out here just to condemn us. Terminate us, perhaps, but I'm afraid I'm getting a little like Charles, I'm wearying of this one-sided vitriol."

Keller tried his most intimidating glare, but finally decided these two expatriate Englishmen had been fouled with the same libertarian thoughts rampant throughout this benighted country. If only Keller had known the two had not just been infected with Americanism, but with *Western* Americanism's even more virulent liking for freedom, he'd have been even more distressed.

The barrister cleared his throat. "We've decided that we must obtain the American mine if we are to maintain our sapphire monopoly. You two are charged with implementing this strategy."

Wells and Gadsden glanced at each other. Gadsden asked, "How much are we authorized to offer?"

"Nothing!" Keller snapped. "But you are authorized to make inquiries and transmit any response by cable. Decisions on purchase price will be retained in London."

"Clear enough," Wells said.

Charles Gadsden mused, "But couldn't this information have likewise been transmitted by cable. Why send you across an ocean and a continent on a mission such as this?"

The malevolence of Edward Keller's grin would've made even Pete Weatherwax shrug. "One either has it or one doesn't. It was decided by my principals that you both need to be reminded that you do not have it. Privately, I can add that for either of you to strive after it would be as futile as an ugly woman applying rouge to her pockmarked cheeks."

Gadsden leaped to his feet to lean his nose only inches from the barrister's eagle beak. "Now, sir, that you've had the immense pleasure of passing on that cutting remark, let me pass along this observation: you do not have authority to terminate either of us, do you?"

* * *

Naseby Ringgold worked hard. His hands blistered and finally turned to calluses. He knew how to use a rocker—after all, he'd watched his mother for most of his thirteen years. But he was hampered by knowing little of Jake Hoover's old claim, so he moved his rocker incessantly, from one bar to another, one bank to another. All in all, the boy recovered three dollars and eighty-six cents worth of gold in July and four dollars and twelve cents in August. Though he could buy a half-dozen of the books he wanted with the money, he was dejected by his failure to recover even half of that recovered by his mother, though he worked at least as many hours at it each day as she.

"Not easy is it, Naseby, this having to work for a living?"

He shrugged. "What else is there?"

She chuckled. "Well, since it don't look like you're going to sprout muscles out of your eyebrows, maybe I'd ought to teach you how to be a right and proper servant."

He turned up his nose. "If it's such a great life, how

come you ain't doing it."

"Because I'd rather be free. And you're not to say 'ain't'."

"What makes you think I don't want to be free?"

"I don't think you don't. But you've not lived yet. And in order to do that, you've got to get outside, into the world. In order to do that, you need a ... uh ..."

"A vocation?" he asked, proud that he beat his mother to it.

"Yes, a vocation. There's nothing wrong with being a servant. Especially if you get to work with folks at the top."

"And you served Presidents?" She could tell he no longer believed it.

"I did. And boy, it don't make no never mind to me whether you believe it or not. But it does make a difference to me whether you're prepared to do the job if ever you're called on for placement." She smiled down at him as he picked a blister on his palm. "And Naseby, it's one hell of a lot less work than shoveling rockers full of sand and gravel on a Yogo Creek gravel bar."

Thus, Naseby Ringgold began training for service to the rich....

* * *

"It's very important, Naseby, that one be attired at all times in a manner of one's position. In your case, we want you to pursue a butler's position, so that means coat and tails, white silk shirt, even at times, gloves."

"Where will I get that kind of stuff?"

"You won't until you stop growing, it's too expensive. But remember what I say. You won't get a chance at a fine position without it." She placed a feather duster in his hands. "The most important thing you do is always look busy. If you're in charge of other servants—and that's where you want to be—they all got to look busy, too. Wash windows, shine silver, dust portraits. Not just the ones you can reach, but the one's you can't. Get a stepladder. Get an extension handle for your duster."

When he moved about desultorily, she grabbed him by an ear and sat him on a bench. "This is no game, young man. You got to get in or get out! If you get in, you'll be drawing up staff plans for the best drawing rooms in the land. That's what you want—responsibility. The more responsibility you get, the more dependence they'll have on you, and the more power you have over them. Remember it, son, the ability to draw up a good staff plan is the cornerstone of any butler's skills. And it's ultimately the butler's position that you want."

As part of his training regimen, the thirteen-year-old became Millie Ringgold's butler, waiter, and coachman (without a coach). It was her good fortune and his that Naseby assumed all those mock rolls, because Millie's health began to decline....

Chapter Six

The American Sapphire Syndicate, mired deeply in red ink, fell into internal battle as the firm struggled to avoid bankruptcy. Matthew Dunn, of Great Falls, finally emerged the victor, barely staving off disaster by investing much of his own capital into a revitalized Yogo American Sapphire Company. But 1907 was not a good year for America as the nation slid into economic depression. As result, scant attention could be spared for an undercapitalized, little known American sapphire syndicate in the wilds of far-off Montana. As it was, the country itself was only rescued when capitalist J.P. Morgan engineered an American banking consortium to bail out the United States Government through emergency loans.

As a matter of fact, the only satisfaction Matthew Dunn found during the disastrous winter of 1907-08 was laughing himself into a stupor at George Wells' approach about the possibility of the English gem firm of Johnson, Walker, and Tolhurst, Ltd. acquiring the Yogo American Sapphire Company....

* * *

Charles Gadsden, as it turned out, had little time for involvement in an attempt to absorb the Yogo American as he had his hands full battling the effects of a bitter winter and a disastrous national economic condition. First, the critical water ditch headgates froze in position and had to be thawed with blowtorches in order to regulate ditch flows. Finally the weather turned so brutal that mining operations had to be curtailed, and finally suspended.

Down in the Judith River Valley, deep snow and the bitter cold halted travel. During blizzards livestock drifted into gullies and fence corners and died there. Farmers and small ranchers were starving. In order to employ miners and help their neighbors, Charles Gadsden armed his crew with shovels and hooked the mine's teams to fresnos and scrapers and sent them out to open roads to Utica and beyond. He even sent miners to haul food from the Yogo's own dwindling stocks to those in distress. And when spring came those same neighbors knew positively that Charles Gadsden was one of their own, and that the English Mine had been instrumental in their salvation.

That's why it came as a shock to the New Mine Sapphire Syndicate when, the following July, Bill Givens and Alvie Pedersen both filed suit against the English Mine alleging that mud from mine waste was ruining their meadows and fields. The ranches of Givens and Pedersen were, of course, closest to the mine's washing pads, and summer was the height of gem washing activity.

George Wells was apoplectic about the lawsuit, but Charles Gadsden made an inspection of the plaintiffs' properties and agreed that the mud was a problem. "I see no other recourse, George, than for the company to buy those two ranches. Their asking prices are reasonable and would probably be less than what a jury would set aside. Besides giving us the property where our overflows would concentrate, as well as the fact that the next property downstream is your ranch, the Syndicate would be immune to any future litigation for any time foreseeable."

After the disaster of the competition from American claims on the sapphire-bearing dike and Wells' abrupt dismissal of the mine manager's advice that the English firm acquire the claims, the Syndicate's President was inclined to listen long and hard to Gadsden's suggestions. The result was the ranches of both Bill Givens and Alvie Pedersen were purchased.

When the sales were consummated, Charles Gadsden rubbed his hands in glee. "Do you have any idea what you've just done, old chap? You may have purchased 830 acres of the most productive land in the entire Judith Valley. You see, I had the mud chemically analyzed and the "fines" flowing over those fields are rich in nitrates and phosphates. Those fields are being replenished on a yearly basis, just as the floods on the Nile did to Egypt. George, you've actually stolen that farmland for little more than a song!"

* * *

Charles and Maud Margaret Gadsden became naturalized citizens of the United States of America only ten days after the New Mine Sapphire Syndicate purchased the farms of Givens and Pedersen. "We're proud to be one of you," Charles said to his assembled mine crew, Maud Margaret at his side. "We're proud to be Americans."

"Hip, hip, hooray!" chanted the miners. "Hip, hip, hooray!"

* * *

An unrecognized rider thundered up to the mine headquarters at dusk on a late August day. "WEATHERWAX!" the man shouted. "WHERE'S WEATHERWAX?"

"He's not here," Charles Gadsden said, coming from the office. "As a matter of fact he's escorting a gem shipment. Can I be of any help?"

"IT'S MILLIE! MILLIE RINGGOLD!" Then the man's excitement dwindled. "She's sick. Up in the Gulch. She may be dying."

Charles whirled to the blacksmith who peered from his shop at the disturbance. "Jeffries! Hitch up a wagon and fetch Dr. Poska. Tell him to bring the wagon as far as he can take it up Yogo Creek. Meanwhile, I'll saddle a horse and ride back with this gentleman."

"Laulis," the man said, leaning down to shake hands. "Don't you remember me? I worked with Weatherwax on washing the stones when the other guy was manager before you. They call me Lawless Laulis. I was up there to look in on my claim and ... you don't have another horse for me do you? This one's about played out."

"Of course. Come on."

"Charles!" Maud Margaret called, running from the office quarters with her riding habit on. "Saddle Trumpet for me, too!"

"You cannot ..." he began, then changed it to, "Come on!"

* * *

They were too late. Millie Ringgold expired five hours before Lawless Laulis returned with the Gadsdens and nearly eighteen hours before Dr. Wyzczek Poska arrived in the wagon. "Up dis creek, the road she is not so good from the mine of the others," the doctor said.

From the moment of the Gadsden party's arrival, Maud Margaret folded the tear-streaked Naseby Ringgold against her bosom and wept with him.

Later, after the two men covered Millie with a blanket and the frightened boy's agony dwindled to anguished sobs, Charles laid his hand on Naseby's shoulder and asked, "Did your mother give you any instructions, young man?"

Naseby twisted away from the hated Englishman's hand as if in terror. Wide-eyed, glancing often over his shoulder, he found Maud Margaret; the woman took him in her arms. Between sobs, he said, "The last thing she said was for me to ... 'remember who you are ... and where you came from. And to remember where you're going ... and how to get there'."

54

Charles said, "Good advice, son. But did she give any instructions about where she wished to be buried?"

Naseby shook his tear-streaked head.

Laulis mumbled that he better get started on "scabbing together a coffin" while Maud Margaret sought a private moment with her husband. "We can't just leave him here, Charles."

He nodded. "I can see that. We'll take him back with us. Perhaps Weatherwax knows of relatives."

* * *

Millie Ringgold was laid to rest in the Utica Cemetery. Out of deference to the service the woman provided to the people of Yogo Village during the influenza epidemic of 1904, Charles Gadsden suspended mine operations on the day of the funeral. Millie's burial provided the social event of the season to the upper Judith Valley. Virtually the entire resident population of Yogo Village attended the funeral, augmented by many folks from the farms and ranches along the Judith's Middle Fork.

Naseby Ringgold left Yogo Gulch riding in a wagon carrying his mother's coffin. He had the clothes on his back, an apple box filled with books, and a bundle of personal belongings bound up in a tablecloth. He was also frightened spitless and, had not Maud Margaret Gadsden sat beside him on the buckboard's spring seat to provide both comfort and an occasional clean handkerchief, the youth might have bolted.

Back at the mining complex, Maud Margaret vetoed the idea that the frightened boy should be given space in the bunkhouse. "Can you not see, Charles, that he must be brought slowly into society. He has no skills with other people at all. To throw him in with all those men would drive him to a far worse and desperate end than I can imagine."

"And what would you have me do, Maud Margaret?"

"Fix him a cot in the office." At her husband's expression of horror, she added, "It would only be temporary, until he became comfortable in these surroundings."

But Naseby Ringgold's place in the office turned out to be not so temporary because the fourteen-year-old youth swiftly made himself indispensable: dusting, straightening, filing papers, keeping the ink pot filled, pen tips fresh and cleaned, window washed, floor scrubbed.

"Good God, Maud Margaret, when I'm there, he's all but invisible. I think I must frighten him, though sometimes I get the feeling that any fright might verge on dislike. But he must be hard at work every minute while I'm away." When she laughed, he added, "And I'll confess that I don't know how in the world I got along without him."

"Perhaps I should bring him upstairs, too."

"Perhaps you should. I don't know how many more scrubbings that downstairs floor can take without wearing through to the joists below."

* * *

It was during one of George Wells' periodic inspections that the New Mine Sapphire Syndicate's President murmured, "Well, well, what do we have here?"

Wells' manager stood to one side, hands clasped behind his back. "I suppose it is difficult to disguise any longer, sir, what with the walls going up. I've told Maud Margaret that it's going to be a new stable, but in truth she is to have a proper home. It's the manager's residence, George. What do you think?" He eyed his boss from an eye corner, without turning his head.

"Har-rumph," Wells growled. "I think it's deserving, yes. But I can't remember this coming across my desk for approval."

"No, sir, it didn't. The brick and stone are surplus here at the mine. So is most of the lumber, ordered for our big expansion of three years ago. I'm paying for the carpenters. They work for me, privately. The only things Johnson, Walker, and Tolhurst will buy will be windows, doors, and interior plumbing. And I had hoped to simply expense those things out over a period of time."

Wells "Harrumphed" again and said, "Invite me to the housewarming."

The new manager's residence was sited beyond the barns, beyond the stables, beyond the bunkhouses, mess hall, and equipment storage sheds. It sat on a spur of land that offered a splendid view of the valley below, the river, the road to the mine, and the mountains in three directions.

Gadsden piped water to the residence; it sported the first water closet in Judith Basin County; and had closet and cupboard doors that clicked shut with magnetic catches. There were five rooms in addition to the water closet: a parlor, dining room, kitchen, and two bedrooms. Three 30" X 48" 12-light casement windows afforded both splendid view and abundant light, while both Maud Margaret's kitchen and dining room contained additional windows.

The parlor displayed a five-piece framed and upholstered parlor suite, a solid oak extension table with matching chairs graced the dining room, while an Acme Regal Sterling range in 46" X 28" main top commanded the kitchen. Though the guest bedroom stood temporarily empty, the main bedroom contained an outsized polished brass bed, a vanity dresser with a large oval mirror and plush Turkish stool. There were also two matching solid oak wardrobes.

When Charles Gadsden carried Maud Margaret across the threshold he thought the wriggling woman would burst with happiness. The event occurred in the midst of a crowd of clapping well-wishers, both invited guests and gate-crashers, all of whom were immensely welcome to the housewarming.

Later in the evening George Wells caught his manager aside and asked, "Are you sure you can expense all of this, Charles? I mean, you have good taste, but this seems, well ..."

"Ostentatious?" Gadsden chuckled.

"Yes, yes. That's the word."

Charles clapped his superior on the back. "Trust me, George. Trust me. To be honest with you, most of it has already been expensed out over the past two years."

* * *

Naseby Ringgold proved a godsend to the Gadsdens during the housewarming and its cleanup, as well as during the move from office apartment to the new Manager's Residence. "He's indefatigable, Charles," Maud Margaret said. "He's up before daylight cleaning, helps me move all day, then cleans again for half the night. The silver is spotless. Our pewterware plates are polished as if they were fine China. He dusts. He mops. He ... do you suppose his mother really did serve America's Presidents?"

"For a fifteen-year-old he certainly does know how to work. I'm going to start training him to be my clerk as soon as everyone gets settled in. He's moving into our old apartment, you know."

She pouted, stamping a foot. "You cannot have him all the time! I'll need him at least two days each week, and any time we entertain."

Her husband smiled. "Perhaps we'll have to ask Naseby to train a helper. Then he could become a proper butler."

She giggled. "Won't Edward Keller's eyes goggle when next he chooses to visit America?"

Chapter Seven

Charles Gadsden's predictions about the productivity of farmlands acquired by the New Mine Sapphire Syndicate proved overwhelmingly true. Also placed in charge of overseeing farming on Syndicate lands formerly belonging to Bill Givens and Alvie Pedersen, Gadsden's farms turned into showplace examples during the first full season of his oversight, producing greater yields of grains per acre, more tons of hay, more potatoes, more turnips, more blue-ribbon cabbages.

Gadsden's success with farming supposedly damaged lands and the growing regard held for the English mine's operation further solidified his standing with the majority stockholders, Johnson, Walker, and Tolhurst, as well as with New Mine Syndicate President George Wells. As it turned out, it was a good thing the man wasn't given to self-satisfaction as arch-enemy Matthew Dunn continued to be a thorn to the stability of the world sapphire market by periodically dumping his Yogo American Sapphire Company's production in an attempt to keep his economically floundering enterprise from total hemorrhage. Then yet another former partner of the British company loomed on the horizon—Simeon S. Hobson.

When the Milwaukee Railroad punched a line through the Judith country, the town of Utica vied for the mainline route to Great Falls. Then the Great Northern Railway system pushed south through Judith Gap. With two railroads crossing within just a few miles of Utica, its townspeople, given considerable aid and comfort from the New Mine Sapphire Syndicate, began a perhaps too premature celebration.

With a Lewistown banker and state senator at its head, a new community of Hobson was formed twelve miles east, siting on one of Hobson's ranches and offering incentives, including a more direct route to Great Falls than the one suggesting a Utica waystop.

The strongest card Utica could play was the fact that the Yogo area's two sapphire mines were nearby, employing a total of well over one hundred men. That argument might have been persuasive, had not Matthew Dunn actively worked to persuade the railroads that any town rather than Utica would be their better choice.

"Dunn is crazy!" George Wells cried. "Utterly crazy! Why his own freight bill to his mine will be higher from Hobson than from Utica."

Charles Gadsden lifted his glass and said, "Cheers." Then he murmured, "I wonder what the bastard has in mind?"

What Dunn had in mind became clear two months into the following year when the Yogo American Sapphire Company threw itself on the mercy of the bankruptcy court. In the interim, however, his work to deny rail service to Utica meant higher freight bills to the English company's mine at Yogo Village.

* * *

"George," Charles Gadsden said as they assembled in London for a meeting with the Directors of the New Mine Sapphire Syndicate, "don't you think Hobson might be in a position to hurt us more than Dunn?"

Dolefully, Wells nodded. "I guess I'm the only one of the original four partners that holds no grudge against present owners."

Gadsden ran a comb through the black brush over his upper lip and wondered about the original lode discoverer. Was it Jake? he wondered. Yes, that's it: Jake. Jake Hoover. The meeting room's double doors swung wide and a servant said, "The gentlemen will see you now. Be kind enough to follow me."

Gadsden studied the usher as the man led them to their seats. Naseby does as well, he thought. Besides this man is quite old. I wonder if there's an age where a servant becomes too old?

"This is not a room designed for entertainment, Mr. Gadsden." It was Edward Keller, the barrister, speaking to him. "We'll be quite pleased to keep distractions to a minimum. Therefore, do tell us the moment you've satisfied your curiosity for Mr. Weystruth."

Blushing furiously, Charles nevertheless stared at and through Keller without responding.

"No tongue?" the barrister prompted.

"No interest, Mr. Keller."

"No interest? Surely you ..."

"Not at all, Mr. Keller. I simply have no interest in having a battle of wits with an unarmed opponent." One might've heard a sparrow's pinfeather squeaking as it drifted in a breeze.

Brownstone Tolhurst shrugged his elephantine frame near the head of the conference table and said, "Move along with it, Edward. If what is being said here is sufficient to duel over, I suggest you two take it up after the rest of us retire."

The subject, of course, was the fact of the New Mine Sapphire Syndicate's primary competitor falling into receivership. "Why," Keller said, "has the other company failed?"

Wells talked for some minutes covering the gamut from demand to marketing to stone quality to production methods. Finally Keller cut him off and asked for Gadsden's contribution.

"My opinion, sirs," Charles said after only the briefest hesitation, "is that their leader, Matthew Dunn, has been engaged in his own journey of revenge, engineered by a vast and intemperate egotism and triggered by a hatred for all things British, with particular focus on a single British-owned sapphire mining operation."

"My," Edward Keller breathed, "we have a philosopher in our midst."

"Shut up, Edward," Ernest Walker said. "If you cannot comport yourself decently, I'll ask you to leave the room."

Keller said evenly, "The chair recognizes the criticism and will henceforth endeavor to be more circumspect."

Brownstone Tolhurst sighed, "That was even tinged with sarcasm."

The ancient Walker, who Charles was mildly surprised to see still among the living, said, "Please continue, Mr. Gadsden."

Charles took a deep breath and said, "I understand nothing of gem marketing, and little about their cutting. But I flatter myself that I do know something of gem mining, and quite a lot about the recovery of stones in this setting. And stamps and crushers and acid vats notwithstanding, it can't be done, either profitably or qualitatively with any known method but ours.

"Dunn has always been, according to George here, too impatient, too opinionated, too egotistical. He failed to listen to experts when your own mining engineers told him stamps and crushers would damage too many stones and would impede the recovery process. Fortunately, Mr. Dunn chose to experiment with his theories with someone else's money in someone else's mine. That fact, in my opinion gentlemen, is the problem with the production end of the Yogo American venture."

A man Gadsden didn't know, sitting next to Tolhurst, waved a hand and was recognized by the chair. "Have you actually been on their ground, Mr. Gadsden? We're given to understand the host dike for the sapphires is badly fractured there. Can you give us any kind of analysis?"

Charles shook his head. "Dunn has given orders to keep trespassers away, even while his company is in receivership. I'm afraid it would take a court order for us to place an engineer on the ground."

"I wasn't talking of an engineer, sir," the man said. "I'm talking about you."

Charles smiled. "And, sir, I take that as a compliment. I can only tell you that—given the opportunity—I would be pleased to investigate the property on this board's behalf."

"Any other ques ..?" Keller began, when Gadsden continued:

"I do believe the vein is less clear, more jumbled than ours." He paused to marshal his thoughts. "One can observe the canyon's far wall from our ditch. And in the specific area where our ditch crosses the presumed sapphire-bearing dike, the canyon is nearly filled with broken and upset boulders and detritus. The Yogo American people even drove a tunnel into the hillside below our ditch, but failed to exploit it. "Therefore I feel they found little or nothing.

"Across the Yogo Creek Canyon from that point is obviously their primary point of operation. It's where their road leads. Several mine tunnels are observable and their rendering operations are located at the lowest surface level."

Ernest Walker's hand fluttered and the principal recognized. "Can you, sir, operate this mine profitably?"

Charles shook his head. "Not the way it's being operated now. But they have sapphires there, make no mistake about that.

And where there's sapphires, I believe I can tell you without equivocation that George and I—and the crew at your New Mine Sapphire Syndicate—can extract gems both profitably and expertly."

* * *

Johnson, Walker, and Tolhurst filed a formal letter of interest in bidding for the bankrupt Yogo American Sapphire Company. Charles Gadsden was given a court order to investigate the property for the bidders. And Johnson, Walker, and Tolhurst, Ltd. terminated Edward Keller's legal services.

By the time Gadsden's investigation was complete, 1910 had spun into 1911. And by the time other bidders had investigated the property, 1911 verged on 1912.

Finally the bankruptcy auction took place. The New Mine Sapphire Syndicate was the only bidder.

Chapter Eight

Naseby Ringgold turned eighteen the month following the English acquisition of the entire Yogo sapphire-bearing dike. Though the slender youth may have been eighteen, he could easily be mistaken for, say, twelve, or thirteen.

Always small for his age, he as yet bore no facial hair and the planes of his face were smooth and unblemished, without pimples or pox. The hair on his head—oddly, given the black hair of the boy's mother and father—was chestnut brown, and curly. He kept it trimmed so short that Maud Margaret more than once said, "Doesn't he look like a little Caesar with those close-cropped locks?" The boy's eyes were small and brown and close-set, the mouth unusually wide with lips fat and, though he kept them pinched much of the time, attesting to an African trace in his heritage.

To a close observer, however, Charles Gadsden's clerk (and Maud Margaret's house servant) appeared to have ancestors from southern Europe, say Italy or Spain, or perhaps Greece. And because he was so reticent, few would-be listeners had the opportunity to detect an accent, even if the silent servant had one, which he did not.

The truth was, Naseby Ringgold dwelled in constant fear. Charles Gadsden was one of the hated English who'd stolen his birthright, though the young man was troubled that the very nice Maud Margaret was married to the thief. From the time of his unwonted arrival at Yogo Village, Naseby's whole aim was to remain as invisible as he could make himself to be. Fortunately it was in that very aim that his mother's training proved of manifest importance.

"First make yourself indispensable," his mother told him

over and over. "Then eventually you'll turn invisible, even when you're standing in front of them."

Millie Ringgold's advice proved true. By making himself indispensable, the lad made a niche for himself within the Gadsden's office and household, avoiding the hard manual labor of others employed at the mine. On the job, he moved noiselessly about, saying nothing, anticipating his employers' moves so faultlessly—uncovering misplaced items or lost items before they were needed, sharpening pencils, replacing worn nibs on pens, refilling ink pots—until both Maud Margaret and Charles shook their heads at the boy's perspicacity and utility.

He became meticulous at filing reports and accessing needed memoranda from forgotten drawers. By the time Naseby had been of service in the office for three months, he'd brought an order to the command center that had not yet been achieved during the thirteen years of its previous existence.

When Naseby was obliged to take meals in the mess hall, as he usually was during those earlier years at Yogo Village, the silent boy was simply a shadow, eating quickly, refraining from conversation—unless accompanied by Pete Weatherwax—fastidiously cleaning up after himself. It helped that his protectors, Weatherwax and the Gadsdens, were considered either the most powerful individuals at the Village, or the most dangerous. It helped, too, that Naseby's mother had been widely esteemed by the men working the mines throughout the Yogo country, and that he himself was deemed inoffensive and perhaps helpless.

That Naseby Ringgold took his role seriously was beyond doubt after the Gadsden residence was finished and he took up duties there as a butler during formal affairs. "Charles!" Maud Margaret fiercely whispered. "You must see Naseby! He's wearing a tuxedo with tails."

"What?" Charles said, breaking off a discussion with a Judith Basin County Commissioner. "What did you say?"

"Go take a look at Naseby. You'll see what I mean."

Charles did, weaving through the crowd, returning minutes later with a huge grin. "I wonder what that cost him?"

"I wonder that he did it!"

"He's an enigma," Charles mused. "But I'm glad he's our enigma."

After the Gadsdens moved to their new residence and Naseby was accorded their old living space over the office, the young man became even more reclusive, usually cooking and eating in his own kitchen. His idle time was spent reading. Already an avid reader before arriving at the sapphire mine, he found Yogo Village a veritable cornucopia of books; certainly so when compared to the Yogo Gulch of his birthplace. There were Dickenses and Scotts and Coopers. He obtained Twain, more Alger. He discovered Robert Service and his poems of the Yukon, where Naseby's father died. The young man read translations of Cervantes and Hugo and even a Tolstoy. Then he ordered a copy of Gibbons' *Rise and Fall of the Roman Empire*.

One day, Maud Margaret visited the office. Obviously the woman had something on her mind. "Uhm?" Charles murmured.

"Look at Naseby," she said. Naseby stopped filing papers to consider the woman. Meanwhile Charles placed one hand flat on his desktop and dropped the report he was reading. "He's not getting enough outdoors air," she continued. "Not enough sunlight. Naseby, dear, you must spend time outside. Otherwise you'll simply shrivel to something less than you are now."

Naseby began filing papers again and Charles picked up his report. She marched to her husband's side and cried, "Don't you see? He's pallid. He needs exercise."

Charles sighed. "What shall I do, Maud Margaret? Send him to shovel muck or work as a teamster? Sending him into the mine won't solve the sunlight problem. I suppose I could put him as a cook's helper in the mess hall, but that'll hardly solve what you see as his need to get outdoors. And it would certainly create problems for me to lose my clerk."

"Naseby, are you listening," she said.

"Yes ma'am."

"You must walk about the grounds. Even if you would just read a little outside in the sunlight it would help."

"Yes ma'am."

"Will you try?"

"Yes ma'am, I'll try."

So Charles began using his clerk as a messenger. Though by then, the mining complex had its own internal telephone system, the manager found ample opportunity to send Naseby on errands he'd normally do himself. By that means Naseby Ringgold learned much of the surface workings of the sapphire mine. The trestle-and-tramway system for ore transportation to the weathering heaps, the heaps themselves, the tailings dams and sluice boxes, the "grizzly" sizing grate, the wooden rocker. He was able to watch the rough stones being sorted by hand. And sometimes he accompanied Charles Gadsden when he led visitors through the mine. He watched the no-nonsense manager complete the tour, then demand that each visitor turn his pockets inside-out. He saw visitors bluster, then try to laugh it off as a joke when highgraded rough stones appeared as if by magic from a pocket. He even saw the short-tempered mine manager grab a local preacher by the throat when the man tried to use his status as a man of the cloth as being beyond approach by mere mortal men. Then Naseby's eyes widened as twin sapphires the size of pigeon eggs turned up in the terrified preacher's pockets.

Naseby visited the barns and stables and storage sheds of the complex. He spent time in the blacksmith shop watching horses being shod and mules' hoofs being trimmed. And eventually a time came when Naseby Ringgold was as familiar as Pete Weatherwax and Charles Gadsden with every above-ground facility and workman of the New Mine Sapphire Syndicate's operation at Yogo Village.

And the young man dreamed. He dreamed that it was all his. He dreamed that he was the one sending strongboxes filled with rough sapphires to be loaded on the Utica Stage. He dreamed that his father were still alive and strolling about Yogo Village, nodding with approval as Naseby flawlessly managed the mine and its workmen, coping with emergencies, overseeing sorting and grading of the precious stones, assigning armed guards to oversee sapphire transport.

The young man's most cogent dreams came of an evening when he poured his own hoard of forty-three uncut sapphires left among his mother's effects and carefully bundled, along with the twelve hundred dollars remaining from the money Jake Hoover had left for Millie and their son, in a tablecloth when his mother's body was taken from Yogo Gulch forever. Sorting through his stones and dreaming, Naseby Ringgold's mind seamed flawlessly on: In his mind he established cutting operations at Yogo Village, bringing in Dutch lapidaries from the Low countries and German gemsmiths from Schleswig-Holstein to facet the stones. It was but a short leap from in-house faceting to jewelry design and manufacture. The Ringgold sales force radiated out from Yogo Village all across America, and Europe, and the Far East. Meanwhile, in his dreams, Naseby's aging father and mother sat in the sunshine of the Yogo's residency porch and nodded their pride at the accomplishments of their son.

* * *

All Maud Margaret and Charles Gadsden's efforts to bring their clerk and servant into early 20th Century society proved of little success. Naseby Ringgold preferred only two things: 1) to work in service to those who held the power, and 2) to be alone to read and dream.

He was, of course intelligent. He read newspapers and magazines, as well as books. But what did "labor unrest in Chicago" really mean? What was an "assembly line" and how did it work? What and why was the growing turmoil in Europe? Geographically, he knew where Japan was, but nothing of the Japanese. Mohammedans? Something to do with Sultans and harems—whatever they were. He knew nothing of trade embargoes, even less about their nationalistic need. He understood the international cry for freedom, but was utterly unaware of the processes of upheaval and violence that attended implementation of that human dream. He knew a great deal about *things*, and nothing at all of their *cause* and *effect*.

Neither did he know about girls, about their cause and effect. True, he admired Maud Margaret and had very much loved his mother, but he hardly noticed the girls attending his mother's funeral and they noticed him not at all. True, the Gadsdens held an occasional social gathering where members of the opposite sex were present, but most were elderly and the ones who weren't so old uniformly failed to take note of the invisible butler who was engaged in a trade in which they thought no respectable American would take.

* * *

It was mid-July of 1914. A U.S. Minerals Survey Pamphlet on gem faceting lay near his right hand, the lamp pulled to the table's center. The smooth-faced young man held his largest sapphire to the light, trying to judge how a gem cutter would facet the stone. He'd read of protruding and receding angles, parallel striate, flanges; he knew some sapphires from other regions carried cloudy or opaque patches and that their removal could considerably lessen the stone's weight and sometimes its color, yet enhance its value. But how to learn?

The door to his apartment swung open. Charles Gadsden said, "Naseby, I need you to ..."

It was as if both men were caught in the sudden glare of an open furnace door. Naseby's fingers were still poised to the light, but his face was swung to the side, to his employer. Gadsden's eyes flew wide, then transfixed his clerk as if he'd thrown a spear. "You bloody little ..." The elder man gagged, but his face turned purple as he rushed forward. "You bastard! A thief in my own household!"

Naseby leaped up, so frightened he barely gasped, "They're mine!"

Then Gadsden had him by the shirtfront, twisting, throwing him onto his cot, growling, "If there's one thing I hate worse than a thief, it's a liar!" The manager turned to the table and swept the sapphires into his hands and stuffed them in his pocket.

Still red, he whirled back as Naseby struggled to his feet crying, "THEY'RE MINE! THEY'RE MINE!"

Gadsden kicked the youth in the pit of his stomach, knocking him back to the cot. "You stay there!" he snarled. "I'll be back in a minute!" And he rushed out, slamming the apartment door on his way out.

Only a few moments later, the manager was back, kicking open the door. He held the Harrington & Richardson Bayonet Revolver in one hand, a pair of handcuffs swung from the other.

But the only thing moving in the apartment was Maud Margaret's embroidered curtains wafting at the open window.

Chapter Nine

It was Charles Gadsden himself who turned steam into the fire whistles, bringing men tumbling from the bunkhouse, the barns, the stable, cooks and their helpers from the mess hall. When the alarmed men had gathered to discover where to direct their firefighting efforts, Gadsden told them they had a thief in their midst and he wanted him collared.

The manager saw Maud Margaret, holding her skirts above her ankles, struggling toward the office. "It's Ringgold," he cried. "I caught him red-handed in the act."

"You can't mean Naseby," someone called from the crowd.

Gadsden raised his voice so there could be no doubt. "I do mean Naseby Ringgold. I caught him with a bunch of raw stones. Obviously he's been at it for some time."

There was a stirring from the rear as a malevolent scarecrow pushed through the throng. "What's this about Naseby?" Pete Weatherwax growled.

"Damn!" Charles Gadsden cried. "How many times do I have to repeat this? Naseby Ringgold was stealing sapphires. He's away into the night and I want him brought back."

The security man pushed his way to the front. Maud Margaret, fist to mouth, followed in the man's wake. "What sapphires?" Weatherwax asked. "Where did you find him stealing sapphires?"

Gadsden actually hopped up and down in anger. "I don't have time for this. Leland, I want you to ..."

The malevolent scarecrow cut him off. "Gadsden, you son-of-a-bitch, where did you find Naseby stealing stones?"

An absolute hush fell over the crowd. Gadsden's eyes

narrowed. He took a step forward and was met by Weatherwax who did the same. One of the security man's eyes was at half-mast, the other stared down his long nose at his boss.

"It was in his room," Gadsden finally said. "He had them on the table and ..."

Weatherwax's voice started somewhere deep within his thin frame and blew out in a roar: "YOU GODDAMNED DIMWITTED BASTARD! YOU ASSHOLE OF THE EARTH! YOU ... YOU ..."

Gadsden leaped forward to grasp Weatherwax's shirtfront and was met by a revolver barrel thrust with force into the pit of his stomach. Gasping, the mine manager released Weatherwax's shirt and stepped back, widened eyes on the gun. "You're fired," he said, barely audible.

"Hell," Weatherwax said, "I quit. I wouldn't work here one more day, now that I know what a greedy stupid bastard I work for." He paused for breath, then blew it out in a mighty roar: "THEM SAPPHIRES WERE *HIS* YOU STUPID BASTARD! DON'T YOU KNOW WHO HE IS? HE'S JAKE HOOVER'S SON! JAKE! THAT'S THE JAKE HOOVER WHO DISCOVERED THIS GODDAMNED MINE."

When he paused again, Gadsden said, "My wife is present, Mr. Weatherwax. I'll ask you to hold your swearing to a minimum."

Pete twisted, thrusting his revolver back into its holster, swept off his hat and said, "Beg your pardon ma'am. It must be goddamned embarrassing to you to have to sleep with such an ignorant sonofabitch as your husband."

Then he swung back to lean his long nose to the manager and snarl, "I gave some o' them sapphires to Millie myself. They were in Jake's things that were returned here when he died in the Yukon. And I happen to know Jake gave her others before him and Hobson ever filed on the claims. How many did you find? Forty? Fifty?"

Gadsden wiped a hand over his face. Though he'd not actually counted the sapphires that were now in his pocket, he suspected the number suggested by his security man was eerily close to the same. Maud Margaret pushed around Weatherwax to grasp her husband's arm. She was sobbing. "I've made a mistake," the manager muttered. Then louder: "I've made a terrible mistake men. I've unjustly accused that boy and he's in flight somewhere out there because of it."

The men shuffled, not knowing what to do. Gadsden met every eye, voice rising, "I called you here to run down a thief. I still want him found. But I want him found now so that I may beg his forgiveness."

Weatherwax started back through the crowd. "Pete!" Gadsden called. "Will you help?"

"Not me," the sinister-looking security man said without pausing or turning. "I won't waste any more time than I have to to get shut of you and this goddamned place."

* * *

Unaware of events back at Yogo Village, Naseby Ringgold, ears filled with the scream of steam whistles, trotted down the road to Utica, washed with hatred for Charles Gadsden and all things British. Flight, as he saw it, was his only alternative.

True, he was innocent. But what did that mean in a court controlled by English justice? Charles Gadsden was the most powerful man Naseby Ringgold had ever known. Earlier that evening the brute had slapped him, pushed him down, kicked him. Obviously he had also assembled the workforce at the Yogo Mine and was, by now, turning all seventy-five of them out to bring the fugitive in. What other course but flight could he follow? He didn't even know if he could call Pete Weatherwax his friend any longer. Certainly Maud Margaret would be aligned against him. He had no other friend, no other champion.

What he did have, though, was nearly twelve hundred dollars rolled up in the pocket of his trousers. Thank God he'd had the presence of mind to jerk it from beneath his mattress before dashing for the window. But what should he do now? Of course the roads would be watched. He thought of circling back around the sapphire mine into Yogo Gulch. Though he knew the lay of the Gulch intimately, all that would do is thrust his neck farther into the Englishman's noose.

What of the railroads? Again he shook his head. Even if he made it to either of the two competing rail lines, Gadsden would have men watching the stations so closely he'd dare not buy a ticket. And though he knew nothing about riding the rails or hopping boxcars, Naseby thought he could learn—except that Gadsden would surely think of that, too.

Now the fugitive's earlier life proved of enormous benefit: raised in one of the most remote locations in a remote region of the unknown West, accustomed to a solitary and exceedingly self-sufficient environment by a mother who insisted that she equip her only child with every tool for survival against odds. Naseby Ringgold not only knew how to survive; he knew how to endure.

Naseby slept in haymows during the days and hiked steadily north, down the Judith Valley at night, stealing what he needed when he needed it from farms and ranches along the way. He was barked at by dogs, chased by bulls. But eventually, three weeks after beginning his flight, Naseby reached the Missouri River at Judith Landing. As day turned to night, the fugitive liberated a weathered, leaky rowboat that had obviously not been used for some time and set off across the river. After reaching the north shore, the rowboat was pushed back into the current to disappear downstream.

He passed through the Bearpaw Mountains by following the route from Cow Island, taken little more than three decades before by Chief Joseph's fleeing Nez Perce. Finally, at Havre, the ragged disheveled youth, spotting no "wanted" poster with his name on it, chanced entering a store. Actually the fugitive visited several stores, for he proved too cagey to purchase more than one or two items from any one store, rightly thinking that a ragged young man like him might arouse suspicion by exhibiting a great deal of money.

After resting a few days while camped near Havre, Naseby Ringgold plodded north, into Canada. He crossed the border far from any customs station, then caught a stagecoach from Willow Creek north to the Canadian Pacific mainline at Medicine Hat. At Medicine Hat, the fugitive purchased a ticket to Toronto and the anonymity of a large city.

During all those miles and all that time, Naseby Ringgold thought of the sapphires stolen from his father, as well as those stolen from him. During all that time, the young man's hatred for the English continued to fester.

* * *

Naseby Ringgold wasn't the only one thinking of stolen sapphires. From the moment Charles Gadsden learned of his horrible mistake, he heard little else but the boy screaming, "THEY'RE MINE! THEY'RE MINE!" And how he'd thrown the boy to his cot, then kicked him back down again as the youngster struggled to his feet.

True to his word, the mine manager sent his men fanning out in every direction—to no avail. He halved the searchers on day two, sending half back into the mine and the other half farther out, to the railroad lines at Hobson and Lewistown.

When he tried to enlist help from the law enforcement agencies of Judith Basin and Fergus Counties, the officers laughed at him, saying "Where's the crime, Gadsden? We bring in robbers and murderers, not runaway kids who are already adults."

Charles Gadsden did not mind that he became a laughingstock to the people of the Judith country. For one thing, he felt he deserved their disparagement; for another, he was too strong-willed to care what others might think. To his mind, public ridicule was but a small price to pay if he could somehow gain the chance to make up to the lad for his great injustice. And most of all, Charles Gadsden was helpless to console his heartbroken wife.

After a week went by, Gadsden advertised for the boy in every newspaper for a hundred miles in every direction. The ad was clearly marked as Charles Gadsden asking forgiveness from Naseby Ringgold. The Yogo Sapphire Mine manager begged to be given the opportunity to make restitution.

Finally, after three weeks, Gadsden quit searching for Naseby Ringgold and focused again on his primary duty: shipping Yogo sapphires to Johnson, Walker, and Tolhurst, Ltd. in London, England.

When Maud Margaret cried, "He was like a son to us, Charles! He must be out there somewhere!"

Gadsden took his wife by the arms and shook her. "Stone the bloody crows, woman, I know that. But we have our lives to live, too. And work to do."

When she sank sobbing into Naseby's old office chair, he leaned against Naseby's desk and said, "I'm trying to bring him back, Maud Margaret. If I could get the boy back I would lick his boots and more than make up for the gems I mistakenly took from him. But suppose we cannot find him; suppose we do not get him back even if we do find him; suppose we fail to make up to him for the great injustice I did to him—what then? Are we to dry up and blow away? Do we return to England and hide in a loft apartment in Pickadilly? Life is for the living, woman."

He sighed. "I greatly regret what was done, stand willing to rectify the injustice in any way possible, pray to do so. But if I cannot, it's not because I will not, it's because I cannot. Beyond that, I—we—must get on with our lives. That means me returning to running this mine with a vengeance. And I hope it means you continuing to stand by my side as you have done for the last decade."

She pushed wearily to her feet and threw herself into his arms.

* * *

Serendipity attended Naseby Ringgold in his travels. Had anyone known the young man carried such a prodigious roll of money, most would've been only too keen to relieve him of it. But in the beginning, he appeared in little more than rags. And when he finally was able to make his first clothing purchase in the railroad town of Havre, the only clothing offered were those of farmers or ranchers or railroaders—workmen's clothing. In addition, the frail young man had to choose from children's sizes. So when he hit the road again, he appeared little more than a yokel on his way home from a visit to the neighboring farm. And in Toronto, Naseby's conversion from yokel to servant to the wealthy was swift and so sure that his appearance again evoked nothing unusual.

If Naseby Ringgold wished to forget about all things English, Toronto, in the province of Ontario, Canada was hardly the place to do so. *If Naseby Ringgold wished to forget.* But he did not. Naseby Ringgold wanted to hate the English, wanted to be consumed by that hatred, wanted vengeance. And one must remember that Naseby Ringgold was a dreamer. All the months he starved and struggled northward—down the Judith River Valley and across the wide Missouri, up through the Bearpaws, up the Milk River into Canada, border hopping into a foreign country, and finally across Canada—the young man dreamed of little else except the vengeance he would extract.

Most of his daydreams were poppycock, of course; the young are given to such dreamworld foolishness. But all of his dreaming was not foolish. Certainly the part of his plan where he would insinuate himself into the households of the men who commanded Johnson, Walker, and Tolhurst, Ltd. was hardly an idle dream. In his training as a servant, Naseby Ringgold had the means to do just that. Now all he needed was proper contact.

The Great War was to prove enormously beneficial in implementing his plan. The Archduke's assassination in Sarajevo that triggered World War I occurred only three months before Naseby's arrival in Toronto. The Dominion was swept with patriotism for the Mother Country and Canada's first draft volunteers totaled thirty-three thousand of their finest young men. The result was that labor was in short supply throughout the Dominion. Especially short was the supply of young men in service industries. And in even shorter supply yet were young men in the service industries who weren't subject to a Canadian Army draft.

When Naseby Ringgold arrived in Toronto, he immediately visited expensive haberdashers and outfitted himself with an impeccable line of suitable clothing for service to the rich. His greatest problem, however, lay in a search for the means to acquire proper documents, which, of necessity, meant counterfeit documents. Here again, strategic planning was the key.

First he ripped three-corner tears in his yokel clothing and picked seam-threads loose. Then he covered himself with filth. Carrying only a few American silver dollars, he made underworld contact along the Mississauga wharves. When sneered at and pushed aside, he shamelessly begged, insinuating that he was a polished pickpocket who could liberate sufficient funds to pay for the documents needed. When told to show the color of his money, Naseby dropped three silver dollars into the contact's palm and promised to have more the following day.

On the morrow, after converting a modest amount of his American money to English pounds, he was back with a twenty pound note. When the contact shook him down for more and found none, Naseby cried huge tears and promised that he would have the final twenty pounds the following day if the contact would produce suitable documents.

The contact tried following Naseby but lost the nimble youth in the teeming street crowds. The following day, the contact met Naseby at their agreed transfer point, in the tower at the Exhibition Park. Naseby examined the documents while the contact nervously eyed passersby. Finally Naseby turned over a last twenty-pound note and took his leave.

This time the contact had two assistants who picked up the trail of the youth who now carried documents with the name Nathan Kenneth Ringling. But Naseby anticipated the attempts to follow him and disappeared amid multiple streetcar transfers and quick back alley dashes.

* * *

Within days, Ringgold, using his new alias was employed as a liveried footman in the household of Sir William MacLeish Macdonald, formerly Chancellor of the University of Toronto and a Senator in the Canadian government. Macdonald was an aging man, appointed to the Senate for life, as were all Canadian Senators of that period. Unfortunately the 'for life' period of Macdonald's appointment had but a few weeks left to run—but not before the grace and efficiency of the Senator's newest servant attracted the envy of his peers.

After Macdonald's demise, Naseby was offered the under butler's position on the Ramsey Douglas estate. And only six months later, the young man known as Nathan Kenneth Ringling took service as a valet butler in the household of Ontario's leading gem merchant, Johann Vincent Abrahamson. In every case the silent, unassuming, discreet young man proved a near faultless tribute to his profession. And when the expert and experienced Nathan Kenneth Ringling determined to take ship for England, he carried recommendations from three distinguished Canadian 'houses', one of which was a leading Canadian wholesale purchaser of finished gems from the most prestigious London merchant of all, Messrs. Johnson, Walker, and Tolhurst, Ltd.

Chapter Ten

One might assume the cutting and marketing of high-quality gems located in The Netherlands because of careful, thoughtful craft development by the stolid Dutch burghers centered around the Low Country estuaries of the Lower Rhine and other nearby streams. But the real truth for establishing the foremost world center for precious gems in Amsterdam is more convoluted, and much farther reaching. It's a story going back to the Jews captivity in King Nebuchadnezzar's Babylon. The tale's threads run throughout the Diaspora as the Jewish people were knocked from pillar to post; the Medes and Persians, Romans and Visigoths, Turks and Syrians; the Crusaders, the Moors, the Spanish Inquisitors. Woe especially unto Jews washed by the Diaspora into Middle and Eastern Europe: Russia, Poland, Ukraine, Germany.

Throughout much of the exile in foreign lands, Jews experienced varying degrees of persecution. Seldom were they permitted to own land, neither were they allowed into most trades; no Jew could be a wheelwright or carriage maker, a potter or chimney sweep. In many countries Jews were excluded from the army. In others they were, each night, enclosed behind walls with locked gates. During the Bubonic Plague that swept Europe during the 1350s, Jews were accused of causing the so-called "black death" by poisoning wells, and were massacred in the tens of thousands by their frightened, paranoid neighbors.

Jewish response to not being permitted to farm or enter a trade has always been to focus on learning. Ironically that necessity led to the production of a fascinating galaxy of minor luminaries within each society: philosophers, physicians, pharmacists, surgeons, mathematicians, cartographers, engravers, historians, dramatists, and poets. Thus it was that the discriminatory practices instituted against local Jewish communities led to their preparation to become leaders in later renditions of those same communities.

Oddly, the discriminatory systems they often found themselves in also prepared Jews to become money-lenders and economic mercenaries. Here's why:

As ironic as we might think it today, Medieval Christian doctrine forbade Christians to accept interest on loans. As a consequence, Jews were the only citizenry both willing and able—and thus permitted—to engage in money lending. Naturally the royal treasuries took a large percent of the profits ... and it was the Jew who bore all popular resentment against "usurers".

Because of their relatively high educational level and necessary practical training, many societies found Jews useful at court and in government. But such positions also found them handy scapegoats when circumstances required.

The Christian Visigoths had all but wiped out Jews from communities in the Iberian Peninsula that dated from Roman times. But when the Arabs overran North Africa and swept into Spain, they proved tolerant in their treatment of Jews. That tolerance led to a flourishing of the arts and literature; a renaissance within a culture. Such cultural flowerings historically occurred when the Jewish community experienced a measure of liberty in the midst of another society.

But problems loomed on the horizon. Muslim religious leaders and many common people resented the authority entrusted by their monarchs to Jewish statesmen and bankers. Then came the Almohads, a fanatical sect from North Africa who took control of Muslim Spain. The Almohads brought with them three choices for the Jews: conversion to Islam, martyrdom, or flight. Many found a precarious refuge in northern Spain, where Christian rulers found Jews useful to them in their efforts to reconquer the peninsula.

All was tolerable for the Jewish emigrants, called Marranos (Spanish for swine) until the last Muslim ruler was driven from Spain and the peninsula united under Ferdinand and Isabella. Marranos who'd risen to high posts as ministers at court were spied upon and harassed. Fanaticism continually stirred Spanish mobs until Spanish and Portuguese Inquisitions came into play during the late Fifteenth Century. Again Jews were given three choices: conversion (this time to Christendom), burning at stake, or flight.

One problem with flight was that Jews were running out of places to which they might flee. By that time, Spain controlled much of Western Europe. What was left was shaky for any Jew. As soon as Christian moneylenders learned how to manage interest rates and collect mortgages, Jews became merely another superfluous minority who was expelled from England in 1290 and France in 1394. In the German states, life was uncertain. In Poland and Russia and the Ukraine it was intolerable.

In 1568 an eighty-years war erupted between Spain and a series of Low Country provinces that became The Netherlands. The revolt was prompted by Spanish King Philip II's insistence on countering a spreading Protestant influence by implementing the Spanish Inquisition on his subjects who were Papal disbelievers. The Dutch were aided in their revolt by an alliance with England. And with the 1588 destruction of the Spanish Armada during Spain's attempted invasion of England, Dutch freedom was secured (though not recognized by Spain for sixty years, until yet another Spanish fleet was destroyed, this time by a Dutch naval force).

A free and independent Netherlands held out three great attractions for the Jewish refugees who, in the early 1590s began arriving from the Portuguese and Spanish Inquisitions:

One was the tolerance afforded by the Dutch state for minorities to openly practice their religions (the Puritans found a home in Holland, too). For the Jews, such tolerance meant they could build synagogues and openly worship in a manner that their forefathers were forced to abandon in Spain and Portugal.

Two was the great economic opportunities citizens were afforded as the tiny country became the world's leading commercial state, as well as a great maritime power.

Three was the cultural flowering accompanying such material prosperity.

* * *

All the foregoing about Jews and the political consequences of their Diaspora is interesting, but thus far there's only a weak connection to why Amsterdam became the world center for high-quality gem cutting and marketing. That secret lies in Jewish history:

Remember the Babylonian bazaar where Abdullah the gem merchant first learned to judge gem weights by measuring them against the weight of carob seeds? Perhaps, too, one will recall how the Jewish people first began their Diaspora by being led into captivity in that same Babylon. Thus the Jews were on hand when the Chaldeans of Babylon became the first great Middle Eastern trading nation.

It's interesting to also note that for most of man's history, India, Ceylon, Burma, and Siam were where most precious gemstones worn in crowns and pendants, belts and rings of royalty originated. To reach the Royal fingers found in the Fertile Crescent, Egypt, and along the Phoenician coast, camel caravans must transport those rough gemstones across Persia, or

86

by trading vessels rounding the horn of India and up the Persian Gulf. Either way, those gemstones passed through Babylon. And either way, those rough gemstones were cut and polished by Babylonians. No matter whether handled by the Chaldeans of Nebuchadnezzar or the Assyrians of Senacherib, the Jews were there, first as slaves, then as craftsmen, and finally as merchants, vendors, and money lenders. When Babylon was overrun by the Medes from Persia, the Jews were there. When Alexander's Macedonian phalanxes came knocking, the Jews were there.

They became experts in appraising, cutting, and faceting gemstones, experts in setting those cut and polished rubies, sapphires, and diamonds in gold necklaces, rings, scepters, and crowns. When the Romans arrived, Jewish merchants and craftsmen were there to provide them with jewels to carry into Egypt and the Orient.

Eventually the Jews left Babylon's crossroads for the Romans and Parthians to slay themselves over, settling elsewhere. And their gemstone knowledge and craft knowledge of appraisal and cutting went with them. They wound up among the Ottoman Turks and eventually followed the Arabs into the far southwest corner of Europe, arriving amid the Iberian Peninsula at the same time Europe passed from the medieval Middle Ages into the luxury and opulence of the Renaissance.

As luck had it, the Jews later discovered a haven from persecution in The Netherlands just as that little nation flowered. What the Jews brought with them was centuries of experience in the gem trade. More importantly, they brought penetration through merchant-contacts into the Ottoman Empire, thus breaking Muslim trade embargoes. In addition, the refugees brought connections to Portuguese traders who held a virtual monopoly on raw gems and spices from India and the Far East.

In short, the Jewish gem cutters and merchants arrived at

the right place at the right time, just as European nations began their domination of world trade.

Amsterdam did not select the Jewish gem traders as much as those gem traders chose Amsterdam. By the time Jake Hoover stumbled onto Montana's Yogo sapphire lode and Cecil Rhodes was assembling his De Beers diamond cartel in South Africa, the city by the Zuider Zee had almost two hundred years of history as the world's leading gem center.

And when precious gems began pouring in like tidal waves, Amsterdam was ready.

Chapter Eleven

In all world history, one would be hard put to identify a more successful commercial advertising and promotional success than that achieved by the De Beers diamond cartel, founded by Cecil John Rhodes in Kimberley, South Africa, beginning in 1888.

Ridiculous one might say, recollecting just a few of the world's most famous monopolies: Standard Oil, the Honourable East India Company, the Dutch East India Company. However, Standard Oil was first with most on the scene of a world-changing new order (combustion engines running on petroleum spawning much of what we know as the Industrial Revolution), and the two State sponsored Indies trading companies were monopolies granted by England and The Netherlands. Each actually began at the top and maintained their position by dominating their rivals through ruthless manipulation and sharp trading practices.

Alfred Beit and Cecil Rhodes merged their two mining companies to form De Beers Consolidated Mines. At the time, the merged company was the sole owner of all diamond operations in South Africa. The De Beers name stemmed from two brothers, Boers whose farm had turned into one of the richest operations in the new company's amalgam of mines. The brothers, who sold their claim, had no involvement with the company that came to bear their name.

That company, De Beers, however, began their gem merchandising career as what could be called also-rans, peddling diamonds in the world of precious stones against more established, more desired colored gems, such as red rubies, blue sapphires, and green emeralds. Rhodes' initial genius was to tie

South African production into one giant cartel until his cartel controlled, at his death in 1902, over ninety percent of the entire world's production of diamonds.

But what might arguably have been the most salient exercise of Rhodes' genius was when he determined to take on the world's taste for colored gemstones with his diamonds. That decision spawned what could arguably be described as the world's most successful advertising and promotional campaign—ever! It's a campaign still going on a century after it began: "Diamonds Are Forever," "Diamonds Are A Girl's Best Friend." De Beers sent promotional letters to European royalty and Oriental potentates extolling the "sparkle" of diamonds compared to other gemstones. They promoted the diamond's hardness over any other gem: "Diamonds will scratch a ruby and sapphire; but only a diamond can scratch another diamond."

De Beers actually had a hand in the birth of an industry devoted to advertising, employing dozens of advertising agencies throughout the world that competed for the diamond producer's favors.

The South African mining behemoth's sales staff fanned out around the globe. Those diamond salesmen struck fertile ground in America, where there was little history of gem-studded diadems or scepters, but whose populace harbored a burgeoning prosperity and a wistful wish to clamber social ladders to social mores set by sophisticates across the broad waters; even to blacken the eye of European pretentiousness. Along the way, diamonds became the predominant gem for American engagement and wedding rings.

Japan proved receptive to diamond sales propaganda, too, thus breaking Oriental resistance to anything but rubies and sapphires. Diamonds therefore morphed into the gemstone of choice for Japanese expressions of love.

Inroads to royal acceptance of diamonds in Europe and South Asia was, initially, an uphill battle for De Beers, but their unceasing advertising and promotional campaigns proved pioneering trail blazers decades before Madison Avenue arrived on the scene. Still, as innovative and earth shaking as the diamond goliath's promotional campaigns were, they could not have been as effective without De Beers relentless, ruthless, monopolistic practices to control diamond supply to the world market.

From their outset, De Beers has been embroiled in controversy: price fixing, antitrust behavior, even the charge that the company withheld industrial diamonds essential to the war effort from allied countries during a World War. The company used it's dominant position to manipulate the international diamond market, including convincing independent producers to join its single channel monopoly, and flooding the market with diamonds similar to those of producers who refused to join their cartel. Finally, De Beers purchased and stockpiled diamonds produced by other manufacturers in order to control prices by limiting supply to the world market.

Politically, the De Beers Company proved heavyweights in South Africa, Botswana, Rhodesia, Angola, and Namibia. And thus far, we've only been discussing the company's more *savory* practices.

The argument could easily be made that the De Beers diamond cartel were accused of following practices that were no different from those most monopolies have pursued throughout history, and it would be true. Except for one thing: Cecil Rhodes and his company operated in a social and political environment without the normal checks and balances inherent in more established environs. Consider the Jameson Raid:

On December 29, 1895, a 600-man armed band of

91

Rhodesian and Bechuanaland police, led by Leander Star Jameson and encouraged by the then Governor of the Cape Colony, Cecil Rhodes, crossed the border between Rhodesia and Transvaal, hoping to incite an insurrection by the primarily British expatriate workers in the gold fields around Johannesburg. The Jameson band was met by hastily formed Boer "Commandos" who roundly defeated the raiders in two decisive battles, killing many and capturing the remainder, including Jameson and Cecil Rhodes' brother, an English army colonel.

The real objective of the Jameson Raiders was to seize the extremely lucrative gold fields of the Witwatersrand. In essence, the withdrawal of police forces from Matabeleland (north of the Transvaal) encouraged the Matabele to revolt, torching the frontier and slaughtering hundreds of European settlers over the next year and a half. Therefore, shocks from the Jameson Raid, spread far beyond the Transvaal. The raid is considered by many to be the actual first skirmish of the Boer War that engulfed South Africa two years later.

Such was the ambition of Cecil Rhodes....

Such was the founding principles of the gigantic diamond cartel he was busily forging....

Chapter Twelve

Unlike the single-minded focus of Cecil Rhodes in creating a colossus with his De Beers diamond cartel, a sapphire monopoly was only fitfully pursued by Messrs. Johnson, Walker, and Tolhurst, Ltd. though their discovery building blocks were remarkably similar. Why?

The firm established by Sir Warfield Anthony Johnson in 1738 was, after all, the world's foremost jewelry manufacturer, as well as the leading wholesaler of precious gems. In addition, it was the claim of Messrs. Johnson, Walker, and Tolhurst that their firm was the world's leading jewelry retailer.

"Should we care who produces the raw stones," Brownstone Tolhurst was heard to ask, "as long as they pass through our hands on their way to market?"

"True," Ernest Walker nodded, adding, "Our objective is wholesale distribution of polished gems, jewelry manufacture, and retail sales. Do we comport ourselves well by becoming involved in discovery and development?"

The complacency of the foremost two principals in Johnson, Walker, and Tolhurst, Ltd. is better understood by knowing their gem marketing system was nonpareil throughout the royal households of Europe and the Near East. Coupling that sales dominance with a precious stone funnel from all around the Orient to Messrs. Johnson, Walker, and Tolhurst's offices at #16 Hatton Garden would naturally provide opportunity for complacency. Then add the firm's very close working arrangement with what was generally recognized as the world's foremost gem faceting and polishing firm of Verenigen Boas Von Den Sprecht at Hogehilweg 12, in Amsterdam and one sees creeping smugness overtaking complacence among the leaders of Messrs. Johnson, Walker, and Tolhurst, Ltd.

That smugness remained in place until the firm's sales staff began returning from abroad with fewer and fewer orders for their precious gems. "It's diamonds, Mr. Tolhurst," Ludwig Earhardt complained after returning from Saxony and Thuringia. "I'm afraid De Beers is having an impact by focusing on one stone."

Tolhurst growled, "We have diamonds among our selection, Mr. Earhardt. We're capable of supplying every gem need."

"That's true, sir. And I made some diamond sales to Prince Georg in Saxony. But it's almost as if no one is even *looking* at the reds or blues; instead, they're being taught that diamonds are more sparkling, that they have more luster ..."

"That's nonsense!"

"Indeed, sir. But are you aware of the advertisements going to the royal houses from De Beers?"

Brownstone Tolhurst drummed fingers to his desk. "I'm aware of no De Beers retail outlets."

Earhardt shook his head. "No, sir. But the efforts they're putting into promoting a product whose production is ninety percent under their control means lots of other sellers are carrying De Beers diamonds to satisfy a growing demand." A brief silence fell, then the salesman added, "And that growing demand comes at the price of falling demand for sapphires and rubies and emeralds and topazes from Johnson, Walker, and Tolhurst."

"But European royalty has always held a fondness for sapphires!" Ernest Walker exclaimed when Brownstone Tolhurst told him of a growing trend. "Surely you must believe the fervor for diamonds to be a fad that will soon run out of steam, sir; run its course."

Tolhurst first dipped his massive head, then shook the jowls. "It's time for us to face reality, Ernest. There's a tidy profit in producing our own sapphires, but we've never achieved the rewards we anticipated. I remember how we celebrated right here in this office when that bastard Rhodes went to his just desserts—that's why we authorized reopening our mine for production."

"And we expanded our sapphire markets," the elder partner murmured.

"We did. Yes, we did. But we continued to meet stiff competition with De Beers diamonds, even after Rhodes was no longer in the picture. Then came the worldwide panic. We both insisted to the board that we should continue blithely on. But when the panic eased and an economic upsurge resulted, our sales remained dissatisfying."

Walker, who'd never seated himself, said, "What are you trying to say, Brownstone?"

"That we must meet De Beers promotion. If they promote the hardness of their stones, we must with equal emphasis promote the history of ours. If they promote their gems' sparkle, we must promote the depth and dreams inherent in ours. We must go head-to-head with them!"

Ernest Walker shook his head. "Can we win? They have no other obligations except to promote diamonds. We have the world's greatest jewelry retail establishment to run. We have a manufacturing arm to ..."

"We have to meet our competition, Ernest."

"Why? Why not simply buy rough stones from De Beers and send our people out with polished diamonds? I fail to see why we must compete with the Africans at all?"

"Because," Tolhurst growled, "if we don't, we may be

sitting atop the world's greatest sapphire deposit and it'll be worth nothing."

Walker shuffled to the door, paused with a hand on its knob and said, "I simply find it difficult to believe any thoughtful man or woman will turn away from the deep colours of real gems for a piece of clear glass."

* * *

English royalty remained loyal to sapphires and rubies and emeralds. The late Queen Victoria's German and Russian court relatives followed suit: the Royal Houses of Prussia, Russia, Hessia, Saxe-Coburg, and Mecklinburg. But the lesser nobility in many European states were more and more entranced by the sparkle of diamond tiaras, diamond necklaces, and diamond rings. By 1912 it was apparent that Ernest Walker was wrong as the sale of diamonds captured an ever-growing slice of the retail market for gemstones of all persuasions.

Walker's error became even more apparent when deliveries of raw stones from Messrs. Johnson, Walker, and Tolhurst, Ltd. must wait in line behind ever-growing stockpiles of South African diamonds for polishing by the draftsmen at Verenigen Boas Von Den Sprecht, Hogehilweg 12, in Amsterdam.

North African rulers, royalty from the Middle East and Oriental potentates, however, remained loyal to the colored gems marketed by Johnson, Walker, and Tolhurst. The firm's problem in marketing sapphires to the Orient, however, was that Oriental markets were historically conditioned to the supposition that all highest-quality sapphires originated in the Orient. It was a premise Johnson, Walker, and Tolhurst easily solved by simple expedient of dropping the Yogo sapphires origin and calling all the firm's sapphires *Oriental*.

Messrs. Johnson, Walker, and Tolhurst, Ltd. also remained the world's leading manufacturer of high quality jewelry products, as well as the top retail jewelry store in England.

They even recouped some of their former position in wholesale gem marketing by swallowing their revulsion and incorporating a broader selection of diamonds in their gemstone offerings to European buyers. The transition for Messrs. Johnson, Walker, and Tolhurst, Ltd. to take part in a growing public infatuation with diamonds was made easier with the advent of Ernest Oppenheimer.

* * *

"A gentleman to see you, sir," Johnson, Walker and Tolhurst chief usher said, gripping the office door with both hands.

"Weystruth, are you all right?" Tolhurst exclaimed.

"Quite all right, sir. The gentleman's card is right ..." The servant stared at his empty finger and muttered, "Terribly sorry, sir. I must have dropped it. So sorry. But he says he has an introduction from ... from ... I cannot remember from whom, sir. But I do recall his introduction is from someone I'm quite sure you know."

Weystruth was sweating, even though snow lay in the streets and the office's inside temperature was struggling to reach a comfortable level. Brownstone sighed. "Show him in, Weystruth. Then take the remainder of the day off."

"Thank you, sir, but I'll be perfectly all right." The door clicked softly.

Ten minutes later, Tolhurst pushed his corpulent self to his feet and strode to the door. A few feet down the hall, a stranger bent over a prostrate Weystruth, wiping the servant's brow with a handkerchief. The stranger smiled. "You must be

Mr. Tolhurst. Mr. Dunkelsbuhler said you were the only gem dealer in London who could match him for size."

"What's wrong with Weystruth?" Tolhurst snapped.

The stranger shrugged, then unsnapped Weystruth's collar and dabbed beneath. "I can't really say. One of your clerks is after water, as well as bringing assistance to help the poor man to a chair." He stood and extended a calling card. "I picked this up off the floor where you butler fell. In case you never received it, I'm Ernest Oppenheimer, from Kimberley, in South Africa."

Just then three clerks clattered down the hall with damp rags and smelling salts.

Brownstone Tolhurst took the stranger's card and said, "Please follow me."

Inside Tolhurst's office, the managing partner of Messrs. Johnson, Walker, and Tolhurst, Ltd. shook hands, offered a chair to his visitor, remained standing, and said, "What can I do for you?"

Ernest Oppenheimer crossed his long legs and leaned back, apparently at ease. He was thin and appeared double-jointed, dressed in finely cut Aberdeen wool, well-polished shoes with spats, a silk shirt, and cravat. He said, "I have a letter from Anton Dunkelsbuhler, should you wish to see it, sir."

"That won't be necessary. Just state your business."

Oppenheimer smiled. "That's simple and to the point. I wish to sell you some diamonds."

"We're not in the market."

"Oh, I believe you are, sir. You see, I own the Premier Diamond Mine, as well as being a principal in Consolidated Diamond."

"Never heard of them, sir," Tolhurst growled.

Oppenheimer flashed a broad smile beneath a pencil

moustache. "Surely you jest." He paused for three beats of Tolhurst's wall clock, then added, "P'raps, then, you've heard of the 'Cullinan Diamond'? It came from my Premier Mine."

At mention of the largest diamond ever discovered, Brownstone Tolhurst stomped around his desk and eased into his chair. He studied the young man seated across from him before saying, "We already have a supplier for our diamond lines."

Oppenheimer nodded. "Of course you do; and you are dissatisfied at the De Beers prices, as well as their shoddy treatment of customers. Everyone is. I'm here as a competitor to the De Beers cartel. With better prices. Now do we have grounds for continuing?"

In reply, Brownstone Tolhurst pushed to his feet and strode to a wall-to-ceiling bookcase, pushed an unseen button, and when a door swung wide, stuck his head into the exposed adjoining office and said, "Ernest, would you be so kind as to step in here for a moment and meet another Ernest?"

Chapter Thirteen

Europe mobilized for such a war no one could imagine. Nation after nation threw the cream of their manhood into battle against gigantic engines of destruction. Generals, every one of which had no experience in this new kind of warfare, ordered their minions to dig holes in the ground, trenches across entire landscapes, then unroll thickets of barbed wire before those trenches, and crouch in those trenches for what little shelter might be afforded from salvo after artillery salvo of mind-numbing procession. Many—or perhaps most—of those minions failed to return home. At least not whole in body or mind.

One year. Two. Male youths between the ages of sixteen and forty virtually vanished from the streets and farms and businesses of England and all of Europe. Such was the circumstances at #16 Hatton Garden when an apparently confident, well-dressed, dark-complexioned young man pushed through the huge double doors of Messrs. Johnson, Walker, and Tolhurst, Ltd., passing a calling card and a note to an inquiring clerk and asked to see Mr. Brownstone Tolhurst....

* * *

To the raised eyebrow of the jewelry showroom clerk, Naseby Ringgold, known by his engraved calling card as Nathan Kenneth Ringling, swept off his black Dunlap-style hat and said, "It was recommended to me by Mr. Johann Abrahamson, Canada's leading purchaser of rare gems from the firm of Johnson, Walker, and Tolhurst that I should, upon my arrival in England, offer my services first to your firm."

"And what may those services be?"

"I was Valet Butler to Mr. Abrahamson." The still

suspicious clerk stared hard at the card. Naseby murmured, "I have a letter from Mr. Abrahamson, as well as other recommendations from some of the most prestigious gentlemen in Toronto."

The clerk started to hand back Naseby's card. "I'm afraid ..."

Naseby smiled winningly. "I can see it's presumptuous of me to ask for Mr. Tolhurst, but perhaps there's someone more appropriate with whom I might leave my letters of recommendation?"

"Do you have the letters with you?"

Naseby nodded. "I do. Might I be able to display them to the appropriate person?"

"Please wait here, Mr. Ringling. I'll see if Mr. Herrelback is available."

The clerk was gone only a few moments. "I'm sorry, Mr. Herrelback is engaged at the present. But his assistant, Mr. Dawson can spare you a bit, if you'd be kind enough to follow me."

Naseby trailed the clerk down a narrow hallway to a back office not much larger than a broom closet. The owl-eyed man sitting behind the cluttered desk glanced up as Naseby and the clerk entered. "Here is Mr. Ringling, Mr. Dawson. He says he's from Canada, with recommendations."

"Thank you, Leeper." Owl-eyes flashed a wan smile and dismissed the clerk with the observation that "there's hardly room in here for three." Then he stared up at his visitor. "You are seeking employment, is that it?"

Naseby stood rigidly, hands coupled at his waist, holding his Dunlap derby. "One might say that, sir. What I'm actually looking for is a position. I'm trained and experienced in service, recently employed as a Valet Butler to one of the most prestigious gem retailers in all of Canada. Who, by the way, recommended that I call on Johnson, Walker, and Tolhurst first, upon my arrival in England."

"I'm told you carry recommendations?"

"Yes, sir, I do." Naseby reached into a coat pocket and pulled out a ribbon-bound sheaf of papers.

While Dawson loosed the ribbon, unfolded the letters, stacked them neatly, then began to read, Naseby studied the man and his cluttered desk. Obviously he had been engaged with ledgers before the interruption. The tiny, meticulously inked numbers indicated that he was some sort of an accountant. His glasses looked as thick as the bottoms of clear liqueur bottles, and the brown spots on the backs of his hands said he was older than first impression. He wore sleeve garters, too, above the elbows of a light-colored, pinstriped shirt. And leather cuffs. The man's hair was thin and a very light shade of blond, except over the ears.

"Do sit down," Dawson said, waving at the room's only empty chair, a wooden ladderback of dubious reliability. He laid one paper aside and picked up another.

Naseby sank carefully onto the chair, sitting stiffly, hat in lap, hands on knees and mirror-shined black shoes tight together.

Dawson finished reading the second letter. "Why did you come to England?"

Naseby held his interrogator's eyes. "When one is in service, the Continent seems the pinnacle of such profession. To one from Canada, England seems preferable."

Dawson picked up a third letter. When he finished reading, he swiftly strode from the room, returning a few moments later with a blank application and a pencil. "Be kind enough to fill this out, Mr. Ringling. I'll return in a moment."

While Naseby waited, he took in the row of file cabinets on one wall, the sliding doors on another. One slider stood half-open, disclosing a row of shelves. The shelves held ledgers similar to the one open on Dawson's desk. Still sitting rigidly, Naseby looked more closely at the open ledger's entries; he thought they were statistics on gemstones: type, weight in the raw, after cutting, where faceted, for what end purpose ...

"It's quite possible Mr. Herrelback might see you, but unfortunately not today."

Naseby came easily to his feet, grateful that Dawson was at his back and could not have seen him scrutinizing the ledger. "Then, perhaps tomorrow?"

Dawson picked up the application, quickly scanned it and nodded. "He will expect you at ten-thirty in the morning."

"And my letters of recommendation? They are my only copies."

"Ah, yes," Dawson said. "Mr. Herrelback wishes to review them. Will tomorrow be sufficiently timely for their return?"

Naseby nodded. "Yes, of course. Thank you, sir, for an opportunity to present myself."

* * *

If Gideon Herrelback ever smiled, Naseby Ringgold thought his present face gave no such indication. Sleek dark hair, parted in the middle. Hooded eyes that seemed to peer down the man's continually elevated nose. Vertical troughs between the eyebrows and down both cheeks. Pinched lips. Tufts of hair springing wild from ears and nose. High starched collar and deep gray four-in-hand tie, dark seersucker jacket. Obviously stern.

"Why here?" stern-face said.

Naseby shifted forward in the overstuffed chair to which

he'd been directed. "Yes, sir. As I told Mr. Dawson yesterday, my last Toronto employer, Mr. Abrahamson suggested ..."

"That's not what I mean, ah, Ringling. Why England? There's a war on over here. You might be safer in Canada."

"Yes, sir. But again, it's as I told Mr. Dawson, if one chooses service as a career, Europe is where one finds the better service people."

Herrelback studied the young man to which he'd been introduced as Nathan Kenneth Ringling. "Are you running from the draft?" he said at last. "Or do you have some physical impairment that's not obvious? All others your age have been drafted to die like dogs in France."

Naseby's smile was quick, then gone. "But I'm not eligible for the draft, sir. I'm an American. I believe my application will show that I was born in Detroit to American parents. If the application is not clear on that point, my passport will certainly clarify it. Would you like to see that, sir?"

Herrelback shook his head, picked up the Nathan Ringling application, stared at it. "Why, then, Canada, Mr. Ringling? Were there no service positions in the United States?"

"Oh, yes indeed. But Americans do not view being in service in quite the same manner as the English. I quite frankly went to Canada in order to polish my professional performance. If I might be allowed to say so, sir, I believe my plan to obtain those necessary skills succeeded."

Still staring at the application, Herrelback said, "Tell me about your background, your training, your ethnic origin."

With barely a pause, Naseby Ringgold continued his well rehearsed lie; the one he'd concocted while still in flight, on his way to Toronto; the one he'd lived with and polished for the last eighteen months: "As the application illustrates, sir, I was born in Detroit, in the United States, on the first day of

April, 1894. Both my mother and father were in service to the household of William Ward Randolph, who owned a small fleet of transport schooners on the Great Lakes. My mother was employed as a household maid, my father as a gardener. Unfortunately I can't tell you much about my father because he died of yellow fever in Cuba when I was four—apparently he was caught up in the Spanish-American War furor and enlisted in the Army to seek adventure. At any rate, I barely remember him.

"Naturally, growing up in the household I did, I absorbed a certain amount of training as a matter of course: cleaning, dusting, carrying serving dishes, and the like. Actually I more or less grew into the profession, came to respect it, decided it would be my career choice. Then my mother's health failed, and she died when I was eighteen years old, I decided there was nothing holding me back from developing more skills and refinement in Canada. Thus I crossed the river to Windsor, in Canada and made my way from there to Toronto."

When Naseby paused, Herrelback said, "And what of your ethnic origin?"

The young man shook his head. "I have no idea, sir. Ringling is, of course, English. I do remember that my father was of a somewhat dark-complexion. But anything beyond that observation died with him."

"What of your mother?"

"Irish, I was told. But I was also told that her family—as did the family of my father—dwelled in America for several generations. Actually, may I ask, sir, are such searching interrogations normal for all your interviews?"

Herrelback peered down his nose at Naseby's vexation. "For your information, Mr. Ringling, the firm of Johnson, Walker, and Tolhurst is one the most prestigious in all the

British Empire. It would be a dereliction of our duty were we to do anything less than thoroughly examine each of our prospective employees. My advice to you, young man, is to remove that chip from your own shoulder, rather than look for someone to knock it off for you."

Naseby squared his shoulders, met Herrelback's eyes head-on, and said, "I'm sorry, sir." When the other failed to respond, he said, "Is it appropriate for me to ask if that means you're considering a place for me with your firm?"

"We might. I was prepared to present your papers to Mr. Brownstone Tolhurst until your pique."

He should trim the hair from his nostrils, Naseby thought, rising to his feet. "Then, sir, if I'm no longer under consideration, I would like you to return my letters of recommendation so that I may present them elsewhere." He knew he was throwing down a gauntlet, but he had to divert Herrelback from searching for the applicant's ethnic background.

To his relief, the interviewer laid his hand flat atop Naseby's papers and said, "We'll hold on to them for a few days, if you please, Mr. Ringling. Mr. Tolhurst is due to return next Thursday. At which time I'll ask him to review this information. Can you call in on, say, next Monday?"

"Yes, sir. Might you suggest a time?"

"Today's time should be appropriate."

* * *

Naseby Ringgold's feet barely touched as he skipped across the Hatton Gardens paving stones! He felt certain to be accepted, though he had no inkling as to his position. Perhaps as an usher or a footman; he might even start as a swamper or washing windows—but he didn't care. He was soon to be employed at Johnson, Walker, and Tolhurst, Ltd—a company for which his hatred had no bounds! Soon he would be engaged

106

in taking his first step toward revenge against the English for stealing his birthright.

Right now, however, the young man known in England as Nathan Kenneth Ringling had the better part of six days to spend exploring the largest city in the world. He wished those explorations to take him first to the Tower of London, so steeped in medieval history, where kings, queens, nobles and commoners had died by the dozens. He wanted, too, to visit London Bridge (where his disappointment was keen when he discovered the present London Bridge was merely the sixth in line of bridges on the site, dating back as far as the first constructed by Roman Legions to the present 19th Century model that replaced the one built in 1747 and pictured by woodcuts in many books he'd read.)

So he walked to Westminster Cathedral with guidebook in hand, and then stood outside the fence at Buckingham Palace, to admire the military synchrony of the changing of those red-coated, bearskin-hatted guards.

Because he was such a voracious reader, Naseby Ringgold wanted to peruse some of the bookshops supposed to be congregated on Charing Cross Road, then regretted that he'd not chosen another day than Sunday for his visit.

Then it was Monday.

* * *

Naseby Ringgold would've been even more pleased had he known the outcome of the discussion about him between Johnson, Walker, and Tolhurst Office Manager, Gideon Herrelback and the firm's Managing Director, Brownstone Tolhurst:

"Do you mean to tell me you've not yet employed this man?" Tolhurst peered over the top of the sheaf of papers he'd been handed. "My God! Are you daft?"

107

The Office Manager peered down his nose. "He's to return Monday for our dispensation, sir. I thought it better to apprise you of his credentials before actually engaging him."

The gargantuan managing director shuffled through the papers again, then muttered, "There's such a thing as being too cautious, Herrelback. We haven't seen anyone with these credentials since this bloody war started." Throwing the papers to his desk, he added, "And he's young, experienced, and outside any future government draft. You must have been addled not to snap him up the moment he appeared. How do you know he hasn't already been employed elsewhere?"

Herrelback reached to pick up the sheaf of papers. "These are guarantees he'll return, sir. I kept them in order to insure that."

"All right, then, why the hesitation? You know our staff is aging." Tolhurst drummed his desktop in annoyance, muttering, "And even my residential butler grows feeble, too. So, once again, Herrelback, what was your hesitation to immediately employ this new applicant?"

"Perhaps his appearance, sir. There was something about his appearance—oh he was neat enough, well groomed, well dressed, articulate. But he's quite dark complexioned; at best, Mediterranean, Southern European, perhaps even Turkish. You know, sir, one cannot be assured of any sort of purity when it comes to Americans. Or even Canadians, for that matter. 'Melting pots', they call it—I call it mongrels." The man wagged his head. "That was my hesitation. I simply wanted to apprise you of his appearance should you wish to view him first."

"I don't care if he's Swahili if he can perform. Or haven't you noticed our staff weaknesses, even before Weystruth's illness?"

"Which brings us to the point, sir: where should we put

him? Until we ascertain if, in fact, he possesses the qualifications he listed, we can't be assured he'll perform to our standards. Should we start him at entry level and advance him as he proves meritorious?"

"I understand Weystruth is to attempt a return?"

"Yes, sir. He wishes to do so. But I have grave reservations that he'll be up to it."

"Then make this Ringling fellow Weystruth's assistant. That should give us ample opportunity to assess both their performances."

"But what about Isaacson, Mr. Tolhurst? Won't he take placing someone else before him badly since he's temporarily replaced Weystruth?"

Brownstone Tolhurst sighed and waved an impatient hand. "May the gods protect me from ineptness. If by now you haven't deduced that Isaacson lacks sufficient competence and dignity for the role he's futilely trying to assume, then you, too, are in a role beyond your own ability." The corpulent managing director of Johnson, Walker, and Tolhurst, Ltd. noted with some satisfaction the rising color on the face of his office manager. Tolhurst's smile held little warmth. "I don't expect Weystruth to be able to perform in a manner that should be required of our chief usher. And I bloody well recognize that Mr. Isaacson cannot do so. Therefore, Mr. Herrelback, who else do you suggest? Have we anyone else in this office you might think capable?"

Gideon Herrelback murmured, "Loomis was being groomed for the role sir, until he was called into the Army."

"Great Christ, Herrelback!" the big man thundered. "Eighteen months ago this office was crawling with young, bright, ambitious young men, all of which are presently in ditches in France, either dead or alive. I'm not asking what our

109

staff was like *yesterday*! I want to know what we're going to do *tomorrow*!"

"Right, sir!" Herrelback replied, picking up scattered papers and folders. "On Monday, when he returns, do you wish to see him?"

"I do not. Not unless he's following Weystruth, acting as the old man's assistant. Now, get out of here."

* * *

Naseby Ringgold was early. He knew he was early, but wished to establish an image of promptness. Besides, by arriving before his appointed time, he thought he might have a chance to browse about the display room a bit. That plan was dashed by Mr. Herrelback's immediate appearance. The surprising thing was the young man known as Nathan Kenneth Ringling had yet to announce himself.

"Ahh, Mr. Ringling. You're early—an admirable trait in one who wishes to be in service."

"Indeed." Naseby barely had time to remove his single-breasted topcoat and hat before the Office Manager's appearance. But he smoothly transferred both to one arm and limply grasped Herrelback's extended hand.

On their way back to the manager's office, Herrelback instructed a clerk to see that tea was served. "Or would you prefer coffee? Or perhaps chocolate?"

"I'm quite content with your choice, sir."

Herrelback rolled his desk chair out near the armchair to which he directed Naseby. "I'm sure you'll be pleased to learn that Mr. Tolhurst has approved your joining our firm." Pausing a moment to search the younger man's impassively controlled face, he added, "Unfortunately we're unable to offer a position commensurate with your obvious experience ..." At that point, tea service arrived and Herrelback busied himself pouring.

"One lump, or two?"

"None, if you please."

"Good. You're a man after my own heart: hot and black, that's the only way."

Herrelback said to the hovering servant, "Dooley, please take Mr. Ringling's hat and coat. The rack in the corner will do. Then be kind enough to bring a tray of biscuits."

They both sipped. "As I started to say, sir, we're unable to start you at a level your experience warrants, but I harbor few doubts your performance will lead to rapid advancement." Again, he waited for some sign from Naseby. Receiving none, he said, "Actually our chief usher is rather old, and recovering from a recent mishap. We've decided he needs help ..." The tray of cookies arrived. Herrelback took one, offered the tray to the interviewee and was politely refused. "... with his duties. Mr. Tolhurst and I decided to create a position as an assistant chief usher and offer it to you." Again he paused.

Naseby nodded, "I see." But he said no more, neither did he give any indication whether the offer was acceptable.

"I presume you're interested in knowing what the position receives in regard to remuneration." Not even a nod. "Since this is a new position, Mr. Ringling, we've not yet established a fair and equitable rate, but you can be assured we'll do well by you."

Naseby took another sip of tea. "I assume that to be true, Mr. Herrelback. And as long as my letters of recommendation are returned, I think they will provide adequate alternative should my expectations not be met."

"I assume that means you accept."

"I do. I presume there'll be an introduction to your recovering chief usher ..."

"Weystruth. His name is Mr. Weystruth."

"… as well as a list of duties you'll expect of me."

"And we'll assign a clerk to give you a tour of the premises."

Naseby stood. "When should I start, Mr. Herrelback?"

"I can arrange for your tour right now. Or tomorrow, if you'd prefer. Or next week. You choose."

"Perhaps we should ask Mr. Weystruth about my starting time."

Chapter Fourteen

It took every bit of reserve that Naseby Ringgold could command not to leap with elation as the clerk, Timms, conducted him through the vast showroom and labyrinthine headquarters of Johnson, Walker, and Tolhurst, Ltd. He was in the heart of the thieves' lair! Now, if he could control himself, control any emotional display, he could familiarize himself with the principals, staff, and establishment layout, then begin planning how he could avenge himself on the thieves who stole his birthright. The new assistant to the chief usher hardly glanced at the myriad faceted gemstones displayed in the locked glass cases, contenting himself merely to rub his handkerchief down the sides and backs of the cases and gaze contemplatively at any dust that might return with the handkerchief. Exceedingly reserved, he never frowned, never uttered a critical word, never bothered even to meet his escorting clerk's eyes.

But he was observed.

His obvious pleasure in the tidiness of the establishment's kitchen was observed; how he studied the assortment of liquors and nodded in affirmation at the selections of fine vintage wines available to serve honored and valued customers was observed. It was observed how he paused upon exiting the cellar to examine the range of serving trays, clucking disapprovingly at their low-luster polish, and picking up several wine glasses by their stem to closely examine for water marks or discolorations. He even snapped at one with a fingernail and nodded when it chimed its coveted Waterford ring.

"I'm hardly qualified to judge, Mr. Herrelback, but he acted more like a critical butler than even Mr. Weystruth. He said nothing—not a word throughout the entire tour, except to exchange pleasantries with Mr. Dawson ... apparently Mr. Dawson interviewed him first?" At Herrelback's nod, Timms continued: "But he clucked disapprovingly at the state of polish of our serving trays in the wine cellar. And he discreetly examined our showroom display cases for dust. Even went so far as to don a glove and checked the sanitation of our hallway corners and carpeting edges against the wall paneling."

"And he never said anything? Even about the jewelry and gems?"

"I'm not even sure he saw them, sir—he was looking for fingerprints or dust. He seems like a fine gentleman, but strange if you ask me."

* * *

When, two days later, the new Weystruth assistant was introduced to the returning chief usher, there appeared a certain degree of aloofness. In the interim, Naseby disappeared in plain sight. Without prompting, he sought brooms and mops, dust cloths and silver polish. Never pausing, he scrupulously polished the glass and wood of display cabinets (dwelling longest on sapphire displays). He swept and brushed out hallway corners that had had little attention for weeks. He obtained a key to the wine cellar, where he spent a full afternoon polishing the silver serving trays and cleaning wine glasses to a level of readiness that satisfied even the most fastidious eye.

The new hire, known to the staff of Johnson, Walker, and Tolhurst as Nathan Kenneth Ringling was so unobtrusive that he attracted little attention—except from the chief usher's temporary replacement—Mr. Isaacson, who saw the new hire as a competitor for the chief usher's position. The problem for Isaacson was that he failed to elicit any emotion from the stoic newcomer. If he objected to the way Naseby polished wine glasses, Naseby simply nodded and with no apparent emotion, continued polishing—no smile, no frown, no hint or word of demurral; just continuing on as though Mr. Isaacson was a wall ornament, or a bust of Disraeli or Wellington, or even Queen Victoria.

With Halstaff Weystruth's return and the subsequent introduction, along with Mr. Herrelback's explanation that Mr. Tolhurst himself felt that Weystruth needed an assistant "until you get back fully on your feet", the chief usher stared through Naseby with weary eyes, shook the newcomers hand, then turned away to shuffle to his "pantry" where he sat at his chief usher's desk and wheezed. Meanwhile Naseby stood outside the open pantry door for over an hour, until Mr. Herrelback came and instructed Weystruth to take Mr. Ringling on a tour of the administrative floor.

"And, Weystruth, do remember tea for Mr. Walker and Mr. Tolhurst while you do so, won't you? I'm sure Ringling will be pleased to carry the service for you."

* * *

It was how deferential Naseby was to Mr. Weystruth that won the old chief usher over to his young assistant. "May I bring the tea service, sir?" Naseby asked the befuddled elder usher, upon Herrelback's departure. And when Naseby returned a few minutes later carrying the service, he helped Weystruth to his feet and dutifully followed the old man's shuffle to the broad staircase leading to the owners' upper floor offices and twin conference rooms.

The clerk, Timms, had not, of course, conducted Naseby on a tour of the largely forbidden upper floor, so the young man was in a state of alert as Weystruth knocked politely on the double doors leading to Ernest Walker's office, opened one a crack and said, "Tea, your honor?"

"Do come in, Weystruth. We're glad to have you back."

115

Weystruth turned to take the tray from Naseby who folded his hands before him while remaining outside the room. The glimpse he had of Mr. Walker's thin cadaverous frame and kindly face, along with his obvious consideration for the elderly usher, told him this might be a difficult man to dislike. And he hoped his face did not mirror his inner turmoil at being in the inner sanctum of the thieves who'd stolen his birthright.

Mr. Walker eyed Weystruth's assistant, but contented himself with asking about the elderly usher's family. Upon their exit, Weystruth handed Naseby the service, though it was but a few steps to what proved to be the double doors leading to the managing director's office. Again, Weystruth knocked twice, opened one door a crack and said, "Tea, Mr. Tolhurst?"

"Come in, come in, Weystruth!" a deep baritone voice boomed. "We're happy to have you back."

Weystruth pushed both doors wide before turning back for the tray, exposing Naseby. "And this is your new assistant? Come on in, young man. I've heard and read some good things about you. Ringling, isn't it?"

The man beckoning to him was huge, monstrous in fact; and red-faced, big-bellied, and small-eyed. But he was smiling broadly. "I've been told you're an American who worked in service to Abrahamson in Toronto—I believe he provided a glowing letter of recommendation?"

Naseby was uncomfortable standing by Weystruth's side while the old man poured, yet his eyes focused on a window beyond the huge managing director. "Yes sir, Mr. Abrahamson was kind enough to do so."

"Well, young man, his loss is, hopefully, our gain. Two lumps Weystruth. And a dash of cream, if you please."

When the old man handed the saucer and cup to Tolhurst, the big man thanked him, remarking on how much better

Weystruth looked than when he last saw him lying on the hallway floor. "I suppose it was the bloody flux—it's been going around I fear."

"I'm quite fine now, sir," Weystruth said, handing the tray to Naseby. "I've never felt better."

"Good. But you must allow Ringling to help you wherever you can."

Outside the office, after gently closing the double doors, the old man leaned against the wall and wiped his brow with a handkerchief. Naseby took his elbow and led the chief usher to the grand staircase, and thence down to his office pantry. After Weystruth was again seated, the assistant took the tea service to the kitchen, then, not knowing the chief usher's normal duties, he stood outside the pantry door until Weystruth noticed him. "Um, yes, Mr. ..."

"Ringling, sir."

"Yes, I was about to find it. My normal station is just inside the lobby entrance, unless otherwise serving the owners, or keeping my logs to date."

Naseby said, "I see. Should I take up that position, sir? And what are my duties? Am I greeting customers as they enter? Or will a clerk be so engaged?"

* * *

It was a role into which Naseby grew. Standing at station at the entry doors may once have been Weystruth's duty when he wasn't otherwise engaged. But it could not have been one he frequently filled. After outlining the role's expectations the chief usher was not seen there again. Though his instructions had been sketchy, the young assistant proved a natural, smiling and greeting customers cheerfully and courteously, inquiring if they wished to merely browse or needed any particular attention.

Standing for hours near the entry doors might have

seemed onerous to one not so obsessed as Naseby Ringgold in getting "even" with the people who'd stolen his birthright. But the position afforded the young man with ample time to evaluate the firm's actual daily operation. And it permitted him to dream. He eventually requested (and received) a standup desk for his purposes, because by then he'd became such a recognized fixture that both Edward Walker and Brownstone Tolhurst wondered why they'd not thought previously to avail themselves of a "greeter".

At the beginning, Naseby served little as Weystruth's assistant because his elderly chief saw the younger man as a potential replacement. The problem was, however, that he was also someone who could be called on for assistance as needed. Soon after Naseby acquired his standup desk, Weystruth had an electric buzzer installed on it to save the old man from having to walk out onto the showroom floor to beckon for his assistant to help with the tea service, or to perform other duties, as needed.

The buzzer was one-way only, however. And when a person of merit requested an audience with Mr. Tolhurst or Mr. Walker, Naseby was required to fetch Weystruth to make the evaluation and eventually the presentation, as the chief usher insisted on being the sole servant to the owner's offices. Problems arose, however, between the shuffling chief usher's arrival, his wearisome evaluation and approval, and his tedious staircase ascent as he led visitors growing resentful at what they saw as an onerous process. Complaints were made.

Office manager Gideon Herrelback tried to diplomatically persuade Weystruth to give up more duties to his younger assistant without any apparent gain. Finally, before Herrelback could take more positive action, Weystruth once again fell ill, effectively transferring his duties to those of the chief usher designate.

118

It was a dream come true for the young man known as Nathan Kenneth Ringling. And, so they thought, for the owners and administrators of Johnson, Walker, and Tolhurst, Ltd.'s wholesale and retail establishment.

"He's exactly the lead usher we need," Brownstone Tolhurst said.

"As good as Weystruth was before his illness," Ernest Walker said.

"Better."

"Are you aware that he is closely overseeing the dusting and polishing of display cases and wall hangings."

"And don't forget his interest in the silver service and our crystal ware."

"Just the other day, I saw him with a stepladder examining our chandeliers."

"I saw that; saw him and Durgiss up there polishing them, too."

"He's never still—always searching for ways to improve our shop appearance."

"Herrelback says he's prompt with his reports."

"Are they neat?"

"So Herrelback tells me. Much more legible than our former chief usher."

"Unfortunately, his zealous assumption of Weystruth's role leaves a hole he was filling so adeptly as a greeter."

Tolhurst nodded, stroking his chin and shifting his bulk. "True. He did present an image we'd do well to continue. But …"

"He's too essential as Weystruth's replacement."

"So let's ask Ringling to find a replacement for the entry desk, then task him with the duty to properly train the new man. What say?"

* * *

Brownstone Tolhurst motioned to him to take a seat across the desk from him. The firm's managing director seemed to have a twinkle in his eye. "Ringling," he said at last, "Mr. Herrelback tells me you wish to install Miss Applestrom behind the entry desk."

"Yes, sir." Tolhurst felt as though his seated chief usher was still standing at attention. The young man's face was entirely devoid of any emotion. He stared straight ahead, without deviation.

"A woman?"

"Yes sir. You asked me to find the best possible replacement. I tried to find a gentleman Mr. Herrelback could approve. But sir, there are none. It takes someone young to stand in one place all day without tiring. Such a person must be young to remain cheerful in the face of a tiring role." Tolhurst saw Ringling's eyes shift to burn into his. Other than the slight shift of focus, there was still no change in expression. "There are no such young men left in England, sir. I may have been the last."

"But a woman?"

"Sir, Miss Applestrom is young, cheerful, and of proven commitment to this firm."

"In the kitchen. As a woman."

"But diligent, sir. She excels in anything she's tasked to do. Just last week I assigned her to all the polishing of our silver and crystal. It is now kept to my standards."

Tolhurst was smiling as he shook his head. "But a woman."

"Sir," the chief usher said, "This is 1916. It isn't the Dark Ages. In times such as these, when suitable men are not

120

available, it seems appropriate to consider such a woman as Miss Applestrom."

The smile faded from Brownstone Tolhurst's face, replaced by a thoughtful frown.

Naseby, still seemingly emotionless, said, "Sir, my mother was in service to some of the most powerful men in America. And she served them flawlessly."

"In what role? Don't tell me as a butler. Or a chief usher."

"No, sir. But she could have had she been given the opportunity." It was then that he dropped his head to stare at his feet. "She did train me in those roles. And I flatter myself that her training was exemplary. But," he raised his head to again stare at the huge red-faced man before him, "if you have reservations, sir, I'll explain that fact to Miss Applestrom."

Tolhurst slapped his desktop. "Oh, go ahead and try it. Herrelback will have apoplexy when I tell him. But let's see if you're right. Let's see if a woman can fulfill such a role. It certainly would ease some of our employment problems while French trenches continue to eat the cream of English manhood."

* * *

She performed near-flawlessly from the first.

"You must not be too, cheerful, Miss Applestrom. Never personal." Miss Applestrom leaned on every word of the man she knew as Mr. Ringling said. "The key is to be entirely professional. Help those who enter. But never give the impression of familiarity. Never remark on their personal appearance, no matter how tasteful the cut of their attire."

"Oh indeed, Mr. Ringling. I do entirely understand."

"Your role should be to put them in touch with the proper person to help them as quickly as possible. If it's a clerk to help them examine our fine jewelry, or if it's the chief usher to apprise them of upper management availability, you must remember that you're only there to help, and not become their friend."

"Utterly. And if the person they seek is unavailable, I must be courteous and apologetic."

"While still maintaining that difficult air of strict, but pleasant, professionalism."

Naseby counseled Miss Applestrom on her appearance. "Grooming is very important, of course. I wonder if it's appropriate for your hair to be down? Might it look too frivolous? Yet would a tight bun be too austere?"

"Dark skirts and light blouses, perhaps with a matching jacket, would seem sufficiently professional, might it not?"

"Comfortable shoes, well polished, but with ankle support, you'll find best suited for your new duties."

"You will find, at times, your duties to be somewhat tedious, Miss Applestrom. But in my experience, that can be expected in any form of service. Above all, even when tired, or bored, or wishing you were elsewhere, you must stay alert. Always. Simply present your best front. Be *professional*."

"Yes indeed, Mr. Ringling. Please be assured I love my new position and will always be grateful to you for putting me forward."

* * *

In fact the experiment with Miss Applestrom proved so successful that it attracted the approving attention of those majority owners who wisely recognized the specialized training the new greeter received from their chief usher. "One wonders if Ringling might be of even more value," Brownstone Tolhurst Mused while discussing their retail operations with Gideon Herrelback, "should he be given more responsibility."

Herrelback nodded while asking, "What kind of responsibility?"

"Perhaps in staff oversight—training, for instance."

"He certainly proved quite effective in training Miss Applestrom. But really, sir, the man has only been associated with Johnson, Walker, and Tolhurst for just a few months. Usually one would prefer to properly assess another's performance over *years*, instead of mere *months*."

The big man leaned back in his swivel chair and said, "In a perfect world, Herrelback, in a perfect world. Unfortunately today's world is hardly perfect. And until this bloody war ends, there is little likelihood of it returning to normal. Meanwhile we must do the best we can with what we have at hand."

The office manager gathered his notes, preparing to leave. At the double doors to Tolhurst's sanctum, he paused to observe, "The young man does seem a godsend, sir; the ideal sort, war or no war."

* * *

The young man thought of by his handlers as the ideal sort was, at the moment, standing some five steps behind Miss Applestrom's work station as a greeter for visitors to the retail store of Johnson, Walker, and Tolhurst. One might assume Naseby Ringgold was observing Miss Applestrom's work habits with a view to improving the woman's performance; after all, the firm's chief usher was near enough to catch every detail, yet far enough to discourage idle conversation.

Having the man responsible for her new position so closely observing her performance made the young woman exceedingly nervous, though she hid any apprehension behind a façade of stoic professionalism, just as her observer had taught.

The truth was, Naseby Ringgold, though appearance might lead one to believe otherwise, hadn't even noted Miss Applestrom or her performance. Instead, his was a sightless focus on developing a plan for exacting revenge on the Englishmen who'd stolen his sapphire mine birthright. Shrewdly, he spent much of his planning time while appearing to be attentive to store detail: polishing display cases and chandeliers, checking kitchen and wine cellar, trolling for errant dust and tidying showroom appearance.

For instance, he knew in which drawer display case keys were stored and, after all jewel trays were removed upon closing, where their locked vault was located. He'd learned where uncut stones were stored: sapphires, rubies, emeralds, diamonds, topazes. He'd even been conducted on a tour of the firm's workshop, where necklaces, bracelets, rings, diadems, and scepters were forged, engraved, and inserted with such jewels as ordered.

He knew also of the security staff; knew all three men were basically detailed to monitor possible staff or workshop theft, leaving any outside robberies to London police apprehension....

"... Mr. Ringling!"

Naseby Ringgold glanced to his side to see Mr. Herrelback. "I'm sorry sir. And how may I be of service?"

Herrelback's smile was brief. "I called you before, Mr. Ringling. But your concentration was so total I fear you must not have heard."

"I'm sorry, sir. I was merely observing Miss Applestrom at her station."

Herrelback smiled again. "I'm sure observing Miss Applestrom is a duty worth engaging, Mr. Ringling. However, would you accompany me back to my office? I have a matter to discuss with you."

Flush-faced, Naseby trailed his immediate supervisor.

In his office, Herrelback told Naseby his work had been

exemplary. "So much so, young man, we're advancing your salary another ten pounds per week." He was told, however, that his duties would also be expanded to include some rudimentary training of clerks regarding demeanor and appearance.

"I'm sorry, sir, but I have no sales training or experience."

"It's their dignity that we're after, Ringling. It's something that you have in abundance. It's a "something" that you are able to impart to others, as you've so ably done with Miss Applestrom. Now we'd like you to try to establish that same dignity in others of our staff. If so, you'll be instrumental in helping us to establish a superior image that will set the firm of Johnson, Walker, and Tolhurst above other firms marketing fine gems and jewelry to influential houses all over the world."

"Is it appropriate for me to ask for clarification, sir?"

"Yes, of course."

Naseby, with hands clasped behind him, rocked gently on his feet. "How much authority will I have with the people I'm to train? Such success as I may have enjoyed with Miss Applestrom was directly attributable to the fact that she thoroughly absorbed my every suggestion. Whether she succeeded or not was in my hands and hers, and she knew it. But should I not question whether I'll have that kind of attention from others I'm to train? Especially if I haven't any authority over them?"

"You shall have it, Mr. Ringling. If there's any problem, let me know and I will take care of it."

Naseby nodded, as if he was satisfied. "Then I assume you would deem it appropriate for me to develop a training program and submit it to you for approval?"

Mr. Herrelback nodded, then harrumphed. "There are more duties coming your way, also, Ringling. With an increase in pay and more authority there will be increased responsibility."

"Sir?"

"Mr. Tolhurst and Mr. Walker want you to monitor the removal and securing of our jewelry cases each evening. As well as the opening and re-establishing of our display cases before openings in the morning."

Naseby's heart leaped, but his face displayed nothing. He said, "I will endeavor to do my best, sir."

"Mr. Dungess of our security staff will provide the keys to our display cases, as well as access to the vaults. But you will accompany him to the vaults, and he will monitor your handling of the display cases."

"I see, sir. Again, I'll do my best."

Herrelback eyes roved beyond the chief usher as he rambled on. "Two men are needed, you see. And heretofore we've depended on two of our security detail to handle such sensitive gem displays." Naseby nodded, still standing erect and attentive. "But we've always been uncomfortable with that process." Again, Naseby, without any clear invitation to comment, nodded. "I used to monitor the process myself, you see, Ringling? But my duties as office manager threaten to overwhelm me. That's why we've gone with two security people. However two ties up two thirds of our security staff and we feel vulnerable in other places, like in jewelry design, for instance, or with petty cash drawer, or in our records department. That's why we thought of you."

Naseby cleared his throat. "I'm sure your faith in me will not be misplaced, sir."

Mr. Herrelback chuckled. "I'm sure it won't, Ringling. And I'm sure your salary increase won't be misplaced either."

No flicker of emotion crossed Naseby Ringgold's features. But as he walked from Herrelback's office, there was a calculating gleam in his eyes.

126

Chapter Fifteen

Though still without a plausible plan for exacting revenge on Johnson, Walker, and Tolhurst, Ltd for "stealing" his father's sapphire discovery, Naseby Ringgold was pleased that he was moving into a position of responsibility within the firm. By doing so, he reasoned that when he did actually devise a plan for revenge, it would be easier to execute as a trusted insider, rather than from outside the serpent's lair. And he took pride that thus far during his time with the firm, that he'd made no apparent mistakes.

Still, risks persisted. One was that Nathan Kenneth Ringling would be exposed as the Naseby Ringgold he really was. His greatest fear, of course, was that the Yogo mine manager, Charles Gadsden, or the New Mine Sapphire Company President, George Wells, might suddenly appear from America and recognize him. That's why the new chief usher sought to stay abreast of incoming gem shipments through his contacts with the sorting and storage departments. And it was through that knowledge that Naseby was able to avoid George Wells when, after ore-heap cleanup, the rancher-agent escorted the year's delivery of Yogo gemstones to England.

By the time of Wells' arrival, Naseby had so nearly altered his appearance that he might well have escaped recognition by the Montana ranch owner, in any event. He did so by growing his hair longer and parting it in the middle, by adding a pencil-moustache, by gaining weight, and by affecting eyeglasses.

It was also the fear of exposure that sent Naseby Ringgold in a surreptitious search for a master forger to draft new identity papers on the off-chance he might once again be required to bolt.

He followed train schedules and stayed abreast of steamship departures, considering both to be potential transportation avenues should flight become imperative. And he weighed destinations for future escape: the Hebrides, Ireland, Scotland. However, no matter what destination he chose, both trains and a seaborne escape would entail peril, depending on how fervent the pursuit—quite unlikely to be especially vigorous at present. But when (not "if") he actually began taking back the fortune stolen from him—and he was discovered—then the hounds would be after him in force.

* * *

"Tea, sir."

"By all means. I didn't realize the time had so slipped by." As Naseby poured, adding two lumps of sugar and a dash of cream, he felt Brownstone Tolhurst's eyes on him. Then when he set saucer and tea, along with a napkin, before his employer, the big man said, "Glanding, out in the fabricating room, tells me you display considerable interest in proper carving of the stones?"

Stepping back two paces, the chief usher said, "Yes, sir. I wish to learn as much as I can about gems and their preparation for the market. It's an interest I acquired in Toronto. With Mr. Abrahamson."

Tolhurst sipped, then blew across the surface of his teacup. "Good! We like to see our key personnel take an interest in why we're here."

As Naseby picked up the tray to leave, he asked, "Will that be all, sir. I believe we have some fresh biscuits in the kitchen."

"None for me, no. But Ringling, if you really do have an

interest in learning more about gems and their cutting, perhaps I can provide you a tour from the sorting and cutting people. Would you like that?"

"Very much, sir."

"And how is the staff training going? I saw your training plan—it looked splendid."

"Thank you, sir. Of course we've just begun, but there seems to be interest there from all levels. Mr. Herrelback clearly established that management is interested in improving our staff image in customers' minds." When Tolhurst solemnly nodded, Naseby added, "For which I'm quite grateful, sir. It is very important to have such unstinting support."

* * *

Over the years, Johnson, Walker, and Tolhurst, Ltd. began to rebuild their sales of precious gems and fine jewelry to former levels, based, at least in part, by a ready supply of rough, top quality diamonds supplied by the Premier Diamond firm of Ernest Oppenheimer, undercutting the monopolistic tactics of the De Beers cartel. By late summer of 1914, the fact that Johnson, Walker, and Tolhurst offered a full range of gemstones, as opposed to the singleminded focus of De Beers on diamonds was proving a benefit instead of liability.

"Thank the Good Lord for Ernest Oppenheimer," Brownstone Tolhurst proposed as a toast to fellow partner, Ernest Walker.

Walker, sipping thoughtfully, said, "I understand the man has political aspirations?"

Tolhurst chuckled. "Mayor of Kimberly. S'pose it provides some form of local political control over the diamond districts, hmm? P'raps shrewd on his part. I'm surprised De Beers would take it lying down."

Both men were silent, thinking. Then Walker mumbled,

"He was indeed a godsend to us, Brownstone."

"Indeed, he brought De Beers to heel."

"Now it's this bloody war! It's difficult to consider fine jewelry when big guns are booming outside your castle turrets."

Tolhurst nodded. "Were it not for the upsurge in the purchase of concealable, negotiable, precious stones in bulk, we might be altogether damaged."

"That, and our swing to the Orient, where peace still reigns."

"I wonder how De Beers is faring in today's market? Quite well, I presume. After all, color makes little difference when one wants something portable and marketable to carry in his pouch."

"Or sewn into the seams of his coat."

Just then, Gideon Herrelback knocked and entered. "Sirs, the *Times* has just reported that Premier Diamonds has merged with De Beers!"

* * *

Ernest Oppenheimer, born a cigar merchant's son in Friedberg, Germany, began his working life at age seventeen with Dunkelsbuhler & Company, a diamond brokerage in London. The young man's work was so exemplary that in 1902, at the age of twenty-two, he was sent to South Africa to represent the company as a buyer in Kimberley, where he eventually rose to lead one of South Africa's leading diamond mines.

With his London connections, and an engaging manner the young man entered the diamond markets as a competitor to De Beers' near-universal control. Eventually, Oppenheimer entered South African politics and became even more of a thorn to De Beers. Then, in a bewildering move—and for a seat on De Beers' board of directors and a significant block of De Beers stock—the young man joined his Premier Diamonds with De Beers, positioning himself to eventually mount a "palace" coup that took him to Board Chairman and Chief Executive Officer of Cecil Rhodes' former company.

* * *

Brownstone Tolhurst and Ernest Walker took the Oppenheimer defection to the enemy in some dismay, but their most pressing concern was focused on the damage inflicted by the Great War on their sales of precious jewels and jewelry to what formerly had been their most reliable market: European royalty. As the Great War morphed into the Great *World* War, virtually every country in Europe was dragged into the conflict on one side or the other. Besides embroiling the major antagonists: Germany, Austria, and Turkey on one side; and France, England, Russia, and Italy on the other; Poland, Belgium, Romania, Greece, was eventually forced in. Then Australia, New Zealand, Canada, and South Africa joined in support of England. Finally, the United States of America, tipped the balance.

But the losses! Entire component principalities within the embattled protagonists: a dozen German states, such as Hessia, Saxony, Prussia, Mecklenburg; Naples, Florence, and Genoa in Italy all drew within themselves; as did Serbia, Bulgaria, and Hungary in the crumbling Hapsburg Empire. Literally dozens of other peripheral, smaller, perhaps still pretentious dynasties were affected: Estonia, Latvia, Andorra, Liechtenstein, Luxembourg. The Great War not only gobbled up the cream of much of the world's youth, it also consumed their natural resources, and their economic wealth as well.

Even if jewel merchants could find their way across battle lines to display wares, and even if the royal lodgings— castles, turreted townhouses, country manors—were still intact, and if the owners still inhabited the place and had not fled elsewhere for safety, they largely presented the image of bastions under siege, filled with wary, frightened people who eschewed contact from outside their enclave. Even those fortunate enough to be far from the guns proved extremely conservative, hoarding, unwilling to consider investments in luxuries—unless it was in small, portable jewels to hide for future emergencies.

"We must cut expenses to reflect reduced revenues," Ernest Walker said to Managing Director, Brownstone Tolhurst, who nodded.

"I've already issued orders to Ramsey to cut our sales forces by half—most of the European, including Hadstrom in Sweden and Finland. I disliked doing that to Hadstrom, you know."

"We must curtail our acquisition of raw gems, too. And gold and silver."

"Obviously. What about our American mine?"

"At least cut out one shift, and reduce the pay for the surviving miners."

Tolhurst made a note, then brought up cutting. "Do we dare bring more stones to London?"

Walker propped his head into two fingers and a thumb, pondering. "It's a risk. Amsterdam is still safe from war, it seems. But aren't you fearful we'll lose Von Den Sprecht should we remove all of our stone cutting to England?"

"We could use the war as an excuse."

"True. And it's one they must respect. But having access to Von Den Sprecht craftsmen is of considerable value. One wonders if, in our absence, De Beers makes more inroads into Von Den Sprecht cutting operations, where that would leave us in the future?"

"If our own English cutters could do the work for us, why should we care?"

"Ahh, and that's the point: can they?"

Now it was Tolhurst's time to ponder. At last, he said, "No. Any truly extraordinary stones should be handled by extraordinary cutters. Do you believe the Claremont and Ward people can ever match the talents of those at Von Den Sprecht?"

Walker shook his head. "Unfortunately no. That means we must keep intact our access to the Dutchmen."

Thus, at the beginning of 1916, the London jewelry firm of Johnson, Walker, and Tolhurst, Ltd. extended an invitation to Amsterdam's Verenigen Boas Von Den Sprecht to relocate their famed gemstone cutting operations to London, to "escape the vicissitudes of war". The offer included a prime location facing Hatton Garden, along with a pledge to assist the gem specialists in building to suit their needs. The Dutch politely thanked Johnson, Walker, and Tolhurst, but excused themselves based primarily on the fact they felt no pressure from the distant war front.

So Johnson, Walker, and Tolhurst suggested a satellite cutting operation located at 16 Hatton Garden, with a guarantee of complete independence to the Dutchmen, should they accept. Again Verenigen Boas Von Den Sprecht politely declined. So, the foremost gemstone cutters in the world remained at Hogehilweg 12, in Amsterdam.

* * *

Naseby Ringgold, as Nathan Kenneth Ringling, was peripherally aware of his employers' attempted negotiations with the Dutch gemstone cutting firm. As chief usher he'd both guided Dutch representatives to the sacrosanct meeting rooms of Johnson, Walker, and Tolhurst, Ltd., as well as served those august presences during their meetings.

But Naseby Ringgold really didn't care about his employer's gemstone cutting negotiations. He didn't care who accomplished the faceting as long as he had a chance to observe and to learn. And in this regard, Brownstone Tolhurst had been true to his word by assigning Wellesley Glanding, in charge of Johnson, Walker, and Tolhurst's in-house jewelry fabricating, to share faceting knowledge with the young chief usher.

Naseby took to the jewelry fabricating environment quite readily, spending as much time as his regular duties allowed. Yes, the young American understood that the gemstone cutters from Amsterdam were the best at their trade in all the world; that their mastery was much farther advanced than that of the men employed in the Johnson, Walker, and Tolhurst fabrication room. But at this stage, Naseby Ringgold wasn't as interested in learning how the best gem cutters in the world applied their trade as much as he wished to know how *any* cutting was successfully accomplished, even though performed by relative amateurs. Why? Because Naseby Ringgold had spotted a way to get even with the thieves who'd stolen his Yogo sapphire birthright. And to do so, meant that he must learn to facet gemstones.

Chapter Sixteen

Actually the man the principals of Johnson, Walker, and Tolhurst, Ltd. knew as Nathan Kenneth Ringling was, in the owners' eyes, proving a valued asset to the firm: an accomplished chief usher and valet butler, unusually effective at staff assignments and training, trusted handler of valuable display cases at opening and closing times. And the mere fact that young Ringling seemed eager to learn about every facet of gemstone preparation and marketing, from rough stones through cutting and merchandising proved that the young man was a "comer" who might well be slated for future development and advancement.

Theirs was not a trust based on instinct, but observation … and investigation. Brownstone Tolhurst and Edward Walker admired Nathan Kenneth Ringling's quiet efficiency while performing his duties, as well as the man's self-effacing demeanor in relations with all others, whether superior or inferior within the firm, or customers from without. But in order to employ the young American in ever more trustworthy roles, they charged Gideon Herrelback with scrutinizing what Ringling did with his outside time. To do this, the office manager for Johnson, Walker, and Tolhurst employed a Bow Street Runner from south of the River Thames.

A loose amalgam of professional confidence men of the lower sort, Bow Street Runners specialized in investigative techniques ordinarily frowned upon by Scotland Yard, but often overlooked if methods employed were for supposedly beneficial purposes to benefit reputable employers. And few could be more reputable than the fine jewelry firm of Johnson, Walker, and Tolhurst, Ltd., of #16 Hatton Garden.

The "Runner" Bill Harms began his investigation by tailing the man he knew as Nathan Kenneth Ringling as he left #16 Hatton Garden after the shop closed each day for two weeks. What his report disclosed was that the man he investigated usually swung by Central London's Markets, sometimes stopping at a green grocer, sometimes at a meat market, and sometimes for bread. Other than that, the target spent the rest of his free time in his third floor apartment some twenty-one blocks away, off St. John Street, on Compton.

On his return each morning to Johnson, Walker, and Tolhurst, Ltd, the target invariably followed the more direct route of Aylesbury-to-Clerkenwell-to-Hatton Garden, arriving punctually an hour before the shop opened to the public.

It was during this period that the jolly fat butcher asked Naseby if he still had the Bow Street Runner following him?

"I ... I beg your pardon, sir."

"The Bow Street Runner. The knob that's been following you—I wonder that you didn't know?"

"Do you mean someone has been following me?"

"Aye. Even followed you into me market a coupla. Wanted t'know what you picked up, I guess." He winked. "Maybe he wanted t'know should he invite hisself to dinner."

When Naseby learned more about the Bow Street Runners, he knew he was being investigated. That's when he placed the tiny piece of paper to fall inside should a dresser drawer be opened without his knowledge. Same with a hair on a piece of luggage in his closet.

It was on day three after Naseby had prepped his apartment with telltale signs of intrusion that he discovered the torn piece of paper still inviolate, but in a slightly different spot than where Naseby had placed it. The hair had disappeared from his luggage. Going over his rooms minutely, he discovered the throw rug by his bed had probably been moved, then slid back in place—evidence that the intruder was looking for loose floorboards that might conceal a hiding place. And the bed, though carefully remade, was not prepared quite as tightly and in exactly the same manner as he always did it.

The surprising thing, however, was that the twenty-pound note was still in its envelope in the dresser drawer where Naseby placed it—the same dresser drawer where he'd placed the torn paper strip. The motive, then, for entry was not robbery. It had to be that Johnson, Walker, and Tolhurst was having him investigated. But for what purpose? Did they know the last of the money his father Jake Hoover gave to his mother before leaving for Alaska was in a bank's saving account on Farringdon Road? And did they know of the empty safety deposit box he'd established in another bank?

Naseby had to assume "yes" to all the above questions. But again, to what purpose? He wondered about the extent of their investigation? Had his real identity somehow reached England? Would his employer's queries reach as far as Canada? To Toronto? He felt safe there, but what if the investigation followed to Detroit? And to the supposed Great Lakes Shipping firm of William Ward Randolph, a man who would search his memory forever without accounting for anyone named Ringling in his service.

So, should his charade be revealed, he reasoned. So what? Thus far, his only crime in England was in presenting false identity—hardly a hanging offense. And even if the false charge that he'd stolen rough stones at the Yogo mine somehow followed him to England, he now knew that rough stones—especially *small* rough stones—were considered of minimal value by his employers. If they were turned from "stones" into "gems", however, that was something else! That's why Naseby

137

Ringgold breathed a sigh of relief that he'd not yet begun his plan. And since he'd also not divulged his strategy for vengeance to another soul, he *had* to be in the clear.

This close surveillance, then, was for another reason— but what? Had someone else within the firm stolen, and this investigation was routine for all the floor personnel?

It occurred to him that, if it focused on him alone, that he might be under consideration for a position of even more trust within the firm ... now *that* would be an interesting development! If true, Naseby reasoned, it could only mean more access to items of value at Johnson, Walker, and Tolhurst: money on hand, the jewels themselves, opening and closing vaults, record keeping....

Naseby changed the amount and number of notes enclosed in the drawer's envelope, reset the strip of paper where the intruder had placed it, then added a fine hair plucked from his head in a far corner. Then he raised his bedstead on its far side and slipped the caster from the bottom of the pipe forming the headboard. Taking a piece of wire with a hook on one end, he reached into the pipe and pulled out the wadded tissue paper he'd used as a plug. Then, by gently shaking the hollow pipe, its additional contents fell into his hand: a number of bank notes of varying denominations, and a second forged passport in the name of "Norman (none) Richards."

Then the young man smiled and, complacently assuring himself that all was in order, patiently composed himself to await the purpose of his investigation to be revealed.

* * *

"He looks clean to me, Mr. Herrelback," the Bow Street Runner Bill Harms reported. "Cablegrams across to Canada bear out what you've told me about his letters recommending him. Nothing in his room to show he's more than he seems: neat, sticks pretty much to himself, not a whole bunch of clothes, but what he has is clean and folded neat, or hung in his closet. Tidies up his bed every morning before he leaves. Cooks in his rooms. Eats sparingly. Don't smoke. Only one bottle of booze in his cupboard: Jamaica rum, and it looks like its only been hit once or twice—the cork was near stuck in. No ale. Neighbors all say he's quiet, behaves himself. Stays pretty much to his own company. Punctual, like as if he's on a time clock. Leaves here almost to the minute every day, swings by the Charterhouse Market most days to pick up whatever he plans on eating, I guess. Lights go out every night by nine-thirty. Lights go on at five every morning. Steady as a rock. Plumb boring, you ask me."

"I assume, Mr. Harms, that you will put that all in writing."

"Yessir. I'll do that right away, unless you want me to look into him further. Trace him back from Canada, say. Or watch him more."

Gideon Herrelback peered down his nose at his investigator. "I should think your investigation complete, Mr. Harms. Thank you. Go ahead and file your written report, and submit your bill with it."

The Bow Street man stood, nodding in affirmation. "There's just one little thing that sticks in my craw, Mr. Herrelback, sir."

"And what is that, Mr. Harms."

"Well, see, he had this little piece of paper stuck in a drawer so's it would fall out if anybody else opened it; like he expected to be burgled and wanted to know about it if it happened. Yet he left some money in that drawer. That don't make sense to me, unless he knew he was being investigated. Is it possible somebody from here told him?"

Herrelback chuckled. "Not likely, Mr. Harms. Perhaps the man was merely being cautious—a trait we like in all our employees. But do make a note of it in your written summary. Now, good day, sir."

* * *

"Do you mind if I call you Nathan?" the fabricating room supervisor asked the man he knew as Nathan Kenneth Ringling.

The chief usher for Johnson, Walker, and Tolhurst was in the room where jewelry was crafted so often he became a familiar sight to those employed therein.

"Not in the least." Naseby Ringgold replied. "I would prefer it."

"All right, Nathan, I thought today I would attempt to explain what we look for in rough stones, in order to determine the proper cutting angle." Wellesley Glanding strode to a row of locked bins, unlocking and opening the topmost, the one holding small rough diamonds, picking two at random and holding out one to his visitor. "Let's begin by carefully examining stones in the rough, look for flaws and imperfections that require removal during the cutting process." He held his stone to the light. "Aha, this one contains a 'feather' that would make the finished gem cloudy and less translucent." He held the rough diamond out so Naseby might hold it to the light.

Naseby peered closely at the stone without expression. "I see," he murmured, handing it back. Then he murmured, "Peculiar, perhaps, but I prefer sapphires."

Glanding chuckled. "I've noticed that about you, Nathan. Most people of taste prefer sapphires." Dropping the two diamond roughs in their proper bin and locking it, he opened another, this one containing rough sapphires. "Because of your interest in sapphires, perhaps I should explain the difference

140

between sapphires from America and those from Australia and the Orient—you do know there's a difference, do you not?"

The chief usher shook his head and moved closer.

The cutting room head held out a rough sapphire stone he said was around three carats. "This one came from Burma. Note the color variations in it, the rainbowing effect." He dropped the stone in Naseby's hand, continuing: "I don't believe we'll be able to do much with it; the blue is lusterless, and the pinkish streak not very translucent. One wonders, if one was to cut it, how one would do it, do you see?"

Thoughtfully, Naseby asked, "And the Yogos?"

"I beg your pardon?"

"The Yogo sapphires? Ones from America."

"Oh, you mean ones from our 'New Mine' in America." Wellesley Glanding stared curiously at Naseby.

Cursing himself for his slip of tongue, the chief usher said, "And the sapphires from America are different?"

The fabricating supervisor nodded. "Back in a shake," he returned to his sapphire drawer for another stone. Upon returning, he dropped a second rough gem in Naseby's hand. "That's an American stone, Nathan. Note how true its cornflower color is and how flawless—no occlusions of any kind. Hold it up to the light, then hold the other. Do you see?"

Naseby did see. He held the stones one in each palm, staring at first one, then the other. "But," holding out the larger Burmese stone, "this one is less valuable, do I understand, because of its cloudiness and color variations?"

"There you have it, Nathan. Truth is, the larger one won't even cut out as many carats as the smaller American stone because so much will be wasted in trying to salvage something of value from it."

Naseby returned both stones to Glanding. As the shop

superintendent returned them to their drawer, he said, "That's the important thing about the American stones, the quality of those coming in." He paused after locking the drawer and murmured, "If only they weren't so dastardly small."

"Small? Are American gemstones all small?"

"Aye. When it comes to sapphires, unfortunately yes. Not all of them, understand. But a high percentage."

Naseby, breathing easily now after his blunder at dropping the 'Yogo' name, asked, "You mean there are no large sapphires coming from America?"

"All too few, I'm afraid. But some. And nearly all, small or large, are consistent in color and clarity." The man peered not unkindly at his visitor. "I say, are you familiar with the paper from Claremont and Ward?" When Naseby shook his head, Glanding said, "They're experts in evaluating precious gems and how to engrave them. Known round the world. Consulted by most of the Hatton Garden jewelry merchants, and even into Germany. We must've asked them to assess our New Mine sapphires. They wrote up their evaluation. Makes for top-notch reading. If you know Mr. Herrelback or Mr. Tolhurst well enough to ask them to let you read it, I'm sure you'll find it uppers."

The man known as Nathan Ringling nodded. Then the visitor pulled a watch from his vest pocket, glanced at it, and murmured, "Thank you, Mr. Glanding ..."

"Wellesley," the other said, smiling.

"... But I really must be returning to the showroom. You've been most kind, and I'm looking forward to learning everything you would care to divulge."

Chapter Seventeen

Messrs. CLAREMONT & WARD

EXPERTS IN GEMS & LAPIDARIES

LONDON

Write of the "NEW MINE" SAPPHIRES thus : --

We have recently cut from the rough upwards of 11,900 carats of these beautiful "New Mine" Sapphires, and we have, during the progress of our work, taken the greatest pains to compare them, in every way possible, with those Sapphires that come to us from Burma, Siam, Ceylon, Australia and elsewhere.

Sapphires, like all the other corundum gems, crystallise in forms belonging to what is known to crystallographers as the Hexagonal, Rhombohedral, or Monotrimetrical system, and assume the forms of Hexagonal pyramids, Hexagonal prisms, Rhombohedrons, Scalenohedrons, etc., or more or less complex combinations or modifications of these figures.

It is, however, comparatively rarely we meet with a crystal of Sapphire perfect in shape, as these gems come into the market generally in broken or water worn fragments, which show upon examination just a characteristic indication of the system to which they belong. This fact is due to the thousand and one vicissitudes encumbent upon such a precarious existence as gems are subject to, from the moment of their formation to their appearance in Hatton Garden or some other gem centre as marketable products.

Now a very noticeable feature of the "New Mine" Sapphires is that they are more often found in the perfect geometric form designed by Nature than are Sapphires from other parts of the world. True it is, however, that the figures even of crystals of Sapphire which reach us from the other hemisphere in a perfect crystallographic condition are often of such a complex nature that the task of deciphering the relationship of one face with another requires a crystallographer of no mean ability, and we have nothing but admiration for the vocabulary equal to adequately describing the wonderful and beautiful surface markings of these precious stones in the rough—protruding and receding triangles, parallel striae and flanges, and a dozen other interesting effects, all of which are intimately connected with the Hexagonal system.

All kinds of gems, as everybody knows, sometimes contain flaws, feathers and other imperfections, the successful removal or reduction of which depends upon the skill and judgment of the lapidary. The most difficult imperfection with which the lapidary has to contend with in Sapphires is the presence of cloudy and semi-opaque patches within the stone, often occurring in parallel lines which generally form a series of hexagons or triangles one with the other. This defect often mars the beauty of a costly gem, and by its removal immense loss of weight is incurred, not unfrequently accompanied by deterioration of colour.

The "New Mine" Sapphires are absolutely free from this tiresome defect of cloudyness, which is undoubtedly the reason of their great brilliancy and luster.

With regard to the colour of these gems—they range from the palest steel colour through all the different shades of blue until they reach, in the fine specimens, that lovely tone called "cornflower blue," which, until

144

comparatively recently, was associated only with the Sapphires of Burma and Siam.

Moreover—and this is particularly striking to a practical gem-cutter—the colour is always quite evenly distributed throughout the stone, and never is found in patches as is the case with all other Sapphires; therefore the "New Mine" Sapphires, when cut and polished, cannot possibly appear "parti-coloured."

These gems also, when cut, are very seldom "dichroic" in effect, as the principal axis of the crystal is generally so very short that it is almost an impossibility for these Sapphires to be cut in any direction except that which gives the true blue colour.

Naseby Ringgold handed the *Claremont & Ward* "New Mine" appraisal paper back to Johnson, Walker, and Tolhurst Office Manager Gideon Herrelback with a polite "Thank you, sir, for allowing me to read this important document." Herrelback took the paper and laid it on his desk with only a nod. The chief usher wheeled with near-military precision and left the manager's office. Though no shadows crossed the chief usher's features, he seethed inside.

Not only have they stolen my sapphires, he thought, but they're the best sapphires in the entire world!

* * *

He stole his first gemstone on a Thursday, at high noon. He was visiting fabrication and had asked Wellesley Glanding if the man could help him understand how an expert cutter could determine the best faceting for individual gemstones. Glanding unlocked the sapphire bin and the two stood examining different

145

stones, with the shop foreman pointing out planes and flaws within a stone that might influence the cutting. "Understand, Nathan, that I'm hardly the right tutor for you to get the most solid understanding. For that, you'd have to learn to speak Dutch. Ha, ha."

The chief usher smiled, spreading the palm filled with sapphire gemstones he'd just dipped from the bin, stirring them with his finger.

"I'm to understand they let you read the Claremont and Ward paper?" When Naseby nodded, Glanding said, "They've got some pretty experienced cutters over there. And they're only a few minutes up the street. P'raps with your connections upstairs, Mr. Tolhurst or Mr. Walker could arrange you a tour of their cutting room."

While Naseby looked thoughtful, Glanding plucked a stone from his hand and held it up to a gas light. "You do know about 'crown' and 'pavillion', do you not?"

"I've read of them, yes. But to really understand—no."

"Hmm," the fabricating room man mused. "It's difficult to explain with a rough stone ..." Then he snapped his fingers, striding to a stand-up desk and rummaging through a drawer. Upon returning, he handed a paper to Naseby. "Here's a diagram of a finished gem. It has each of the cuts outlined on it, and marked."

Naseby took the paper, dropped his palm of rough sapphires into the proper bin—all except one that was concealed in the bottom crease between his index and middle finger—then studied the paper, murmuring, "Yes. I see. The crown is not merely the top of the jewel, but the *top part*, above the girdle, which is the widest part of the entire finished gem. Is that right?"

"I believe that correct. And you'll observe the pavilion?"

"That's the part below the girdle?"

"Mmm-hmm."

"Then the actual height of the stone controls the angle of the pavilion facets?"

"No, it's not that easy, Nathan. And it's here that I'm weak; you see, it's not the length of those pavilion facets, but the angle of them compared to the angle of crown facets that produces a jewel's maximum reflective attributes."

Naseby shook his head in obvious confusion.

"In order to demonstrate more clearly, young sir, we would needs examine a polished gem. And that's something ... wait a minute! Trebas is working on a necklace right now. Follow me."

They moved to a table where a workman labored over a filigreed-gold necklace, already studded with several diamonds. Two other gems glistened nearby. Wellesley Glanding picked one up to hand to his visitor. Holding the paper in one hand and the polished diamond in the other, it was easy to pick out the table, the crown, girdle, and pavilion. But he was still confused over the many 'facets' revealed on the gem, each at a slightly different angle: main crown facets, break facets, star facets, main pavilion facets, pavilion break facets. "How do they know to do all these angles, Wellesley?"

"That's the secret, m'lad. That's the difference between them and us. They know how to design their cuts in order to get the right angles to bring out each gem's best brilliance." The foreman took the stone, held it to the light, then handed it back. "Now look at the jewel from the top down—that's how it'll be viewed when it's slipped around a pretty neck. See how the light is reflected back? That reflection—its brilliance—results directly from the faceting angles; the actual design determined beforehand by the cutter." He shook his head. "Their skills in reading raw stones are why they're paid so well."

He directed Naseby to place the diamond back at the fabricator Trebas's elbow. "And it's why the best cutters in the world are still found in Amsterdam."

* * *

Over the course of three more weeks, the man known as Nathan Kenneth Ringling pilfered six more raw sapphires by concealing them between his fingers in much the same manner. By the very nature of his method of theft, the chief usher was limited to stealing only gemstones of limited size. But, he reasoned, most of the raw sapphires stolen from him in America were small, and his first objective was to replace what the thieves of Johnson, Walker, and Tolhurst had stolen from him.

Then another shipment of raw sapphires arrived from America, and the already committed Naseby Ringgold managed to take six more stones, including three in the mid-range size (two of four carats and one five).

The larger high-graded stones were missed! But since the man known as Nathan Kenneth Ringling only accompanied the shipping containers to their underground vaults (and one case to replenish the fabricating room bin), any suspicion of the chief usher was dismissed. Bow Street Runners were called in to investigate, however, and in the course of their investigation, Naseby Ringgold's room was examined for the second time.

He noted the entry when he discovered his dresser drawer had been opened. Again, everything was in order, including the envelope with petty cash in it. His clothes were all neatly folded and in place, socks arranged tightly, side-by-side and by color. The slip of torn paper was also in place, more nearly approximating the position he'd placed it. But the hair was gone. The drawer had been opened.

Alerted, he paid close attention. Someone else had remade his bed to a close approximation of his neatness, but not

148

quite as meticulously done.

He smiled; especially since he'd only two days before removed his back-up passport and the earlier pilfered gems from the hollow bedpost to join his most recent acquisitions in the new "Norman (none) Richards" safe deposit box, located at the staid old King's Cross Bank, off Farringdon Road.

It was the following morning when Miss Applestrom joined the man she knew as Mr. Ringling on his walk to #16 Hatton Garden. It was barely daylight, and fog drifted in from the river. At first, Miss Applestrom's appearance startled him, though he gave no indication. "This cannot be either your regular time, or regular passage, Miss Applestrom." He paused, then added, "Your parents do dwell in Bloomsbury, do they not?"

"I took the trolley, Mr. Ringling. I wanted to talk to you." When he turned to continue his walk to Hatton Garden, she hurried to catch up. "This is not something I'm comfortable with discussing at our place of employment."

He stopped, turning. "Whatever can you mean, Miss Applestrom. Is this something unrelated to Johnson, Walker, and Tolhurst?"

Her chin was up and her eye firm—the young lady was nearly as tall as he. "No, Mr. Ringling. It has to do with our employment. But I'm afraid to bring the subject up before others." He waited while she seemed to gather courage. "I fear some gems have gone missing, Mr. Ringling. And I have reason to believe I may be a suspect in their disappearance."

"That's ridiculous! Where could you get such an unfounded idea?" He resumed walking. This time she strode at his side.

"Mr. Ringling, these men came to my mum and pop's home to inquire about me! They filled out a paper with a lot of questions, all about me, my history, schooling, previous work,

149

then asked mum and pop to sign it. Like they were Bobbies, or something. Then they wanted to go through the apartment—as 'part of their investigation'—they said."

"Did your father and mother allow that?"

"They didn't know what to do! This kind of thing never happened to them before."

"So they permitted it?"

"My mum went with them into every room. And mum and pop was both there when they went through my room."

He stopped to face her, smiling. "I presume they found no missing jewelry?"

"Mr. Ringling, you're actually smiling!"

"That must have been quite a search—silk stockings and under garments."

"Mr. Ringling, do you realize that I've never before seen you smile."

He set off walking once again. "Don't you feel you're being a little ridiculous, Miss Applestrom? Surely you must know you have nothing to worry about." They paused at Farringdon Road to let a carriage go by. As they crossed, he said, "Presuming you have no cause for alarm, I can safely tell you that indeed some raw stones have gone missing. I don't know how many or how valuable they were. But I'm sure Mr. Herrelback and our security people are alarmed. There's reason to believe they may have employed some Bow Street Runners to investigate all our in-store people."

"But my mum and pop ..."

Again Naseby paused, this time taking her by the elbow and turning her to face him. "Miss Applestrom, those men had no authority to enter your parents' home. If your father had rang for the police, those men would've left." She was wide-eyed, obviously leaning on his every word. "But under the circumstances, since obviously you have nothing to hide, by them searching your home, you're beyond suspicion."

"Mr. Ringling, I like it very much when you smile."

His face went blank and he dropped her elbow to continue on his way to Johnson, Walker, and Tolhurst, Ltd. They crossed Clerkenwell, then were at Hatton Garden. As they neared the imposing front of #16, Naseby Ringgold said, "I'm sorry, Miss Applestrom, but I'm sure security won't allow you in the shop while we're stocking the display cases." He paused to gaze inquisitively on her.

"Oh that's quite all right, Mr. Ringling. I understand. I'll just pop on down to the Smithfield's and order a cup of chocolate." When he nodded, she said, "Thank you so much for putting my mind at ease."

"Think nothing of it, Miss Applestrom." Then he smiled and added, "I'm only sorry I wasn't the one permitted to rummage through your dressing table." And he spun around to ring the bell and stood facing the huge double entry doors.

She hesitated a moment, then hurried off down the walk, her heels clicking a tattoo on the tiles.

Chapter Eighteen

"You wish to purchase flawed stones, Ringling? Is that what you just said?"

The chief usher had just poured tea for the managing partner of Johnson, Walker, and Tolhurst, Ltd. Brownstone Tolhurst pushed the cup and saucer aside with fat fingers and stared inquisitively up at the servant, who stood before the great man's desk with the tea tray in hand.

"Yes sir, I did. As you know, sir, I have a profound interest in products sold by our firm, particularly precious gems. And, as you've so graciously allowed me to visit our fabricating room to view stones and metals in design and completion, I've become even more intrigued by the cutting and faceting process of precious gemstones. Mr. Glanding—your fabricating room supervisor—has been very kind in showing me the process of design and producing your ..."

Tolhurst shook his massive porcine head. "That's all very interesting, Ringling, I'm sure. But why would you wish to purchase flawed stones? *That* I don't understand."

Naseby took a deep breath. "To experiment, sir. I'm especially fascinated by how gemstone experts arrive at how to cut and polish rough gems to bring out the best in finished jewels. Mr. Glanding has been kind enough to explain the theory behind the process, but unless one could actually try carving on real crystals, I doubt I'll ever fully understand." The young man paused, then added, "Sir."

Brownstone Tolhurst picked up his tea cup and blew across the top, staring all the while at his servant in thoughtful speculation, until Naseby blurted, "I've already tried cutting a glass bottle, sir."

"With what success?"

"None." Then the young man shook his head. "Actually, I found one could score it, and break it; and if I used small enough bites with a small wire, I could flake off small bits. But facet? No."

"So you wish to learn to cut and polish real corundum?"

"That's my thought, sir."

"You realize flawed stones are sold for industrial purposes."

"Yes, sir. But I'm given to understand sale prices for industrial stones are relatively nominal."

Tolhurst sipped, sipped again, all the while staring at his chief usher. Finally, "You know, Ringling, what you really need do is tour a real cutting room—like the one at Claremont and Ward."

"Yes, sir. I'm sure I would like that very much."

"There, you can see real lapidaries at work." The big man seemed to be staring through the servant, instead of at him. "The equipment we have in our shop is quite primitive, and your opportunities to learn from Glanding and his minions would be limited."

"Yes, sir. But they do have *some* tools, even if they are limited. And my thought is, sir, that theory also has limitations that only hands on experimenting can expel."

Brownstone Tolhurst abruptly dropped his empty cup into its saucer and pushed both forward while reaching for a sheet of paper. "Please be kind enough, Ringling, to pour another cup of tea. And this time, don't forget the sugar."

* * *

*This authorization is to provide Nathan
Ringling with up to ten pounds of flawed industrial*

153

stones for his purposes. He is also to have access to
our cutting equipment when it is not otherwise in use.
                                                    - Brownstone Tolhurst

Wellesley Glanding whooped as he read the Johnson, Walker, and Tolhurst Managing Director's note. "This doesn't say a thing about charging you for them, Nathan. This means he's 'gifting' you ten pounds of flawed stones for you to experiment with—that's wonderful!"

Naseby chanced a quick smile and received a broad one in return—he was starting to understand the inherent value of the occasional smile; it was almost as important as the imperturbable stoic expression he most often employed. The unexpected smile could be winsome, ironic, disarming, or infectious, as long as it remained unexpected and—most important—infrequent.

* * *

Brownstone Tolhurst was in Ernest Walker's office when Naseby Ringgold, known to the two jewelry firm's principals as Nathan Ringling, served tea. Both men occupied window seats and were gazing out over Hatton Gardens. Naseby served the long-faced older man first, then poured for Mr. Tolhurst, spooning in the requisite two spoons of sugar. When he handed his cup and saucer to the managing director, Tolhurst abruptly said, "Claremont and Ward turned down my request to allow you to visit their cutting room, Ringling. The blighters."

Ernest Walker coughed delicately into a handkerchief, then said, "They did? Why ever for?"

Tolhurst said, "They claimed they're in the process of restructuring their cutting room. But I believe they're wary of letting someone tour the premises whom they might think we're grooming as our own cutter."

154

"And they won't even grant a favor to one of their best customers? That seems bad form, don't you think?" The old man's bloodhound face appeared to sag even more as he turned his sad countenance on their chief usher. "Well, as a principal in Johnson, Walker, and Tolhurst, they can hardly refuse me a tour of their cutting room, now can they? I'll have Herrelback ring for an appointment for mid-afternoon tomorrow."

Tolhurst murmured, "Ernest, Ernest, don't you think the extent of that tour would be too much for you at your age."

The long bloodhound face actually brightened. "Oh I believe I shall be all right, especially if I can lean on Ringling's arm throughout." He peered up at Naseby. "You will be able to set aside a bit of time to assist me during the tour, won't you Mr. Ringling?"

As the chief usher withdrew, he overheard Brownstone Tolhurst suggest that their firm send over an issue of uncut sapphires prior to Walker's arrival, so that Claremont & Ward could have the assortment on a table for analysis when Ernest and Ringling toured....

* * *

Nathan Ringling, Chief Usher for Johnson, Walker, and Tolhurst, Ltd. assisted one of the firm's principal directors Ernest Walker from the carriage they'd taken for the two blocks from their offices to the Claremont & Ward "Experts In Gems and Lapidaries." The sad-faced older man, hobbling with a cane and accompanied by his servant, met by Theodore Claremont, were first led into a conference room and offered tea (which was abruptly declined).

Claremont, a pained, cadaverous man with muttonchop sideburns and an obsequious disposition that was obviously so seldom displayed that he struggled in deference to his firms primary customer, led the way out onto the cutting room floor, followed slowly by Mr. Walker (ably assisted by his cautious and watchful servant).

Naseby's overview was quick and encompassing. But there were so many people doing so many things on so many different machines that he was soon lost trying to absorb it all.

"Where are the stones we sent over yesterday?" Walker asked.

Claremont nodded and waved them to a well-lit corner table where two men wearing magnifying eyepieces were analyzing and cataloging each stone. Both bent nearer their work as their visitors loomed over them. "What are they doing?" Walker demanded. Claremont murmured to one of his workmen who turned to explain. Ernest Walker waved his servant nearer, then said to their guide, "Alas, Theodore, I'm rapidly tiring. Perhaps I'll be unable to complete this tour. However, my Chief Usher, Nathan Ringling, knows what it is that I need to know."

He turned to Naseby. "You do have the list, Ringling, do you not?"

Naseby met his employer's guileless gaze and nodded, "Of course, sir. It's right here in my pocket." And he pulled out a folded piece of paper with which he'd intended to take notes. "I'm sure I can get answers to everything you wanted to know, sir."

Walker nodded and waved Claremont away, saying, "Perhaps I will have a spot of that tea, sir. So nice of you to ask. Perhaps a biscuit, too."

And as the two shuffled away, Ernest Walker had the other's elbow, saying, "I'm sure Ringling will be all right, but if you would prefer not to leave the man to his own devices, perhaps you can assign someone to guide him around and answer his questions."

Naseby Ringgold stayed by the table spread with

sapphires from *his* Yogo mine—the one stolen from his father. But his primary interest was no longer revenge as much as absorbing as much as possible about the gemstone cutting process. He learned about the sides of an octahedral crystal, and that those sides are harder than those of dodecahedral planes. He was told that the relative ease with which a facet can be introduced into a gemstone depends "on its orientation to the crystallographic planes of relative hardness."

"You do understand," one of the crystallographers said, "that some stones—diamonds, for instance—rate higher than sapphires on a hardness scale, but not nearly so hard on the toughness scale."

"I don't understand ..."

The man—elderly, but with a touch of humorous frankness to his features, said, "When we talk of 'hardness', laddie, we mean you cannot scratch it, you see?" He drew the point of a sharp knife across the face of stone. Naseby nodded. "But when we talk about 'toughness', a hammer could easily break it—cause it to shatter. Steel is much tougher, eh?"

"Billy, Billy," the second man muttered, "You're making this much too complicated. All the gentleman really wants to know is how stones are faceted."

But Billy wasn't to be diverted. "You can even shatter diamonds," he said, "which is the hardest material on earth—with a bar of lead, which is soft. But that same bar of lead can be beat to death and all that might happen to it would be that it would dent, never shatter."

Naseby nodded, murmuring, "I see." But he didn't. Again, the other crystallographer came to his rescue.

"Get to your point, Billy."

"My point ... my point?" he appeared strangely perplexed.

The second man said, "Billy's point is that corundums and diamonds can be cleaved provided the crystallographer strikes it on the right plane."

"And how is that determined?" inquired Naseby.

"That's what we're doing here, mate—grading these stones for angle and plane." He held one out. "Hold it to the light and see if you can catch the octahedral face within ..." His explanation drifted to nothing as he spotted Naseby's puzzlement. Then he said, "Aha!" and whipped off his magnifying eye loupe and handed it to his student. "Here, screw this into your eye socket and see if that'll help."

It did. "Yes, I believe I'm seeing a very slight shift there. Is that your 'plane'?"

"Aye. If you were to place that stone in yonder cup, tighten it down to the correct angle, then strike it with the mallet and chisel, it would most certainly cleave at that angle." To the nodding Naseby, he added, "I could show you, but we're not through studying and grading these stones, and it might not be the proper application to get the most from the gem. Right?"

Naseby handed the loupe back. "Of course. I understand. But do these 'planes' exist in all stones?"

Just then a burly, black bearded man in overalls paused at the table. "You're Ringling? I'm Georgeson. Mr. Claremont asked me to show you through the workshop; said you were to do some research for the gentleman from Johnson, Walker, and Tolhurst."

Quickly establishing his authority, Naseby said, "Yes, that would be Mr. Walker, the senior director at Johnson, Walker, and Tolhurst."

"I see. Mr. Claremont said the gentleman provided you with a list of questions?"

"That's correct."

"Perhaps I could see the list?"

"Just a few quick notes. Most of them are in my head."

Another man, this one in a tweed suit, drifted up. The burly man said, "Ah, Mr. Ward. We're just about to get this young man moving." He turned again to Naseby and said, "All right, sir. What's next?"

"I'd like a little better understanding about the grading system used for our sapphires, Mr. ..."

"Georgeson. And surely by now you've run the table on that question, long as you've been here already."

Guessing that he was treading unstable ground, Naseby said, "Then how about a tour of your implements and machines. Mr. Walker said an inventory would disclose to him whether Claremont and Ward are actually among your industry leaders."

He smiled tightly as Georgeson glanced angrily at Mr. Ward, who hesitated, then gave a brief nod and turned away.

So it was that the one-time Yogo waif, Naseby Ringgold was shown most of the up-to-date cutting tools utilized in one of the foremost gem cutting and faceting rooms in all of England: the wheels and quills, bruting machine, dopping cups and pins, the diamond saw, and three different polishing rigs. He learned about collecting diamond dust and how it was mixed with very fine oil for polishing.

When the machine tour was complete, he thanked Mr. Georgeson, then snapped his fingers and said, "Mr. Walker specifically asked if he could view the various 'cuts' available for our gems?"

Burly said, "Oh I don't know about that—is it Ringling? I'll have to ask management if I can show you that."

Naseby turned to stare unseeingly out over the workroom of Claremont & Ward. "Thank you, Mr. Georgeson. Please do. I'm sure Mr. Walker would be vitally interested in getting a deep understanding about all the capabilities you people are able to provide."

Burly returned a few minutes later to ask Naseby to follow him. In Theodore Claremont's office, he was handed a thin folder containing drawings of the various gem cuts produced by Claremont & Ward, along with four actual jewels (sapphire, diamond, ruby, and emerald) displayed on a square, velvet covered board.

Naseby analyzed the drawings, then murmured, "I see a rose cut sapphire and two table cuts in the ruby and emerald, but I'm unsure of the diamond. Can you illuminate me on that cut?"

"Theodore Claremont said, that is one of the newer ones—we call it an 'oval brilliant'. Do you like it?"

"Very much. Do you have others not listed in these drawings?"

"We're experimenting all the time, sir."

He raised an eyebrow to Burly. "What else, Georgeson?"

"How about the 'Briolette'? And the 'Shield'?"

"Ah yes. As I said, we're experimenting all the time. Next week there may be another new one."

Naseby held out his hand to both gentlemen. Then to leave Claremont and Ward with a note of uncertainty he said, "I don't see anything here on Oriental cutting. For instance, the 'Moghul'—do you gentlemen experiment with any of those gem forms?"

Chapter Nineteen

Miss Applestrom flashed her best smile upon his entrance. "We're glad to have you back, Mr. Ringling. Mr. Walker asked specifically that you call on him upon your return."

"Thank you Miss Applestrom. I do imagine he's anxious for his tea."

"I believe Mr. Hayes served Mr. Walker and Mr. Tolhurst in your absence, Mr. Ringling."

"Thank you again for your information Miss Applestrom."

As he turned and started for the broad staircase to the upper floor, he heard her whisper, "Still no smile, Mr. Ringling?"

He knocked.

"Do come in," came the muffled reply and he pushed one of the double doors open to slide inside.

"I've been given to understand you've already been served your afternoon tea, sir?"

The sad face drooped even more as Ernest Walker peered across his immaculate desk. "It is well past tea time, Ringling."

"Yes, sir. And one could say I found the shop at Claremont and Ward so intriguing that time slipped away from me—if permitted I'll try to make it up by working extra hours, or during my day off, or ..."

The senior director waved dismissively. "Please sit down, Mr. Ringling, and give me a thorough report. You were treated well, I hope?"

"Yes, sir. You laid the cornerstone quite well, Mr. Walker. I sensed they didn't like it, but I received a gratifying— if all too short—tour. I even had a chance to talk to a few of their workmen. Saw stones polished, one was even cut using a saw they said was state of the art. And I believe it—the cutting head was circular and ran through a tray on its bottom that contained a mixture of light oil and diamond dust. Ran in and out on a rail they said was true to one thousandth of an inch, and could be ratcheted around to any desired angle, as could the stone being cut. It was amazing, sir."

"No doubt. Might be something that would interest me, do you think?"

Dampened a bit by Mr. Walker's apparent lack of enthusiasm, Naseby changed course: "I even received a cursory report on how to sort, as well as how to analyze stones for their most beneficial cuts."

Ernest Walker had propped his sad and wrinkled face between both hands, elbows resting on the shining desktop.

Naseby slid the folder he carried across the desk. "I even brought these drawings of many of their various finished products, sir."

Walker opened the folder, shuffled through the pages, then slid the file back. "Did you inquire about their cutting room restructuring—I saw none while there?"

A bemused smile flashed, then was gone. "No, sir. I saw none. But I'll confess it never occurred to me to ask."

When Ernest Walker seemed satisfied with his report, Naseby said, "I'll always be grateful, sir, that you and Mr. Tolhurst found a way to further my gemstone education. I do want you to know I find the entire process exceedingly fascinating."

The countenance drooped even more than normal. The Johnson, Walker, and Tolhurst partner waved an idle hand and said, "Go. Do."

* * *

162

Days followed days. The chief usher for Johnson, Walker, and Tolhurst spent as much time as his duties allowed in the firm's fabricating shop, experimenting with those rudimentary cutting and polishing tools found there, carefully grinding, cutting, cleaving and polishing the ten pounds of rough throw-away stones he was allotted by Brownstone Tolhurst.

One day, Wellesley Glanding dropped a large, rainbow-colored corundum stone in Naseby Ringgold's palm. "Here's one for you, Nathan. Came in with a shipment from Brazil, probably as ballast. Leastwise we're not likely to pay for something as parti-colored and milky as it is." As Naseby turned the stone over and over, Glanding chuckled. "Looks like it tried to make something of itself, but couldn't decide on what shade to go for: green, red, yellow, or blue."

"And I may have this?"

"Far as I'm concerned. None of us could see any value in spending any kind of time trying to cut worthwhile gems from it. The cloudiness alone says the only thing it's good for is to grind up for cutting powder."

Still staring at the multi-colored rock, turning it over and over and over in his hands, Naseby murmured, "Would I be allowed to take this home?"

Glanding chuckled again. "I can see no reason why not. It may put you over the ten pounds that Mr. Tolhurst allotted, but it looks to me like they don't care that much about waste material—especially if it goes to you."

Naseby moved to a light table, screwed in an eye loupe and studied every angle of the stone. He identified a plane and struck a sliver of cleavage from it, then another. Finally he pocketed the five-inch stone and returned to his own workplace as chief usher for Johnson, Walker, and Tolhurst, Ltd., London's foremost jewelry firm.

* * *

Days followed days into weeks. As far as any observer could see, the chief usher they knew as Nathan Kenneth Ringling was the utter epitome of an English butler: stone-faced, always watchful, closely monitoring sweepers and swampers, clerks and cashiers and greeters and clerical.

Office Manager Gideon Herrelback breathed in relief to have Ringling directly below him in the command chain; the man appeared tireless and efficient, but Herrelback couldn't help it, Ringling puzzled him. The man demanded nothing, but assumed as much responsibility as was thrust open him, always acquitting himself to perfection. He was punctual to the moment in his duties; nothing escaped him:

"Mr. Pendergast, you were three minutes late reporting for duty this morning."

"Mr. Hadley, I noticed the dust and cobwebs I asked you to remove three days ago still fouls the southwest corner of the wine cellar. I will not ask you again!"

"Miss Applestrom, are you missing a cuff link on your left sleeve?"

"Mr. Fowler, the firm has identified a counterfeit twenty-pound note that came from your register. I was given to understand that you have already attended the class for identifying counterfeit bills provided by the Bank of England. Am I right?"

* * *

Miss Applestrom was almost prepared to admit defeat—she simply seemed unable to attract Mr. Ringling's attention. Each time the young man ventured near her workstation, she smiled, usually eschewing a spontaneous pleasantry that she had

164

long prepared, "Good morning, Mr. Ringling." "My you look as though you are on a mission, Mr. Ringling." "Have you noticed that I'm wearing two cuff links today, Mr. Ringling?"

Never a comment. Never a flicker of emotion. Seldom ever a glance in her direction.

Only twice had she seen the young man smile. So transformational, yet so elusive!

Then one day she arrived at Johnson, Walker, and Tolhurst at her proper time, went directly to the cloakroom, shed her coat and scarf, then returned to her workstation as the man she knew as Nathan Ringling unlocked the massive front doors to the public. There on her workstation perched a triangular tube of faceted, clouded, multicolored corundum about five inches long, by two inches wide at its base. Puzzled, she picked it up, turning it in her fingers. On one side was carved the word:

APPLESTROM

Miss Applestrom leaned against her stand-up greeter's desk, eyes wide as saucers, staring around. There was absolutely no one watching! No one even glanced her way! No clerk, no Mr. Ringling, no Mr. Herrelback. She placed the beautiful nameplate stone back atop her desk and, with considerable effort, composed herself.

After a few minutes, she turned the stone so the name faced her.

But when the first customers entered a few minutes later, she turned the stone so her name would be customer-visible.

All day, Desiree Applestrom stared in wonder at the gemstone with her name carved on it, flipping it back in its proper direction when customers approached, but flipping it back when alone. Gradually, she worked out that the stone must have been the result of the man she knew as Nathan Ringling's generosity. But when she could actually tear her eyes from the stone to search for Mr. Ringling, he appeared only at a distance. Never did he so much as glance in her direction.

Once, however, opportunity knocked. But she was so entranced by her name stone that Nathan Ringling passed right by without her notice until he was ten feet past. "Oh Mr. Ringling!" But apparently he didn't hear. Or chose to ignore.

* * *

"What is that, Miss Applestrom?" It was Gideon Herrelback, preparing to leave his office for the day; unconsciously she'd been fondling her gift, stroking it, turning it over and over, and end for end.

"Oh, Mr. Herrelback! You surprised me."

"I daresay. I also asked you about the thing you are holding."

"Yes, indeed, Mr. Herrelback. It seems to be a stone with my name carved into it. It was here on my entry desk when I arrived this morning. I wondered if you might've left it?"

"May I see it?" She handed the carved and faceted stone to him; he turned it over and over in his hands, then dropped it in his coat pocket.

Her distress was plain. "Is it not mine, Mr. Herrelback?"

"That remains to be determined, Miss Applestrom."

"But it was left at my station, Mr. Herrelback! It has my name on it!"

Gideon Herrelback peered down his long, thin nose. "I'll concede your point, Miss Applestrom. What I won't concede at this time is that it belongs to you. Messer's Walker and Tolhurst may wish to make that decision."

Desiree Applestrom was sobbing when she followed Gideon Herrelback out the doors (which were locked behind her) a few minutes later.

166

The tears had ceased, but the woman's eyes were still red and her cheeks contained a rosy flush when a half-hour later, the man she knew as Nathan Kenneth Ringling let himself out of the ornate carved doors of Johnson, Walker, and Tolhurst, Ltd. "Miss Applestrom!" he said in surprise. "What ever are you doing standing out here? You'll catch your death."

She took a deep breath. "It was yours, wasn't it, Mr. Ringling. You carved my name into that stone and left it for me, didn't you?"

"An accusatory tone hardly becomes you, Miss Applestrom."

She seized his arm with both hands, clinging tightly. "Oh why do I do and say everything wrong!" She began sobbing again. "Please! I'm *accusing* you of nothing! It ... it was the most splendid gift anyone ever, ever gave me. Ever!"

He used his other hand to prise her fingers loose. "May I suggest, Miss Applestrom, that you control yourself. It was merely a bauble. Had I any idea you might become so emotional, I wouldn't ..."

"HE STOLE IT!" she cried, tears gushing.

"Who stole what?" Naseby Ringgold asked, taking a step back from the prostrated woman.

"That awful Mr. Herrelback! He asked to see it, then kept it, pocketing it. He said Mr. Walker and Mr. Tolhurst would decide if it was mine or theirs."

He reached up and pinched his lips, then stroked his chin for several moments. At last, he sighed and took the girl by the arm, propelling her along the sidewalk. "Come, Miss Applestrom, I'm dying for a cup of chocolate and I'm sufficiently extravagant to suggest one for you."

On their way to Smithfield's market, she tried: "Aren't you afraid they'll suspect you of thievery, Mr. Ringling." Or, "I

167

can't help it, Mr. Ringling, I'm so worried about you." But he said nothing throughout their ten-minute walk. No flicker of emotion.

Finally seated on a sidewalk bench, steaming cups of chocolate in their hands, he said, "I'm afraid, Miss Applestrom, that your worries are for naught. The gemstone you so obviously cherish is actually worth very little. It was given to me by Wellesley Glanding from the company's fabrication shop."

Naseby actually fidgeted on his bench: she sat so near, her widened eyes so obviously adoring as she leaned toward him to assure that she caught every word, every nuance.

"You see Mr. Tolhurst authorized Glanding to supply me with a limited amount of flawed stones so that I might experiment with cutting and polishing them."

"Then why did that awful Mr. Herrelback take the stone you gave me?"

His smile flashed, then was gone as he took her hand. "I suppose it's possible that Mr. Herrelback was not privy to Brownstone Tolhurst's authorization for me to obtain a few flawed gemstones. When he finds out—as he will as soon as he brings the stone to Mr. Tolhurst's attention—you will get your namestone back."

She drained her cup and laid the empty in her lap so that when he made to remove his hand she clasped it with both of hers. "It is so comforting to talk to you, Mr. Ringling. You must be the most intelligent, practical man I've ever known. And just a moment ago, you smiled! Do you have any idea how handsome you are when you smile?"

He tried to withdraw his hand, but she clung even more fiercely.

"Please, Miss Applestrom. Your parents will be worried about you."

"I think the stone with my name carved in it is the most precious gift I've ever received ... *Nathan*."

He jerked. "Are you so surprised that I called you 'Nathan', Mr. Ringling?" When he didn't reply, she said, "I go to sleep almost every night counting how many ways I can say 'Nathan'. Does that surprise you, Mr. Ringling?"

He stared across the sidewalk at busy shoppers entering the greengrocer. "Indeed it does, Miss Applestrom. But even more so, it embarrasses me."

"Desiree."

He managed to retrieve his hand, but she transferred her grip to his arm.

"Say Desiree. Not Miss Applestrom. My given name is Desiree. It would give me so much pleasure if you were to say it, Nathan."

He chanced a glance at her while saying, "If I do, then will you promise to release me?"

She nodded.

"Desiree."

She released him, sighing, "A smile and my name, all in one day—actually within just a few moments of one another." Her laugh tinkled. "Mr. Ringling, that's an enormous amount of progress for you."

Chapter Twenty

A week passed. Then another. Naseby Ringgold had expected to be queried, but nothing happened. Yet Miss Applestrom's engraved stone had not been returned. The young lady dripped distress; so much so that the man she knew as Nathan Ringling felt compelled to frequently pass her greeter's station and wink. Or smile. Or, if no one else appeared to be watching, simply give her a thumb's up. She smiled bravely, wistfully, even proposed another cup of chocolate after work— which he feigned not to hear.

It came as no great shock when his room was searched once again, this time less reconnoiter than ransacked. This time his drawers were left opened, bed unmade, clothes jerked from closets and left strewn at random on the floor. Of course his twenty-pound note was gone.

He called the police. It was while the investigator was still in his rooms that Mrs. Ferguson, the landlady said the two characters that'd been in his room had also discovered his cellar corner where Naseby had his grinding wheel, cutting table, and tools. "They took some bright stones from your workbench, Mr. Ringling. I saw them! Just scooped up ones you had in a tiny dish into their hands. Even swept some fragments from the floor. Bow Street runners, if you asked me." A tear trickled down her cheek. "I couldn't stop them, sir. I tried, but they just shoved me to one side."

Naseby patted the landlady's shoulder and asked the inspector what his recourse might be? The man held a notebook and pencil. "A bit impolite if you ask me. Took money out of a dresser drawer, hey? How much?"

"Several 20-pound notes," Naseby replied. When the inspector inevitably asked the amount, the ransacked apartment dweller appeared vague. So the inspector addressed the landlady: "You say they took some gemstones from a basement workroom owned by ..." he rifled back through the notebook "... Nathan Ringling—this gentleman. What, sir, are you doing cutting gemstones in a rooming house cellar?"

It took some doing. But finally, Naseby explained that jewelers Johnson, Walker, and Tolhurst employed him, and that his company allowed him to practice faceting skills on worthless stones.

At last the inspector left with this parting advice: "Keep your money either in the bank or on your person, young man. Leaving it in a desk drawer for any passing guttersnipe is poor form."

Naseby sighed and, helped by Mrs. Ferguson, restored his room to order. After they finished, the landlady asked Naseby Ringgold if he'd care to trot downstairs with her for pie and coffee.

* * *

He knocked at the conference room opening off Brownstone Tolhust's office. He'd expected the summons. No real surprise, either, at the three people seated at the big conference table: Tolhurst, of course, and Ernest Walker, with Gideon Herrelback. Miss Applestrom's engraved corundum stone was the sole table ornament.

"Sit down, Ringling, if you please," said the gargantuan managing director of Johnson, Walker, and Tolhurst, Ltd., waving at a chair directly across from him.

The chair slid out easily on casters. It was plush, leather upholstered. Naseby eased down, perching on its edge, hands on knees, back stiff. He thought about saying something trite, like,

"You wanted to see me, sir?" but decided against it. He was clean—unless they'd discovered his safety deposit box under an assumed name, and he knew they hadn't because he'd checked its security after the ransacking of his room. He raised his eyebrows, peering directly at Brownstone Tolhurst.

"Yes, well, Ringling, Mr. Herrelback brought this stone to our attention and we'd like to ask you about it."

"Yes, sir?"

"This is your work?"

"Indeed it is, sir."

Ernest Walker, sitting next to Brownstone Tolhurst, leaned forward to pick the stone up, rolling it over and over in his hands. Finally he held it to the light, then replaced it on the table and leaned back in his chair.

Tolhurst glanced for a moment at Gideon Herrelback. "Yes, well, as soon as Mr. Herrelback discovered the stone on Miss Applestrom's desk and drew a few logical conclusions, he brought in some private investigators to look into your activities."

"I'm aware of that, sir. Someone had investigators into my rooms twice before. Previously they've been discreet and tidy, even leaving the money that I purposely left in a drawer to see if those men breaking and entering were in fact thieves. But this last time, sirs, they trashed the place, stole my money, abused my landlady, and took some of the unfinished stones you had already placed at my disposal; they took them from a cellar work space that Mrs. Ferguson was kind enough to let me use. I must say I'm somewhat disappointed in anyone who would order such disgraceful activity without regard to law or ethics, sir."

Both Brownstone Tolhurst and Edward Walker stared pointedly at their office manager. A flushed Gideon Herrelback

172

stammered, "I was never aware that management had sanctioned your access to our gemstones."

"Only flawed gemstones, sir."

Herrelback threw up his hands. "Any gemstones, Mr. Ringling. I'm really not qualified to pass judgment on gem quality."

"Did you then think to ask those of our staff who are qualified, such as Wellesley Glanding, sir? Before you sent in agents to trash my private dwelling space!"

"ENOUGH!" thundered Brownstone Tolhurst, slapping the heavy oak tabletop with the flat of his hand. "Mr. Ringling, Mr. Herrelback, control yourselves."

The chief usher and the office manager both subsided into their chairs, one red of face, the other outwardly impassive. Tolhurst continued: "That Mr. Herrelback was not informed of our wishes"—he gestured at Ernest Walker—"is our fault for not doing so." The huge man reached for Miss Applestrom's nameplate stone. "Be assured, Mr. Ringling that Wellesley Glanding apprised us that he'd entrusted this piece of flawed corundum in your care and, in fact, watched you do some preliminary carving on it in our fabrication shop."

When he paused, Naseby murmured, "Thank you, sir."

Ernest Walker cleared his throat and, without looking away from his folded hands, said, "Do you wish to say something, Mr. Herrelback?"

The office manager murmured, "Yes, indeed. I wish to apologize to Mr. Ringling for my jumping to conclusions and ordering his person investigated. Obviously not only was my conclusion in error, but my selection of a new investigative team was flawed."

The man the others knew as Nathan Kenneth Ringling sighed. "Thank you, Mr. Herrelback. I, too, am sorry if, during

173

this exchange, I might've said something to give offense." He scooted forward in his chair and turned from Herrelback to Tolhurst with a raised eyebrow. "Might that be all, sir? May I return the stone to Miss Applestrom?"

"Not yet, if you please." The big man's tone was gruff. "Perhaps now we can get to the point of this meeting."

Naseby Ringgold retreated back into the luxurious conference room chair, still with a single raised eyebrow. Tolhurst seemed unable to keep either eyes or fingers off the Applestrom stone. "This is what I wish to talk about, Mr. Ringling." He looked up inquisitively. "And you did this yourself?"

Naseby leaned forward again, eyes searching the big man. "Yes sir. I'm sorry I couldn't accomplish what I would've liked to do with the stone, but my equipment is quite primitive—much more than even that found in your fabrication shop."

Brownstone Tolhurst nodded, bemused. "Yes, we have a thorough understanding of the equipment found in the shop in your lodging house basement: the treadle from a sewing machine adapted to a small grinding wheel, isn't it? And a tiny circular saw designed to run through a cup filled with cutting dust and light machine oil."

"That didn't work very well, Mr. Tolhurst. I'm sorry to say."

The huge man turned Miss Applestrom's stone to face his chief usher. "The font—what is it, Ringling?"

"Yes, sir. It's called 'Desdemona'. It's new. I chose it because it appears Grecian, and because it is composed of mostly straight lines that I thought I could cut largely with my saw, such as it is."

Tolhurst smiled at him. "And how did you finish the

174

carving, Nathan? Our investigators found the stencil that you obviously fashioned by hand—quite creative, sir, if I might say so."

Naseby nodded. "Thank you, sir." He reached for the Applestrom corundum, peering at it closely in the room's weak gas light. Then he returned it to Brownstone Tolhurst, saying, "If you'll examine the upper left of the second 'P' you can discern a rough spot." Tolhurst studied the carving, then shook his head. Naseby continued: "Never mind, sir; it's there, and will become more clear in better light. But frankly, I was tiring. I used a handmade stylus, made from a twenty-penny nail, along with a little bit of diamond dust Wellesley Glanding was kind enough to share with me. That, and a little oil, and a significant amount of intensive labor allowed me to complete the project, at least to the point you see it now."

"And what of the facets, young man? How did you determine and implement those?"

"Determination was no problem, sir. The stone makes those for you. I did some cleaving, of course, to get the shape of the stone that I wanted. Any facets that were made prior to its polishing was purely for decorative purposes, because the rainbow cloudiness within kept the stone from any significant reflective properties."

Gideon Herrelback cleared his throat and asked if he might be permitted to leave? A wave of Tolhurst's hand was the sole attention received during the man's exit.

Ernest Walker leaned forward to ask, "Where did you pick up such gemstone terminology, Mr. Ringling?"

"Why from you, Mr. Walker." Then Naseby shook his head. "Well, not necessarily *from* you sir, but *because* of you. Claremont and Ward contributed a lot. And I would've not had access there, had it not been for you. Then there's Mr. Glanding, who has been most sharing. And I shan't forget Johnson, Walker, and Tolhurst who've been altogether generous in permitting me to learn about precious gems and their cutting."

Still holding Miss Applestrom's stone, Brownstone Tolhurst reached into a vest pocket and slid a key across the table to his chief usher. "Mr. Walker and I have decided such talent needs all the support it can get, Mr. Ringling. You obviously have a God-given gift with rough gemstones that needs to be encouraged. The key before you will allow you access to our fabrication shop any time you choose. Access, of course, will permit you to use our equipment, such as it is. Certainly our equipment, while not state of the art, is better than what you have in the cellar of your lodging establishment."

Naseby picked up the key in wide-eyed wonder. "This ... this requires a great deal of trust on your part, good sirs ..."

"And a great deal of responsibility on yours, young man."

Naseby Ringgold bowed his head. Peering at the floor, he asked, "What constraints do you wish to place on me in the use of this key?"

"Only that you notify the watchmen when you plan to enter. We will instruct security to keep a record. You are empowered to work with any flawed stones Mr. Glanding chooses to permit. He, in turn, will be required to leave a record of the carat size, flaws, and a loose description of each stone. Then we wish to see what you're able to achieve, Mr. Ringling." Naseby, still staring between his feet, nodded. "In that manner, we wish to track your progress, Mr. Ringling. The sapphires from our American mine might not be the only gem we garner from the New World."

Naseby's eyes found the shrunken orbs of his overweight boss. "I will endeavor to acquit myself in such manner to make you proud, sirs."

Brownstone Tolhurst handed the corundum stone across the table. "Please tell Miss Applestrom how pleased we are that she permitted us to view her very lovely gift."

Halfway to the door, Mr. Walker called him back. Peering up from his long, hang-dog face the senior partner dolefully said, "And, young man, if you ever come into additional such suitable pieces, I'm sure both I and Mr. Tolhurst would admire having our own namestones."

Chapter Twenty-One

Wide-eyed speechless joy exploded in Miss Applestrom when the man she knew as Nathan Ringling gently laid her nameplate stone on her greeter's desk. "Perhaps you might join me at Smithfield's for chocolate in celebration after our day is complete," the emotionless chief usher murmured.

She started to accept, then sobered. "Oh, Mr. Ringling, can we do so tomorrow? I must hurry home today to help my mum. I promised."

"Tomorrow then," he said turning away.

* * *

She waved to him from the middle of a sidewalk bench between the refreshment center and the greengrocer. A shopping bag took up a space to her left, which was placed at her feet when he carried their steaming chocolates. He simply couldn't remember—ever—a lady so beautiful, even his mother.

"Please, Nathan—may I call you Nathan?"

"Please ... what ... Desiree?"

The radiance of her smile nearly enveloped him. "I want to know *everything* that happened to allow you to return my stone!"

Instead, he peered over the cup's rim into her wide green eyes and said, "I once knew a man—you would've thought him sinister with his black and pointed handlebar moustache and cadaverous body—who used to say, 'Now that's a tall subject.' But he wasn't sinister at all." He lowered the cup and his dark eyes took on a far-away cast. "He was one of the finest persons I ever knew ..." Then he shook himself and said, "Mr. Walker and Mr. Tolhurst seemed intrigued by my work on your stone,

178

even complimentary. Mr. Walker also asked if I could make namestones for them."

She started to clap, but spilled her chocolate instead. He jumped up to grab a handkerchief and hand it to her. She smiled privately to herself as she dabbed, murmuring, "Too polite to mop up my carelessness, Mr. Ringling—Nathan?"

"On your dress, yes."

"Most of it was on my coat."

"What will your parents say?"

She smiled again.

He said, "I'll get another chocolate for you."

But she shook her head. "I'd rather have wine with our dinner."

He raised an eyebrow. "Well, as much as I might wish to oblige you, Miss Applestrom, I'm afraid that's out of the question."

"Oh dear, I hope not. The wine is in the shopping bag at our feet, along with fresh baked rolls and some salad greens I picked up while waiting for you. Now all we need is to pop into the butcher's and pick out a cut you'd prefer, then flounce on to your apartment where we'll have our celebratory feast."

He was still on his feet and she peered up at him with a bewitching half-smile. "You're insane," he muttered.

"For good reason."

He felt his face reddening; the blush crept from beneath his starched collar to pinched lips and narrowed nostrils. He couldn't remember when he closed his eyes, but when he opened them hers were wide and amused. "*Mister* Ringling! I'm going to serve you dinner. And I'm going to do so at your apartment. I've been planning to do so for well over thirty hours now and you will not—will NOT—thwart me!"

Naseby Ringgold was so stunned he seemed transfixed.

179

"So please sir, take our empty cups back and accompany me to the butcher. I believe you once told me you and he got on…?"

He never said a word; not one word at the butcher counter where he only pointed at a thick cut of steak. Miss Applestrom handled everything: the greeting, the crisp order, the pleasantries accompanying the purchase. He proved so inept that she even paid for the meat from her own purse. During the brisk walk to his apartment he was still mute, though she chattered on about 'what?' he could never recall. On their climb to the third floor he was mute, and when he unlocked the door and pushed it open to permit her entry, he maintained a wary frightened silence.

She strode directly into the tiny kitchen space and plopped her shopping bag on his kitchen table. Then she turned to smile while shaking her head at the man she knew as Nathan Ringling, standing in shock just inside his still opened apartment door. "You really are shy aren't you, Mr. Ringling? All along I thought you maintained a certain … well … professional aloofness."

When he stood like an upright log, she walked past him to close the door. "But you really are shy, aren't you?" His eyes followed her as she strode back past him to the couch, to the rocking chair, then on into his bedroom. Upon her return, she said, "Is it because I'm a woman, Mr. Ringling? Have you never had a woman in your apartment before?"

As if someone snapped fingers, he blurted. "You can't be serious, Miss Applestrom. What if someone finds you in my apartment? Like your parents? Mrs. Ferguson?"

Still pacing, she asked, "Who is Mrs. Ferguson, Nathan?"

"My landlady! She …"

"Then let's go ask her. What is her room number? Bottom floor, I imagine. I'm quite sure she would agree that we

180

could at least have dinner together in your apartment. Let's ask."

"Miss Applestrom!"

She stopped her pacing to stand directly before him—the damned insufferable woman was grinning like a Cheshire cat; "Miss Applestrom, you cannot ..."

"Desiree."

"Please, Miss Applestrom!"

She took a step forward and brushed lips against his. He blurted, "You cannot know what you're ..."

She jerked his head forward and gave him a long and sensuous kiss. When she broke off, she murmured, "I've wanted to do that for a long time, Mr. Ringling."

He pushed past her to fling himself in the rocking chair. A minute went by. Two. Then she slipped from her coat, throwing it over the back of the couch. "I'll start dinner."

"NO!" As she paused, he muttered, "I mean no, Miss Applestrom. It would be wonderful were that to happen, but I cannot allow it. You have your reputation to think about. Your family. Johnson, Walker, and Tol ..."

"Nathan, Nathan, grow up." She sank to her knees before his rocker. "I think I'm beginning to understand. You're shy because ... because ... Nathan, have you ever kissed a girl before?" He turned his head to the side, lips pinched. She leaned on the chair's arms to rock him forward. "Look at me, Nathan!" It was a command; he looked. She kissed. He didn't turn away. She kissed again. "Put your arms around me, Nathan." And she kissed him again.

* * *

It was with the connivance of Gideon Herrelback that Naseby Ringgold obtained the eight-inch-long, five-inch-wide, flat piece of Chinese jade. The office manager was relieved when the chief usher, displaying utterly no rancor, laid the drawing before Johnson, Walker, and Tolhurst's office manager and asked if it might be possible for Mr. Herrelback to help? "You see, sir, Mr. Walker and Mr. Tolhurst asked if I might carve some nameplate stones for them."

Herrelback could not possibly be more attentive—after all, this was the young man he had so wronged over Miss Applestrom's corundum name stone, and fouled with unfounded charges before both managing directors. Yet this young man presented the same urbane demeanor he always displayed, unsmiling, but courteous and unfailingly polite. "But I wish to present something creative, something unique. Something like this drawing, sir. I thought perhaps jade would be the ideal stone with which to work."

Herrelback looked at the carefully rendered pen and ink, and gasped at its exquisiteness: a curving dragon standing on its tail on a base nameplate with Ernest Walker carved in a unique Oriental-type font. "This is very beautiful, Mr. Ringling! Extraordinary! But could you do it?"

"I believe so, sir. Especially having access to all the tools presently in our fabricating shop. It would be a challenge, but one I seek to meet."

"And you wish to render this in jade?"

"Chinese jade, sir. But I would need assistance in acquiring a piece suitable for such work."

Herrelback picked up the paper, then laid it down. "Expensive, I'm afraid."

"Indeed, sir. That's why I came to see you. I'm willing to contribute the work, and do so on my own time, in the firm's workshop. But the cost of the material is beyond my own means. Yet to render it in anything less—wood, for instance—seems as if it would demean the end result. It's my belief that Mr. Walker and Mr. Tolhurst, as the firm's leading directors, deserve something at least as impressive as Miss Applestrom's namestone."

"And my role?"

"I'm suggesting you might have some idea on how I might acquire the rough jade without going to Mr. Walker or Mr. Tolhurst."

Herrelback drummed the paper with his fingers. "You wish it to be a surprise?"

"If possible."

"Mmm-hmm. Let me think about it, my boy. I'll get back to you."

"Thank you, sir."

But as Naseby turned to leave, Gideon Herrelback called him back. "What of Brownstone Tolhurst?"

"I'm sorry, sir, but that's not entirely clear in my mind: perhaps a bear or majestic lion standing over a prostrate maiden or an injured hunter. Possibly in ivory."

Herrelback nodded, adding, "If you don't mind, I'd like to keep this drawing while I explore jadestone availability."

"Of course, sir."

* * *

The drawing wasn't the only thing Herrelback wished to have in hand while exploring the feasibility of suitable jade; he also inquired of Miss Applestrom if he could borrow her corundum namestone as an example of the kind of work the man he knew as Nathan Kenneth Ringling could turn out.

Nascby missed the stone on her welcome desk the day it disappeared, although she thought he seldom glanced in her direction. "It was Mr. Herrelback, Nathan ..."

"Mr. Ringling, if you please, Miss Applestrom. Always Mr. Ringling at Johnson, Walker, and Tolhurst."

"... He asked if he could borrow it to show others the

quality of your work. Of course I said yes. He was very polite about it, assuring me that he would return it as soon as he could. But I really do miss it."

"I see." One of his rare smiles. "I'm sure he'll return it, Miss Applestrom. Please don't worry about it."

"He asked me not to tell anyone. But I can't do that. Both Mr. Tolhurst and Mr. Walker missed it when they came in, and asked about it. I had to tell them that Mr. Herrelback borrowed it to show off your work." She drew the fingers of one hand across her brow, hiding her lips as she murmured, "I love you."

No answer, but another smile. So she laid a paper on her desk and asked him something about it. When he bent forward to see where she pointed, she murmured, "Can I have another chocolate?"

He put his own finger on the paper, brushing hers. "Today?" he whispered.

She nodded.

So did he. Then strolled away.

* * *

The piece of jade was larger than needed, and was accompanied by a foot-long, five-inch tall section of ivory from an elephant's tusk. Wellesley Glanding presented both to the man he knew as Nathan Ringling, just three weeks after Naseby had discussed with Gideon Herrelback the possibility of carving name stones for Edward Walker and Brownstone Tolhurst.

"I'm not sure what's going on, Nathan," the fabricating shop supervisor said. "But Mr. Herrelback said these were to be entrusted to your care, but that they must be locked up when not being carved."

One could almost see the mechanical calculator clicking as the chief usher rolled each piece in his hands, lost in some distant creative realm unknown to Glanding or, for that matter, the other shop workmen, each of whom applauded the exchange.

When Naseby paused to knock on the office manager's open door in order to thank him, Mr. Herrelback waved him in, saying, "The initial cost is underwritten by Sir Douglas Cole; Lord Orwell, if you please. He agreed to underwrite the project in the expectation that the entire board of directors will actually recompense him as an award from the board to Mr. Walker and Mr. Tolhurst for superlative service. Lord Orwell sits on the board, you see."

"I see, sir. At least I think I do. Would it be proper for me to thank Lord (he stumbled over the word before hurrying on) Orwell, sir? Or would the carving be sufficient?"

"The carving, Ringling. The carving." He slid Naseby's dragon drawing across his desk to the chief usher. "If you can achieve your dreams, everyone connected will be amply compensated."

"Thank you very much, sir. You've been most helpful."

Herrelback also pushed Miss Applestrom's corundum namestone across the desk. "Would you be so kind as to return this to our young lady with my gratitude for loaning it for a worthwhile purpose."

* * *

Naseby Ringgold set immediately to work on carving the jade dragon, utilizing every bit of free time he could allocate — late nights, Sundays, sometimes during his noon meal time. The dragon began to take shape. It was the worst kept secret in all of Johnson, Walker, and Tolhurst, Ltd. Gideon Herrelback took a constant interest. One noonday hour the office manager was accompanied by a scowling bushy bearded elderly gentleman. "Ringling," he said with preamble, "this is Lord Orwell. He asked to see the work in progress."

185

Nathan nodded, but continued the careful polishing of the claws on one of the dragon's feet. When he was satisfied with the stage of polish, he switched off the machine and said, "How do you do, sir. I hope the work thus far accomplished meets your expectations?"

"So far, so good young man." Then Lord Orwell harrumphed and mumbled, "You are quite a craftsman. Tolhurst might be wasting your talents as an usher."

"Thank you, sir. But I'm content in my regular post, especially as I may pursue this as a hobby."

Herrelback's laugh was high-pitched. "Please, m'Lord, Ringling's present position within the firm is highly valued."

Ernest Walker found time to limp through the shop—according to Wellesley Glanding his first visit in two years. Then Brownstone Tolhurst loomed in the doorway. Both managing partners paused at the table where their chief usher labored over the jade dragon. Neither partner uttered a word about the dragon and its supposed "surprise," but Naseby watched Tolhurst eyes wander around his table, then to the other tables in the shop. So later that evening he cut the piece of elephant tusk to the size needed, then began shaping the grizzly bear and the sprawled hunter; with a broken harquebus off to one side, and a bear cub peering out from behind bushes.

* * *

Compared to working with the jade, the ivory creation went more swiftly—or began so. But the Brownstone Tolhurst creation entailed research unnecessary for Ernest Walker's jadestone. Dragons, you see, are figments of imagination, thus no one really knows what a dragon looks like, enabling considerable latitude in Naseby Ringgold's artistic creativity. Grizzly bears are, however, real wild animals, as were frightened hunters, bear cubs, and an ancient, broken fowling piece. That's why Naseby visited museums to study ancient blunderbusses, and why (sometimes accompanied by Miss Applestrom) he visited the London Zoo with scratch pad in hand to draw American grizzlies and European brown bears.

Compared to others, Naseby Ringgold had advantages unknown to most London frequenters when it came to dredging imagination for grizzly bears: he'd twice actually seen the animals live and in-the-wild when dwelling with his mother along the remote Yogo Creek of his youth. Then there were the true-to-life paintings of his father's friend, Charles Manion Russell, which was even as early as a decade into the 20th Century becoming known in England—one of which even hung in Brownstone Tolhurst's office!

* * *

Subtly, more and more time became available for Naseby Ringgold to work on his jade and ivory projects. "I'm not sure what's happening," Miss Applestrom mused to Mr. Ringling over chocolate late one afternoon, "but Mr. Herrelback asked me to serve tea to Mr. Walker and Mr. Tolhurst today. He said he'd rather not disturb you at the present, and that I might be obliged to serve on additional occasions."

The man she knew as Nathan Ringling stirred his chocolate with a forefinger while asking, "And?"

She said, "May I lick that finger when you're through stirring?" He smiled. She said, "I so love it when you smile." He held out his finger and she, without any seeming embarrassment, licked it despite the strand being crowded with strangers who smiled and strolled knowingly past.

"Mr. Tolhurst and Mr. Walker were very patient and obliging. They each shared with me just how they preferred their tea served—you never told me Mr. Walker liked to have his saucered first!"

"I didn't? No, I suppose I didn't. But, then, why would I?"

"And Mr. Tolhurst wants three spoons of sugar."

"Only two. But they need to be heaping. And he likes a dash of cream."

"He told me three. But he wanted them level, not heaping."

Naseby smiled again. "Same difference, I suppose."

She stared fixedly at the man she knew as her boss, friend, lover, advisor. Then she said, "Nathan, I need your help." He sobered, interested. "Mr. Tolhurst asked what I thought of being given additional duties as your assistant. He wondered if I thought a woman could actually fill the role of an 'assistant usher'?"

"And your reply?"

"No. First I want to know what you think?"

He stirred his chocolate, pensive. Then he once more held out his finger for her to lick. "I hope you weren't hesitant."

"Why? Do you think I should—or even could—do it?"

"I know you could. Certainly you should." He paused. "What did you tell Mr. Tolhurst?"

"That of course I could do it! Especially if I had his support, and support from Mr. Walker and Mr. Herrelback. As well as access to training from you."

He nodded. She stirred her own chocolate with a forefinger, then held it out for him to lick.

Ignoring the finger, he mused, "Your problems would stem from the rest of the staff. To be bypassed would be a slap in the face to some. Others would be appalled to think that a *woman* would be given a role elsewhere reserved for only men."

"The finger, Nathan." He licked. "I'm sure you're right, love. I already had something of a brush from Hewlett Hadley."

He nodded, staring sightlessly through teeming passers-by. Finally he asked, "How much of my role do they expect you to take?"

"That's just it—I don't know. As far as I know, the offer is merely to assist you; to be your assistant."

He took her hand, staring past her. "Seize the opportunity, Desiree. But in the beginning, act only in service to top management. Do not attempt to overtly oversee others. Leave that to me. My advice is to remain primarily a cheerful greeter who also provides tea service to top management. That would help me a great deal if I didn't have to interrupt my carvings at each of the assigned tea times. I will still do my walk-throughs each morning and evening, making suggestions or delivering reprimands where necessary. Gradually, you'll grow into the job, expected to do more and more until you slip naturally into the role." Then for the first time, she heard him laugh aloud. "Finally, you'll become so entrenched in the job they will wish to fire me and hire you as my full-time replacement."

His humor was infectious. "I've already told Mr. Tolhurst that I would be honored to accept. How long do you think I must wait before telling them I'm ready to fully replace you?"

* * *

As the "surprise" carvings for Johnson, Walker, and Tolhurst's two managing directors approached completion, Brownstone Tolhurst proved a regular visitor to the firm's fabrication shop. One day he and shop superintendent Wellesley Glanding paused at the table where the man they knew as Nathan Kenneth Ringling, magnifying glass screwed into an eye socket, put the finishing touches to an exquisite jade dragon. Pausing at their approach, Naseby was surprised when Mr.

189

Tolhurst poured out the contents of a small leather pouch onto the worktable. Three sapphires, a ruby, and two diamonds lay glistening. All six rough stones were of size—at least of six-carats, or more.

He whipped off the eyepiece to peer up into the managing director's beefy face. Brownstone Tolhurst said, "These are 'firsts', Ringling. Both Glanding and I have studied and catalogued them. They've each been weighed and measured for the record. Normally, we would send them over to Amsterdsam for cutting, but we've been sufficiently impressed by your work that we're placing these in your hands to see what you can do with them. Study them. Take as much time as you need. But at closing time each evening, you should return them to Mr. Glanding for security purposes until the next time you request them." Then without even glancing at the jade dragon or ivory grizzly bear, Brownstone Tolhurst turned and lumbered from the shop.

Naseby Ringgold switched his attention to the gems, then to Wellesley Glanding who shrugged, eyebrows clawing for the ceiling. Naseby screwed in his eyepiece and picked up the largest sapphire to hold to the light. "Beautiful!" he murmured.

"They're putting a lot of faith in you, Nathan," Glanding said. "It's a real opportunity. Don't foul it up."

Naseby glanced at the shop superintendent. "Believe me, Wellesley, I have no intention of risking this opportunity." Then he gathered up the six stones, poured them into the leather pouch, and handed it to his friend. Finally he picked up the jade dragon and began polishing a rough spot on one of its scales.

Chapter Twenty-Two

The "surprise" nameplates for Ernest Walker and Brownstone Tolhurst were delivered at the annual spring meeting of Johnson, Walker, and Tolhurst, Ltd.'s Board of Directors, held in the upstairs conference room above the firm's showplace sales store at 16 Hatton Garden.

It wasn't normal to hold quarterly board meetings in such confined quarters, but both senior partners acquiesced to the location suggestion at the urging of influential member, Sir Douglas Cole—Lord Orwell—who was adamant about an undisclosed "special reason" for the request. Naturally, Managing Director Brownstone Tolhurst went along with the "request" without disclosing that he knew all there was to know about the coming presentations.

Extra chairs were brought into the conference room, crowding the lengthy table. Other chairs lined the walls for staff members who might be called to answer questions raised during the meeting.

Alerted to the importance of the huge staff and board meeting, Head Usher, Nathan Ringling had his showroom sales staff display-ready: freshly shaven, hair brushed, collars starched, and suits sharply cleaned. The kitchen staff was as prepared as possible, with copious quantities of tea and condiments, their cooking ware shining like the sun, serving trays and dishes brilliantly spotless.

Miss Applestrom stood at the door, never more sparkling in a new wool suit, pleated white blouse peeking from behind the partially buttoned jacket. Her role, she'd been informed by Office Manager Gideon Herrelback, was to "remain at her station until ten minutes after time for the board meeting to

191

begin, then join Mr. Ringling in serving the board room occupants." (She tingled excitement!)

The imperturbable Mr. Ringling was waiting just outside the conference room door, hands clasped before him, eyes half-lidded, lips clenched, seemingly at total ease. To his right, stood four staff personnel drafted to be porters. Before each stood trays of tea service on folding stools. On tables behind were trays of condiments of all kinds, cloth-covered and properly warmed or cooled, as desired for the specific food dish.

She arrived somewhat breathless. He seemed not to notice. "Here's our plan: We'll enter first, Earl and his staff will follow with the tea service, then return for condiments and to carry out the empty teapots for replenishing. I will serve Mr. Walker, Mr. Tolhurst and Lord Orwell, who're on Mr. Tolhurst's left. You are to begin serving the gentlemen on Mr. Walker's right and progress around the table until we meet. Then we'll pour for the staff seated against the wall as Earl and his people bring in the condiments. You will begin with Mr. Herrelback, who is seated just to the left of the entry door, then progress around the wall in both directions, while I serve the board members condiments. Pay no attention to what's said, except as to any additions to the tea as the persons are being served. Later, after each board member has been served condiments, we will begin condiments to the staff. Understood?"

She nodded, taking a deep breath. He opened the door.

Their service went swiftly, to many admiring glances from the board members. She was surprised to see the fabricating shop superintendent—Glanding, was that his name?—perched in one of the chairs against the wall. So, too, was the accountant, Dawson. There were others she didn't know by name, but thought they were part of the company's overseas sales staff.

Then suddenly everyone was served and Earl and his people brought in additional tea urns before returning to the outside hallway. Nathan discreetly guided her to stand one side of the door while he stood, hands folded, on the other side. After a few minutes he picked up a tea service and approached Ernest Walker, motioning her to begin offering additional tea and picking up empty condiment service.

Brownstone Tolhurst was winding down on a summary of the firm's latest financial statement. "As you can—hurrumph—see, this infernal, everlasting war is continuing to have a deleterious effect on our cash flow. Yes, Lord Orwell?"

The Lord pushed back his chair. "If I might interrupt the flow of business, Brownstone, I, and the rest of the directors, have a presentation we'd likt to offer you and Ernest for your exemplary leadership of our company's ship of state."

Brownstone Tolhurst, a faint smile on his face, asked, "Can't it wait until we've finished with the financial statement, Sir Douglas?"

"I'm afraid not, old chap. Mr. Herrelback!"

Gideon Herrelback, two carefully wrapped packages in his hand, hurried around the table to hand them to Lord Orwell who, carefully placing a previously prepared card on each package, set one before Ernest Walker, the other before Brownstone Tolhurst.

Back in her station beside the door, Desiree Applestrom was nearly beside herself in excitement! She glanced sideways at the man she knew as Nathan Ringling; he seemingly stared boredly across the room, through a window.

Tolhurst opened his card: It said, "In Gratitude," and was signed by each board member. With a bemused smile, the huge managing director nodded at each person surrounding the table. Ernest Walker had already ripped the paper from his jade dragon to hold it aloft in triumph. Still bemused, Tolhurst carefully removed the wrapping paper from his nameplate and studied the finished product. "Isn't that exquisite," he murmured, holding it aloft.

Walker and Tolhurst exchanged pieces, then both dragon and grizzly bears began circulating in opposite directions around the table.

The gargantuan managing director lifted his big head from the tabletop to say, "I cannot possibly imagine a better indicator of esteem than the one rendered Mr. Walker and myself today. Can you, Ernest?"

Ernest Walker shook his head, hound-dog face following the progress of his jade dragon around the table.

Lord Orwell cleared his throat. Everyone turned attention to the man. "The reason I insisted on the presentation at this time, Brownstone, is that I did not want the person whose genius created these masterpieces to slip away before I introduced him to each and every board member. Mr. Ringling, will you step away from the door, please? Come over here by my side if you will."

Miss Applestrom couldn't believe the calm indifference her Nathan exhibited as he stood at Lord Orwell's shoulder, with Gideon Herrelback two steps behind!

"The other stone Mr. Herrelback," the Lord said, holding out a hand as his other arm draped over the chief usher's shoulder. "When Herrelback showed me the work that went into this other flawed piece of corundum in Miss Applestrom's behalf ..." he paused, seemingly to discover the room's only lady for the first time. "Please come around here, young lady."

Face flaming, Miss Applestrom somehow made it all the way around the table to have Lord Orwell hold her namestone before her so all could see. "When Herrelback showed me this namestone and suggested that we commission its creator to do something even more creative for our managing partners, I knew we had an obscure and hidden talent." With that, Sir Douglas started Applestrom's corundum nameplate around the table.

Ernest Walker trapped his jadestone dragon as it started around a second time, and Brownstone Tolhurst placed his ivory grizzly bear in the table's center.

"When I saw the quality of this man's work"—he squeezed the slight craftsman's shoulder—"I decided to underwrite Mr. Herrelback's suggestion that the board consider gifting our two managing directors with suitable samples of our regard for them. Thus, the pieces of jade and ivory that Ringling here turned into such exquisite masterpieces."

The Lord cleared his throat and said, "Now I'd like to make a motion that this board reimburse me for my initial outlay to set in motion our high regard for Ernest Walker and Brownstone Tolhurst." The motion passed without dissention. But during the discussion, it was disclosed that the craftsman behind each of the exquisite works donated much of his own time to his creations, and it became clear that the board was much in favor of some sort of a tangible reward. A member at the table's end held up a hand to ask, "Whose idea was this again, Sir Douglas?"

"Mr. Herrelback's, our office manager." He waved to the man behind, "Step up here, Gideon."

The board voted a two hundred pound bonus to Gideon Herrelback for his idea, and one hundred pounds for Nathan Ringling's actual work.

Desiree Applestrom turned an indignant eye toward Nathan, but received not even so much as a glance in return. She did, however, note that his mouth corners twitched in irony.

Brownstone Tolhurst murmured, "Thank you Miss Applestrom, Ringling, Herrelback. You may return to your places." He raised eyebrows to Lord Orwell. "Are you quite through, Sir Douglas? If so, I'd like to get on with this financial statement."

* * *

Out in the hall, Desiree Applestrom exploded: "Herrelback! Two hundred pounds!"

But the young man waved her down. "Please return to your front door station, Miss Applestrom. I can handle their immediate needs for now. However, plan on returning at three for our afternoon tea." When she demurred, he firmly said, "Miss Applestrom, you *will* do as I say!" Without further attention, he turned to Earl and his crew for a few brief instructions, then re-entered the conference room, quietly closing the door behind. She was nearly blinded by welling tears as she descended the staircase to the showroom floor.

Back inside the conference room, the man known as Nathan Ringling took station alongside the door. Brownstone Tolhurst was saying: "... so by not controlling our gemstone cutting operations, our company loses financial resources through their processing." He paused, then continued: "As per the board's instructions, we approached Amsterdam with a proposed satellite cutting operation, but they declined. Yes, Sir Douglas?"

"What of the cutting firm up the street?"

Tolhurst waved dismissively. "We discussed Claremont & Ward, Sir Douglas. And Ernest and I recently re-examined their work. They're the finest gem cutters in England — unquestionably. But they haven't the spark of genius that exists in the faceting at Von Den Sprecht. Do you wish to add anything, Ernest?"

196

Ernest Walker fondled his jade dragon namestone. "Only that this kind of craft has the potential to alter our thinking."

Several board members glanced at the silent chief usher standing by the door. Brownstone Tolhurst said, "Mr. Glanding, do you have the stones?"

"Yes sir."

"Would you be kind enough to set the samples on the table?"

The fabricating shop superintendent Wellesley Glanding carried the contents of a bag to lie before Johnson, Walker, and Tolhurst, Ltd. Managing Director. It was a black velvet-covered pillow containing several side-by-side cut and polished gems.

Sliding the velvet pillow in a slow circle, Brownstone Tolhurst then pointed to his ivory nameplate and Ernest Walker's jade dragon, saying, "As you all must recognize, there seems a spark of genius in the man who crafted these. And as you're certain to know by now, such creativity, conducted on our premises could not remain a total secret from we principals. So Ernest and I, in conjunction with our fabrication superintendent, Mr. Glanding, selected six high quality rough gemstones of size—stones we would normally send to Amsterdam for processing—and placed them before the craftsman who created Ernest and my namestones, to see what Mr. Ringling could do.

"Though our man had only time to facet three of those gems before this meeting and three of the stones remain in the rough, each of our in-house stones is arrayed with ones of similar size that were cut by Verenigen Boas Von Den Sprecht." Tolhurst paused, took a deep breath while gazing thoughtfully around the table. "It is my opinion—and the opinion of Mr. Walker and Mr. Glanding—that Ringling's ability is easily on a par with that of Claremont and Ward and, while not quite the level of the most master craftsmen of Von Den Sprecht, does indeed demonstrate as much potential."

At that point, Lord Orwell reached to slide the black pillow nearer in order to more closely examine the gemstones perching there. He picked up two, holding them for comparison to light streaming through a window.

"You wish to say something, Sir Douglas?"

"Indeed, Brownstone. First, I can see no difference between these two stones. You say the one faceted by Mr. Ringling doesn't quite come up to the quality of the one from Amsterdam?"

"That is correct, my Lord. Its problem lies in a slightly shallow angle for the pavilion cut. That, of course, led to a bit too-shallow break facets—all combine to slightly limit light reflection back to the viewer. The crown facets appear perfect to our analysts."

"Has Mr. Ringling been apprised of the shortcoming.?"

"He has. And he concurs absolutely. At this point, I think it important for the board to realize these stones were placed in the cutting room care of Mr. Ringling without stipulations in order for us to judge the man's God-given talent. That the young man came this near perfection is remarkable; and it's certainly indicative that he will, with a modicum of training and a little more practice, match the performance of some of the most talented gemstone cutters in the world...."

"Secondly," Sir Douglas Cole interrupted, "I believe I can take credit for being the first to recognize Ringling's talent as something more valuable than as a mere valet butler or chief usher; isn't that right, Mr. Herrelback?"

The office manager's eyes brushed Brownstone Tolhurst's amused smile, taking on the fever of an escaping convict. Still, he had no alternative but to agree—it popped out

198

as a squeak, but he gulped and tried again: "Yes indeed Sir Douglas. You suggested Ringling be elevated from chief usher after examining his work in the cutting room."

"So, Brownstone, I'm pleased to see you and Ernest are also gravitating to my opinion of the promise of this fine young man. And I'm persuaded that the board should be apprised of these new developments. But, my good man, surely you don't need board approval for such an executive decision as to where to place Ringling so he can be of most benefit to Johnson, Walker, and Tolhurst. As a result, I'm somewhat mystified as to the purpose of this agenda item?"

Tolhurst, bemused smile still in place, rolled eyes to the ceiling, the desktop, on the bowed countenance of Ernest Walker, and finally circled the board of directors. "Are you quite through, Sir Douglas?"

"Quite."

"The reason for this item for our agenda is certainly pertinent to the future of Johnson, Walker, and Tolhurst, good gentlemen. It goes without question that we'd like to expand our cutting and fabricating shop capabilities to equal that of any jewelry firm in the world. And you've just seen that we believe we have uncovered some unique and extremely valued in-house talent that might allow us to pursue our long-held dream of taking all phases of gemstones from discovery to development to faceting to dispersal—which we'll cover later this afternoon with sales and marketing. But our problem isn't in our talent, or even limited by lack of knowledge. Our problem lies in our present antiquated cutting room equipment."

The managing director paused to allow board members to absorb his explanation thus far. Then he continued: "We, Ernest and I, believe—as does Nathan Ringling and Wellesley Glanding—that the major reason for our cutter's failure to

199

achieve optimum results lies in that very antiquated equipment. Ringling, frankly, could not be absolutely certain of the angle of his pavilion cut, and therefore his pavilion break facets, because much of our equipment dates back to another age. That's what this board needs to consider: upgrading our gem faceting equipment.

"At this time, I'd like Mr. Glanding to report on his estimate of our equipment needs and the result of his cost-research. Mr. Glanding, please take my place to make your report."

Chapter Twenty-Three

Naseby Ringgold stood as a marble statue while the discussion about him and his work blew about like dust devils before a coming storm. He could hardly believe he was allowed to be present during this discussion—imagined that his being permitted to remain had more to do with English culture than mere oversight failure. And when Brownstone Tolhurst winked at him as the man moved his chair back to allow space for Wellesley Glanding room at the conference table, he knew his presence was intentional.

Perhaps he should've listened to the fabricating shop supervisor's presentation, but he'd already discussed the proposed equipment needs with Glanding, and suggested they make a list of two categories: 1) absolutely necessary, and 2) desired. So as Wellesley Glanding expounded on his research into shop needs, cost, and availability, Naseby's thoughts wandered.

He considered the irony of him standing mute against the wall while his own work was being discussed in such intimacy. He thought his first image as a marble statue inaccurate, deciding he would rather reference himself as a wooden Indian. Thus, his mind whirled back to the first time he heard the name "wooden Indian" from his mother many years ago. The dark eyes softened at the thought of that beautiful woman dwelling alone on her isolated gold claim on Yogo Creek. He thought, too, of his father, barely remembered, but a lion in a young boy's memory bank. And he did remember what his mother said and thought of Jake Hoover, topped off by the utterly high regard his friend, the formidable Pete Weatherwax, had for Naseby's father, the discoverer of the Yogo Sapphire lode.

Staring across the room at the far wall, Naseby's thoughts turned to how the mine had been stolen from his father, ultimately by these very Englishmen. His heart hardened when he recalled how he'd been driven from a life at the mine headquarters by a false charge of stealing rough gemstones that were really his, given to him and his mother by Jake Hoover while that ten-foot-tall mountain man still owned the mine. Like it was just yesterday, he recalled how he'd been beaten and kicked by mine manager Charles Gadsden, but escaped into the night and eluded searchers until eventually reaching Canada and safety.

But Gadsden had stolen Naseby's own cache of his father's gemstones and the fugitive swore he'd someday get even. Though the road had been long, he'd at last reached a point where he could exact revenge. But the idea of revenge no longer burned as intensely as before. When he eventually moved into a position of consequence with the English jewelry firm of Johnson, Walker, and Tolhurst, Ltd, Naseby had discovered the firm's two foremost principals, Ernest Walker and Brownstone Tolhurst, were something less than the ogres he'd imagined. In fact, both had taken their young American employee under wing, providing him unimagined opportunities and commensurate pay increases. What in the hell kind of people are these English scoundrels, anyway?

He considered the gems he'd already pilfered from Johnson, Walker, and Tolhurst—almost enough to compensate him for his own sapphires stolen in America. Yes indeed, packaged in his Kings Cross Bank's safety deposit box under the name of Norman (none) Richards were upwards of twenty rough sapphires he'd spirited undetected from his employer's inventories over a considerable length of time, along with two prized carborundum gems rated as green and pink sapphires.

He'd discovered it possible to retrieve them from the rejected stone from which he'd fashioned Miss Applestrom's nameplate, then faceted into beautiful jewels on his own time. The safety deposit box also contained two pieces of jade and a considerable chunk of ivory that were left over from Ernest Walker's and Brownstone Tolhurst's nameplate pieces.

* * *

Board members were each handed a two-part cost analysis paper for the proposed fabricating shop equipment upgrade, and Mr. Dawkins, the accountant, compared both the "necessary" and the "desired" equipment proposals with the company's cash reserves. When asked about suggested amortization rates and its result on taxation, office manager Gideon Herrelback joined his accountant in delineating the company's most profitable line of approach.

Unable to help himself, Naseby Ringgold yawned.

With Wellesley Glanding's presentation complete and responses to questions delivered, the fabrication shop supervisor returned to his seat and Brownstone Tolhurst again chaired the meeting for the discussion that followed. The board's decision was to authorize purchase and installation of each piece of proposed equipment listed under the "necessary" heading, but tabled further discussion on the less important "desired" level until after the new incoming equipment was installed and functioning.

* * *

It was during a short recess when Glanding met the chief usher in the hallway as Naseby returned with a box of cigars for the conference room. "We should've," the shop supervisor commiserated, "elevated more of our proposed lower level equipment into the 'necessaries', Nathan. We would've had them approved, too." Naseby smiled as he hurried past.

As the meeting resumed, the chief usher busied himself preparing for afternoon tea. He deliberately passed the greeter's desk to ask Miss Applestrom if she was ready to perform her forthcoming service duties?

The lady's head sank and eyes clinched. Then she sighed, widened her eyes and, red of face, said, "Of course. But I still think you were treated unfairly ..."

"Just don't let it get in the way of your performance, Miss Applestrom."

* * *

The skies were darkening when he handed her a chocolate. She exploded! "How can you take their insult so passively? That beast, Herrelback, receiving twice your bonus for a credit he didn't deserve! You! You were the one who suggested the namestones for Mr. Walker and Mr. Tolhurst! Not that insufferable sycho ... sycho ... phooey!"

"Restrain yourself, Miss Applestrom."

"Desiree."

"Restrain yourself, Desiree. First, who ever said the world was fair? Second, I wasn't the one who first suggested the namestones for Mr. Walker and Mr. Tolhurst. That credit honestly belongs to Mr. Walker."

"I hope you stir your chocolate, Nathan. I need something to lick to burn off my anger." Then she asked, "Don't you ever get angry?"

"Only with you."

"Why me?"

"Because you only see the surface. No, the world isn't fair. But look beyond your nose; I'm one hundred pounds richer—unheard of wealth for a poor orphan colonial boy who once beggared on the street. In addition, I stand certain to have the opportunity to advance into a highly skilled profession. If that requires that Mr. Herrelback also advances in order to enable me, then so be it."

"The finger, Nathan. Stir."

He didn't. But he held out his finger for her to kiss. "I don't begrudge our office manager anything. Without him, I may not have had the opportunity to obtain the jade and ivory to make Mr. Walker's and Mr. ..."

"Not true! Not true! You would've found another way— I know you would!"

"... Tolhurst's namestones. Without that opportunity, I may never have had another opportunity."

"What about that awful Herrelback authorizing vandals to trash your apartment?"

His smile was more grimace than amused. "Are you asking whether I trust him? No, I do not. But if you're asking me to refrain from ever *using* him again—*that*, as my friend Pete Weatherwax might've said—is a horse of another color."

"Who is Pete Weatherwax? Tell me about him."

He leaned away from her. "Would you consider joining me for an evening out—say at the *Dog & Duck*—for wine and fine dining? That way I could flash a bit of my forthcoming bonus in celebration."

She took both his hands in hers, smile bewitching: "Only if I would be permitted to end the evening in your apartment."

He squeezed. "Let's!"

* * *

The *Dog & Duck* was a small but established cellar pub off Hatton Garden and Charthouse Street that had been recommended more than once to the chief usher at Johnson, Walker, and Tolhurst, Ltd. He'd passed the entrance many times while on the way to Smithfield's Market, but never had an occasion to drop down the entry steps and push through its heavy wooden entry doors. Thus, flushed with both pleasure and anticipation, Naseby Ringgold held the door open for Desiree Applestrom.

The first person he saw in the dimly lighted pub was a Johnson, Walker, and Tolhurst board member—*is his name Waller, Spinder Waller?* Waller sat a stool near the door, talking heatedly with a man whose back was turned to the arriving couple.

Miss Applestrom pointed to a brightly lighted menu posted on the wall near the door and they studied it long enough that three people entered and two left. Then they found a table in a far corner. She ordered fish and chips, he opted for broasted shrimp. When the waiter brought the bottle of wine, he said, "Compliments of the gentleman at the end of the bar, sir." When Naseby looked, Spinder Waller waved and the second person turned, also to wave. He, too, was a member of Johnson, Walker, and Tolhurst's board. Naseby cursed to himself that he couldn't remember the second man's name.

Soon both men converged on their table. Naseby rose to greet them. Holding out a hand, Waller said, "We just wanted to offer congratulations to a rising star in Johnson, Walker, and Tolhurst's firmament."

"Thank you sirs. I merely hope I can fulfill expectations."

"Oh you will, you will," the second board member said. "The name Nathan Ringling will soon become entrenched in future annals of gem faceting."

Naseby waved to his companion. "You may remember Miss Applestrom; she assisted in serving you gentlemen today."

They both chuckled. Waller said, "Anyone sufficiently fortunate to set eyes on this young lady is unlikely to forget her. Indeed!"

A blushing Miss Applestrom said, "It was most kind of

you gentlemen to provide our wine."

Naseby, out of courtesy (but hoping against hope they wouldn't) asked the gentlemen if they'd care to join their table.

"Hah!" the second gentleman snorted. "We're far too discerning to do that to you young folks." Then he said, "Come, Spinder, let's leave these people to their well deserved privacy."

"Devices, you mean!" They returned to the bar, chuckling at their wit.

* * *

One bottle of wine was hardly sufficient for the jubilance surrounding Naseby and Desiree on this particular evening. So he consulted the wine list, saw that a second bottle of the excellent *Chateau Relaigne* was within his price range and raised his finger for a waiter.

The result was that the couple was a bit tipsy when they exited the *Dog & Duck*. Darkness had settled in as a driving rain engaged in battle with a dense fog blowing in from the River Thames. He turned to shelter her, mumbling that she should wait inside while he tried to obtain a Hansom cab. "Nonsense," she cried. "I'm not made of sugar and neither are you!" And she pushed past to run up the steps onto the street.

He laughed. "Desiree, come back here. You'll drown."

She wheeled to face him, hands on hips, while her fetching hair flattened. "Follow me, love. I'll race you to your apartment. Come on now! We'll hang ourselves out to dry once we reach there." There was little he could do, but wag his head in dismay, then leap up the steps and out into the rain.

They were soaked in minutes. He shrugged from his jacket and tried to throw it over her head, but she fought his attempt, laughing and all but running down the street. So he threw the jacket over his own head and tried to keep pace with her hurried step. Once, she turned in shadow (an absent flame from a faulty street lamp) and kissed him soundly on the lips, then whirled away giggling and eluding his more fervent grasp.

They left a dripping water trail all the way up the stairs and into his room. There he pinned her, wet hair and all, to the wall and planted a long and passionate kiss, which she returned at least as fervently. She twisted away to shrug from her coat, dropping it to the floor. Then she turned her back to him and murmured, "Unbutton the dress, Nathan, please." The dress fluttered atop the coat, followed by her silk undergarment. As she struggled with the snaps on her foundation piece she said, "Are you going to stand there like a dummy in those wet clothes, love. Do take them off as I watch."

He was saucer-eyed, so dumbfounded that he never moved when she stomped closer and unbuttoned his vest, loosed the knot on his tie, and began on the buttons on his shirt. And when he gasped, "Desiree, we ... we can't!" she giggled, "Nathan, we can ... and we are."

She kicked off her flats, then threw away her unsnapped foundation piece as her lovely, blossoming breasts glowed in nippled perfection. Then she removed the bloomers, standing finally revealed in a short satin corset with straps down to snap into silk hosiery. She placed fists to hips and frowned. "Well, don't just stand there, dummy. Get out of those wet slacks—or do you need me to help you once again?"

"You ... you're beautiful!" He was still mesmerized as she moved to unbuckle his belt and unbutton his trousers.

When she pulled the trousers down to the ankles, exposing striped boxer shorts, she said, "It'd be best if you removed your shoes and stockings, Nathan, while I pour us a nightcap of some of that rum you're hiding on your top kitchen shelf. Then you can join me on the couch and take off my stockings."

She did, and he did. Then, while they sipped the sweet, heavy Jamaican extract he said, "You simply cannot do this, Desiree. How will you dress to return home?" (God! isn't she beautiful in her altogether.) "What will your parents say when you do?"

"Silly! I'll stay here all evening. Sometime later, after the rum—and whatever comes next, I'll hang my things up to dry. By morning they'll be suitable for dress. Now, for goodness sake! Will you get out of those boxer shorts so that I may get a look at the lump that's thrusting up beneath!"

It's all a dream—it has to be! he thought as his head fell back against the couch while her fingers explored the delight she discovered when his boxers were removed. "Let me turn off the light," he murmured.

But she held him back. "No, Nathan. No. We've never before had the chance to examine all of us. For this once, I want to drink in your vision so that I can remember it later, when you're not available to touch and feel and taste and see. Come, open your eyes and look at me. Enjoy it as much as I enjoy looking at you." Then he twisted away as he spouted through her fingers. She smiled, as he twisted back, face anguished. "Don't worry dear, we'll clean up later." And she continued to stroke.

When he finally recovered his voice, he said, "I love you."

She laughed aloud, "Good! And I'll pour us a bit more rum, then we can get serious about whether we really are in love." When she returned, she handed him a glass with only a dash of rum inside. Then she threw off hers and straddled him, wriggling so that her right breast was at his lips. With eyes closed and lips panting, she fitted him inside and began moving in slow ecstasy.

Chapter Twenty-Four

The next few weeks were hectic in the fabricating shop of renowned gem dealer Johnson, Walker, and Tolhurst as deliveries of new faceting equipment arrived, one piece after another. Though machine placement was largely the province of shop supervisor, Wellesley Glanding, Naseby Ringgold haunted the building, consulting with Glanding about location, lighting, ease of access, and innumerable other questions arising. Within minutes of each machine's placement, Ringgold (known in the shop as Nathan Ringling) was testing, testing.

As chief usher, Mr. Ringling was absent so much from the sales room and offices of Johnson, Walker, and Tolhurst that Miss Applestrom was pressed more and more into his duties, much to the dismay of other members of the showroom sales staff, not to mention the kitchen cooks and cleaning crew.

Miss Applestrom doted on the challenge, however, performing near flawlessly, a credit to both her sex, and the opportunity the war's demand on England's absent young men afforded her. Besides, Desiree Applestrom was very much in love, and wished to assist the man she knew as Nathan Ringling as he moved forward toward his coming new occupation as a master gem cutter and jewelry designer.

For his part, the chief usher was on hand sufficiently to suppress most sales room criticism of that woman—miss high-and-mighty! Applestrom—lording it over her masculine underlings. Besides, Naseby Ringgold was also in love. And as he stood near her stand-up greeting desk, he felt the ring in his vest pocket and wondered if today should be the day?

Their lovemaking had become frenetic and he worried that their affair might not be as sufficiently discreet as he'd wish.

Could they, in fact, marry? Certainly that would assuage the guilt he felt toward her parents whom he'd never met. Merely engaging to be married would, he felt, be of some help to his wounded conscience.

She must have sensed him nearby, for she glanced behind her workstation, saw him and smiled, eyes shining. "I'll handle this morning's tea, Miss Applestrom. Mr. Glanding is a bit like a wounded owl and invited me to leave the shop so that he might, according to him, 'get something done'."

"My," she said, "that was quite a long speech, Mr. Ringling. Very much out of character for one so reticent as you."

He looked away, fearing that he must let his emotions show. "Irony doesn't become you, Miss Applestrom."

Her eyes swept the showroom; there was no one within listening distance. "May I ask if there is anything about me at all, Mr. Ringling, that does become me?"

He walked away.

* * *

When he knocked twice and pushed inside with the morning tea service, Ernest Walker's patented hound-dog face looked even more despondent than usual. "Tea, sir?"

"Absolutely, Ringling. But you, sir, are a disappointment. As a replacement for Applestrom, you seem a bit lacking."

The chief usher smiled. "Everyone else at Johnson, Walker, and Tolhurst is a disappointment compared to Miss Applestrom, sir."

The sad-faced man nodded, accepted his tea, and murmured, "Look, now. You've slopped it into my saucer. Your replacement, besides being better appearing, seems also to be better trained."

"And more adept, too."

"More polished."

211

"Better disposition."

Not even so much as one wrinkle twitched on Mr. Walker's long face as he saucered more tea back and forth to his cup. Then he glanced up at his chief usher and said, "Do I discern a certain fondness toward the topic of our discussion, young man?"

The chief usher smiled once more, but added nothing as he backed from Ernest Walker's office to knock twice on Brownstone Tolhurst's double doors. Upon entry, he spotted the firm's managing director pacing near the huge bow window, sheaf of papers in his hand. "Ahh, Ringling. Replacing Applestrom today?"

"Yes, sir. Mr. Glanding is harried with all the new equipment arriving and suggested I pursue more worthwhile activities."

Tolhurst pitched his papers to his desk, took his chair, and said, "Well, I suppose we shall have to bear up under the strain of your service instead of hers."

The younger man added a dash of cream and two spoons of sugar before handing the saucer and cup across the desk. "That's what Mr. Walker indicated, too, sir. I may have my feelings frayed if I should choose to pursue this activity."

Tolhurst chuckled. "And how is the new equipment installation going?"

"Very well, I should think. Mr. Glanding is presently clearing space for the new lapidary gem saw. And we're waiting for the bruting machine. It was supposed to have arrived yesterday, but now they're saying it will be next week."

"After everything is in place, I suppose we'll see much less of you in our showroom and offices."

"That's my understanding, sir. Mr. Herrelback suggests that I will be phased slowly out in order to smooth the transition."

"I see. Has Herrelback asked your advice for your replacement?"

"No, sir. I assumed that would be Miss Applestrom."

Brownstone Tolhurst peered at his chief usher for a disquietingly long time before saying, "Yes, I suppose Herrelback has made so many failures in judgment about you that he's reluctant to engage you seriously." He waved a hand "Do set the tea service down, Ringling, and pull up a chair. We need to have a caucus."

Slipping cautiously into a chair, the man known as Nathan Ringling said, "We need to have a *what*, sir?"

"A caucus. A meeting. We need to talk."

"Yes, sir. About what?"

"About your replacement. Beginning with Miss Applestrom."

"Yes, sir."

"You know of our reservations about having a woman as chief usher—it's just not done. Never. Anywhere."

"Yes, sir. The counterpoint to that, sir, is that these times are hardly normal. Sometimes one must ..."

"There is no question as to Miss Applestrom's suitability, Mr. Ringling. If she were a man there could be no question. But whether we could overcome the hurdle of a woman as chief usher is, in our mind, questionable."

The man known as Nathan Ringling shrugged and leaned back in his chair. "Obviously, sir, that is your decision, one that is beyond my province. Except for my suggestion that the lady in question is the most qualified person I know to assume the role, I can add little else."

"Perhaps." Brownstone Tolhurst studied the young man across the desk from him until Naseby actually felt compelled to squirm. "I will tell you this, Ringling: Both Edward and I are in

213

favor of Miss Applestrom's elevation, though we're cognizant of the possible repercussions of doing so. Herrelback is concerned with the firm's image. But the man is also concerned about potential disquiet among other staff members in the wake of Miss Applestrom's elevation."

His frankness caused Naseby to lean forward. "Surely, sir, Mr. Herrelback's suggestion that I be phased out slowly in order to help my replacement grow into the role should respond to that concern."

"True. Unfortunately that's not our only concern."

He sank slowly back into his chair.

"Ringling," Brownstone Tolhurst evenly said, "are you fond of Miss Applestrom?"

He chose to sideslip the question. "I certainly respect her professionalism, sir."

"That's not what I mean, Mr. Ringling. As a vigorous young man in the prime of life, do you find Miss Applestrom, a healthy young woman also in the prime of life, attractive?"

Naseby Ringgold's face reddened, but otherwise remained a mask. He took a deep breath and said, "Sir, I must ask if this line of questioning is appropriate at this time and in this place."

Brownstone Tolhurst's own demeanor seemed patient, but firm. "I believe it is, young man. And our reasons are in the best interest of Johnson, Walker, and Tolhurst. In considering whether or not to advance Miss Applestrom to an even more key position within the firm, we must know she would be available for the duration." He paused, cleared his throat, then continued: "It is, and has always been our policy, not to permit any hint of nepotism to develop within the firm."

"Nepotism, sir?"

"Nepotism. We will not employ two people from the

same family. Neither Ernest, nor myself, will permit members of our own family to be employed at Johnson, Walker, and Tolhurst, nor any members of the present staff. D'you see now why I asked the question. Ringling, one would have to be blind not to see sparks flying between you and Miss Applestrom. Even two of our directors remarked on it."

The man known as Nathan Kenneth Ringling shifted in his seat, stared at the floor. Suddenly the ring tucked into his vest pocket seemed to weight him down. *For God's sake! Is it swelling? Does it show?* He sighed. Meeting Brownstone Tolhurst's gaze head on, he said, "I was thinking of asking her to marry me, Mr. Tolhurst."

Tolhurst nodded. "We were afraid of it! If that were to happen, one of you would have to go. And I think it most fair to tell you that, after spending several thousand pounds on gem faceting expansion committed to a gamble on your development, we would be quite unlikely to ask it to be you."

The chief usher nodded, mostly to himself. "Not to mention her own lost opportunity for career development."

Tolhurst appeared to be enumerating. Gently, he murmured, "Not to mention the pregnancy question; bearing children is hardly the norm among English butlers and chief ushers."

Naseby pushed unbidden to his feet. "May I have a day or two to digest this development, sir?"

"Absolutely! Just don't do anything rash, Ringling. Remember, even we old dogs were known to howl at the moon in nights long past. You have too bright a future ahead of you to muck it up by burying your spike too deep."

"Thank you, sir," Naseby murmured as he pushed through the big double doors, completely forgetting the silver tea service still perched on a corner of Tolhurst's desk.

"We must talk," he said to Miss Applestrom upon his return from talking to Managing Director Brownstone Tolhurst.

"Chocolate?"

"No, Miss Applestrom. I'm afraid this is more serious than that. Can you visit my apartment?"

She shook her head while flashing her spectacular teeth at him. "Oh, Nathan. I promised my mum I'd be home right after work." Then she gripped her desk with both hands and, dimples prominent at her turned-up mouth corners, murmured, "Are you sure you only wish to talk?"

"Desiree, this is really quite serious. We have to stop seeing each other. I'm uncertain how to handle it. We must talk."

Applestrom's eyes widened and moistened, and with cheeks reddening covered a gaping mouth with one hand while steadying herself with the other. "You can't be … be serious!"

"I've never been more so."

She swallowed, then swallowed again. "I really must go home first. May I leave a few minutes early? I'll ride the trolley back to Smithfield and try to reach your apartment before it's fully dark."

"Leave as soon as you wish. I'll cover for you. I'll also explain to Herrelback that you developed a headache."

"I'll bring some cheese, if you'll pick up a loaf of bread."

"I'll get some wine, too."

* * *

The hallway door was open when she arrived. She carried a valise as well as a brown paper bag; obviously prepared to spend the night. He was sitting at his kitchen table, somewhat disheveled, jacket and vest and celluloid collar discarded carelessly on the living room sofa, a half empty bottle of red wine at his elbow and a glass containing but dregs in his

216

hand. She kicked the door closed behind her and said, "All right, Nathan. Tell me what's going on."

He pushed his chair back and reached her a wineglass from the cupboard. Along with the wine, he added a plate with several buttered slices of rye bread, She dropped her valise and set a block of cheddar cheese on his countertop. Rummaging for a knife, she stared accusingly at him. "I asked a simple question, luv. What's going on?"

"They know about us."

"So?" She sliced several cuts of cheese, plopping them atop the bread slices. "They know about us—so what? I'm of age. As are you—unless you've held out on me, my dear. I'm not exactly sure who *they* are. If you tell me it's that bloody prick, Herrelback, I'll tell you I'll stick a stiletto-heeled slipper up has unprincipled ass."

"I'd like to discuss this rationally, Desiree."

"Well, would you now!" She took two big gulps of wine and stuffed her cheeks with rye bread and cheddar. Before she even chewed a little, she blurted, "Of mmph shudden, ooh tell mee oursh is all over." She chewed and swallowed. "That we must talk." She leaped to her feet and paced to the hallway door and back, around the couch and back. "So they know! So what?" She stood before him, hands on hips. "SO WHAT, NATHAN? TELL ME!"

"Please calm down, Desiree. Please."

"Well let me tell you something, luv, they—whoever in hell *they* are—aren't the only ones who know, because I told my mum and pop about us. I told them we're lovers and if I wanted to spend the night in your apartment, I would. And there was nothing they could do about it."

He looked stricken as he filled both their glasses with the last of the wine. Then he drank off half. She did likewise.

217

Finally, he said, "Go ahead and let it all out, Desiree. I cannot begrudge your anger. When you've let it all out and run down, then perhaps you'll listen carefully as I explain our dilemma."

With eyes brimming, she again strode around the apartment. Even into the bedroom. When at last she returned to pick up her wineglass, she said, "Surely this is not the only bottle of wine you brought for this kind of discussion?"

"In the ice box. Getting chilled."

She sat down across the table from him. "All right, explain."

Again, he tossed off another half of his half. "Apparently, they suspected our affair, perhaps alerted by the two directors we met in the *Dog & Duck* a week or two ago. As apparently did you, I suspected it wouldn't matter even if they peered in our bedroom window. After all, as you point out, we're both beyond the age of puberty, beyond the age of consent, so what could it matter?"

She went to the icebox and brought the second bottle of wine to their table, pausing at the sink for the corkscrew.

When she returned, he said, "That's why I was shocked when Brownstone Tolhurst asked today if we were lovers. I told him that I was considering asking for your hand in marriage ..."

"Oh, Nathan!"

"He said, 'We were afraid of that'."

"He didn't!"

"He did."

"Then he, too, is a target for my stiletto heels!"

He held up a hand. "I'm sorry, Desiree, but I get ahead of myself. Tolhurst first asked about the fabrication shop and how the new equipment was coming along? Then he said they recognized that I would soon be leaving as chief usher and Asked if I had any recommendation for my replacement?

Naturally, I said I assumed it would be you."

She smiled for the first time during the evening and reached across the table to squeeze his hand. "As could be expected, he trotted out the standard disclaimers that having a woman as chief usher just wasn't done—had never been done. But when I said, 'Then, sir, if that's your decision I can have nothing else to say,' he said something strange—to the effect that both he and Ernest Walker actually favored you. That it was Gideon Herrelback who was opposed—for several reasons."

"I may really develop a deep hatred for Mr. Herrelback. But tell me, what were his reasons?"

"Possible pregnancy is one. Flouting tradition is another. But the final one was when Mr. Tolhurst asked about our relationship."

She again reached for his hand, murmuring, "I don't understand."

"It's called nepotism. It's against Johnson, Walker, and Tolhurst's policy to have more than one family member employed."

She shook her head, still not understanding. So he said, "Desiree if we were husband and wife, the firm would have to let one of us go." She jerked loose from her lover's hand to cover her mouth as the consequences of the nepotism policy sank in. He hammered that realization home by adding, "Mr. Tolhurst was quick to point out that if it came down to dismissing one or the other of us, a gem cutting professional was far more valuable to them than even chief ushers, especially if the chief usher was considered marginal to begin with."

Her head drooped for several moments as she closed her eyes, then glanced up, pushed the second bottle of wine across the table, along with the corkscrew. "Open it, Nathan. Even then I must tell you that it may not be enough."

*　*　*

They said little throughout the second bottle of wine; perhaps nibbled a little cheese, tore off a few chunks of bread. But come up with any pearls of wisdom to help address their dilemma—no. At last, she asked, "Were you really going to ask me to marry you?"

In silent response, he retrieved his carelessly discarded vest and held out the ring he'd fabricated. It was of hammered gold, set with sixteen tiny sapphires so small no one except she would think it of any value. She took the ring ever so gently and began sobbing. It slipped perfectly onto her third finger. "Oh Nathan ..." Tears ran down cheeks that had but moments before been tight with anger.

He looked away; seemed somehow to shrink. "There's sixteen tiny stones in there, for the sixteen months we've known each other." She leaped up and dashed for his chain-pull commode. He could hear her sobbing and retching. He polished off the rest of their last bottle of wine, swigging straight from the bottle. Then weaving, he headed for her, bouncing from gas stove to countertop to icebox to doorjamb. He found her, feet in the bathtub, cold water pouring in.

"Do heat us a kettle of water, luv," she said. "Then join me."

He heated two kettles. Between the first and second, she shrugged from her remaining clothes and sank under bubbles of suds. By that second kettle, she'd regained her composure enough to quip, "When you get in, the water may become too hot for us."

They'd not made love in the tub before. It was difficult, but not impossible when the heat of passion consumes them.

*　*　*

Later, again clothed and sitting at the kitchen table, they

nibbled cheese and buttered rye bread, drank water, and more lucidly considered their problem. She began the second round by asking if they could marry in secret. He shook his head. "Not hardly, my lady. Herrelback already had me investigated twice. Give him the slightest snitch of scandal and he'd have Bow Street all over us in spades."

"Can we live together in sin? I don't have to flaunt your ring."

"Same difference. We cannot live together, and that's that! Not, at least, if you, too, are employed at Johnson, Walker, and Tolhurst."

"So that's the real question, isn't it? Career or marriage!" She slammed the flat of her hand to the tabletop. "The bastards!" When he only peered sadly at her, she said, "Well, what now?"

"What now?" He took a pinch of cheese, a bite of bread, a swallow of water and said, "Well, Desiree, the choice is yours. I'll go along with whatever you decide. Should you want to pursue your career, I'll understand. Should you feel marriage is more important, the offer still stands. I, of course, do not intend to leave Johnson, Walker, and Tolhurst, no matter what; so the decision is totally yours."

She stared beyond him, turning the ring over and over in her fingers. "Nathan, I'm in a career position most women can only dream of. With a chance for even further advancement."

"I understand. Actually, Desiree, you seem to be making a choice that I, were I in your shoes, would make myself. It's one I expected you would choose."

"But I love you so!"

"And I you."

Her's was almost a scream of anguish: "Why does this have to be so difficult!"

He leaned back in his chair, folded his arms and said,

221

"There's one other potential problem we haven't considered—at least you haven't. But they have: Children. Brownstone Tolhurst made that abundantly clear in the midst of our discussion: they have no need to worry about a male usher becoming pregnant; that they could in no way tolerate having a pregnant chief usher. Or, for that matter, a pregnant assistant to the chief usher. Nor probably even a pregnant greeter."

"Nor a pregnant cook, or pregnant serving maid. Nor a pregnant scullery girl...." She trailed off, then sighed. "Nathan, you are so innocent. Women have had ways to control pregnancies for thousands of years. And this is England, the most advanced society in the entire world. Please! If I should choose my career over a marriage, there could be no way I would allow a pregnancy to jeopardize that decision."

Dawn was just beginning to break across nighttime London when Naseby Ringgold wearily started a pot of coffee. When he returned to the table, he said, "I'm afraid I must ask for a decision, Desiree. I will wish to give them a decision today."

She said, "I cannot give up my career, Mr. Ringling. Henceforth, please refer to me as Miss Applestrom."

Chapter Twenty-Five

The war in Europe continued to spit out horrifying news, perhaps the deadliest conflict in history. "Verdun" became a detested word because of its two great, but indecisive struggles on the central French plain. And on July 1, 1916 the British Army endured the bloodiest single day in its history, suffering over fifty-seven thousand casualties during the opening of the allied drive on the Somme.

The entire protracted Somme offensive cost the British Army some four hundred and twenty thousand killed and wounded, while the French suffered another two hundred thousand, and the Germans around a half-million.

There was considerable trepidation on the Eastern Front as the Russian Czar was overthrown, replaced by a weak provisional government who proved incapable of providing more than confusion and chaos at the front. With the eastern war in virtual collapse, the Russian government had no alternative but to ask for terms from their enemy, in essence releasing several entire German and Austro-Hungarian army groups for use on the stalemated Western Front.

The war situation could hardly have looked more bleak, except for the April, 1917 declaration of war by the United States of America in retaliation for the sinking of U.S. merchant ships by German submarines. Thus, the war's essence evolved into a race between replacement German armies from the East hurrying to crush the beleaguered British and French armies before significant numbers of American troops could arrive.

Naseby Ringgold was vaguely aware of first one war crisis, then another. Even as far removed from mainstream English social life as the reclusive chief usher/master gemcutter was, he could hardly fail to note soldiers recovering from the effects of front line gas attacks—the burns and disfigured faces, or ones hobbling about Smithfield's Market, or riding the trolleys. Once a crippled uniformed soldier and a young girl clinging to him as if she'd never let go, entered the showroom and browsed the selection of engagement rings. (Though they left without purchasing, every clerk in store wanted to assist in bringing trays of new selections; to assist in showing what Johnson, Walker, and Tolhurst had to offer.)

Naseby noted Miss Applestrom quietly wiping her eyes upon the soldier's and his girl's departure. He dropped his handkerchief on the soon-to-be new chief usher's greeting stand, then pushed through the doors to pursue the limping soldier and his girl. When the couple paused at his call, Naseby hurried up to hold out the ring he'd crafted for Miss Applestrom, saying it was a gift from the employees of Johnson, Walker, and Tolhurst, Ltd. in gratitude for the soldier's service. Then he wheeled abruptly and returned to the floor to stroll about and gaze complacently at the staff and attractive displays that he would soon be turning over to Miss Applestrom's care.

* * *

In the fabricating shop, the man known as Nathan Ringling grew ever more engrossed, as he met first one rough stone after another. It was soon obvious, even to a casual observer, that the young man was extremely talented in discerning the planes of each stone, verging on genius in determining proper cleavage, sawing, bruting, faceting, and polishing.

"Mr. Tolhurst," Wellesley Glanding reported (as he was instructed), "he's most near uncanny." Glanding held out a cut and polished gem. "Look at the star inside, sir. Nobody else could see it like Ringling did. I thought it was a flaw myself.

But Ringling! Why he took it, studied it, cleaved it a couple of times, ran a light girdle around it, then stuck all those facets around it and handed it to me for polishing."

Brownstone Tolhurst took the sapphire, held it to the light, handed it back and asked, "What was the size of the stone to begin with?"

"That's another thing, sir! It was just a shade under seven carats. And that one weighs out at a bit over three. Nobody I've ever known would've cut out more than two-and-a-half, and damned few of them—pardon me for my language, sir."

"Thank you, Mr. Glanding. Set Mr. Ringling up with every challenging stone we get. And start considering how we can transfer some of his God-given skills to some of our other craftsmen."

"I'm sorry, sir. Do you mean for him to train them?"

Tolhurst chuckled. "You're damned right I do—and you can forgive me for my language. But let him develop. Let him develop. The idea that he might be able to impart some present or future skills to our other, lesser talented cutters should be kept under wraps for the present time; best kept a secret between you and me. But keep in mind that Mr. Ringling has, in the past, demonstrated considerable skills in training others to his level of perfection."

"Mmm—I guess I see. Yes, I do! If he continues to develop as we all think he will. And if he can share that development with other cutters in our shop, why we may rival Claremont, up the road."

"Amsterdam, Glanding. Don't set your sights too low."

* * *

Naseby Ringgold, the man known at Johnson, Walker, and Tolhurst, Ltd. as Nathan Kenneth Ringling had, for the past

225

several weeks become more and more caught up in his new work, as Wellesley Glanding pushed an ever-growing assortment of raw gemstones his way: rubies, emeralds, diamonds, topaz, sapphires. Requests for more and more jade and ivory pieces were placed on special order for Johnson, Walker, and Tolhurst's new gemsmith to craft. Then one day when the weary gemsmith paused and wiped his eyes, a hovering shop supervisor asked, "What's wrong, Nathan? Do you need to take a break?"

Naseby pinched his nose and swung his head to peer up at the supervisor. "I need more light, Wellesley. It needs to be brighter, and it would be even better if there was an additional row of small single lights along one table edge."

"Tell me what you want, Nathan. Let's lay out a diagram and I'll see that it's done."

The master craftsman pushed away from his worktable. "Is there any coffee?"

"I'll send to the kitchen. Or would you rather have tea?"

Naseby shook his head. "Thank you, but I'll get it myself." When Glanding started to remonstrate, the younger man said, "Look, Wellesley, I know where the kitchen is and I need to avail myself of the restroom at any rate."

As the former chief usher's new role grew to capture more of his attention, Naseby Ringgold spent ever declining amounts of time on the showroom floor. After he drank two cups of coffee, stretched, and visited the restroom, he decided to stroll through the sales premises, evaluating the new chief usher's effectiveness. Exchanging greetings with most of the staff, he was pleased to see their cheerfulness; that the corners were dusted, and the display glass freshly polished and gleaming.

She stood at her stand-up greeter's desk talking with

visitors who'd apparently just entered the building. Beyond her head, Naseby was surprised to see a small window cut into the wall to Gideon Herrelback's office, allowing the office manager a constant showroom view. Herrelback spotted him, leaped from his desk and hurried into the showroom and to the man he knew as Nathan Ringling.

"Ahh, Ringling!" he said, holding out his hand. "Came back to assess your old haunts, eh?" (Naseby saw Miss Applestrom turn at Herrelback's excitement, then turned back to continue conversation with the visitors.)

He nodded at the new chief usher and asked, "How is she doing, sir? The shop looks well. I just took a tour of the kitchen and wine cellar. Noted the good cheer of most of the staff. All looks well from my perspective."

"Fine! Fine. Couldn't be better. Makes me proud that I recommended her." Herrelback must have noticed something in Naseby's narrowing eyes because he added, "As did you. Right?" The former chief usher rolled his eyes, swallowed, and nodded.

"Do you have time to join me in my office for a few moments, Nathan. I'd love to hear more about the exciting new developments coming from fabricating. I'll send out for tea." Noting Miss Applestrom's engagement, Herrelback waved down a passing clerk.

"None for me, sir. I just had two cups of coffee before wandering out here." But Herrelback ignored him, issued the tea request to the clerk, then steered the visitor to his office. Significantly, Naseby thought, the office manager slid an overstuffed armchair over by his own swivel chair and jovially waved his visitor to it.

After they were comfortably seated and Herrelback understood his visitor was unlikely to volunteer information said, "I'm hearing great things about you and the new developments in fabricating." He waited.

"Thank you," Naseby finally murmured.

"Ah, yes. Well. How is the new training program progressing?"

"Training program?" Naseby's eyes flickered in interest. "What training program?"

"The one you're putting together ..." His visitor's stare was blank, so the office manager added, "... to improve the professional level of the rest of our fabricating team."

"Sir, I haven't the foggiest idea what you're talking about."

Gideon Herrelback's laugh was an embarrassed one. "Let the cat out of the bag, did I?" He waved dismissively. "Well, now you know. Our top-level directors are so impressed by your progress that they hope you'll be able to convey some of your apparently God-gifted skills to others in the fabrication shop."

The clerk, Pendergast, bustled in with their tea. After he'd departed, Naseby said, "No, Mr. Herrelback. I've heard nothing of such a proposal. But I suppose I'd be flattered to be so directed."

Herrelback mused, "I imagine you'll wish to put together some sort of training program plan, perhaps like you did when your chief usher's role was expanded, giving you floor oversight. When your plan is prepared, I trust you'll run it past me for approval?"

Naseby laughed. "Mr. Herrelback, until now I heard nothing about any such proposal...."

"Well, you certainly have now."

"... And when it comes, I assume it will come, as Pete Weatherwax used to say, right from the horse's mouth."

"Pete Weatherwax?"

228

"So until I hear from my supervisory sources, I'll have to consider it mere rumor, and not instructive."

"Oh, Ringling, I think you can consider my information as instructive. Think of it as authorization from me to begin developing a plan."

Naseby smiled, flashing extremely white teeth in his otherwise dark countenance; he would enjoy ever so much what he was about to say: "Mr. Herrelback, perhaps neither of us understand the state of our current relationship. I believe I'm working now under the direct supervision of Wellesley Glanding. That means, as I understand it, that my command chain extends from Brownstone Tolhurst through Wellesley Glanding to me. Are you implying that you are inserted with some authority over the fabricating shop command?"

When Herrelback's face turned red, as well as sour, Naseby murmured, "Please advise me, sir, if my understanding is in error."

Chapter Twenty-Six

Nathan Ringgold left Gideon Herrelback's office only moments after challenging the office manager on the assumption that he still had oversight over the man known as Nathan Kenneth Ringling. He left his tea untouched. Miss Applestrom was gone from her stand-up greeter's desk, but she was in her chief usher's cupboard. And when he passed the open door, she called, "Oh, Mr. Ringling!" When he paused, she said, "Won't you step in here for a moment?" When he did, she closed the door.

"What is it you wish, Miss Applestrom?"

"We hardly ever see you any more."

"Perhaps you could take that as a commendation on the fact that I'm no longer needed out here."

She blushed. "Thank you. Apparently the floor passed today's inspection?"

"Very much so. I found the staff cheerful—a very important indicator."

"I'm not having as much trouble there as we expected. Oddly enough, I think Mr. Herrelback's observation window helps a lot. But for the most part, I think the staff simply feel they couldn't handle the job as well as I'm doing."

He shrugged. She said, "Nathan ..."

"Mr. Ringling."

"Mr. Ringling, I'm simply wasting away to nothing without ever the chance to see you again."

"Miss Applestrom I do not think that a good idea."

She pushed to her feet so their eyes—and lips—were of a level. "Perhaps you're right. Yes, of course you are! But would you kiss me?"

"No."

She opened the door, effectively dismissing him.

"Discarded first by Herrelback, then by Applestrom," he murmured as he strode away. "Soon I'll not be welcome in the kitchen or the cellar."

* * *

The man known as Nathan Ringling was welcome in the shop, though. And his every wish very nearly constituted a command. His worktable was quickly illuminated so brightly that a screen was set up to shelter other nearby machines and worktables from the light.

Noting the benefits of better lighting, Wellesley Glanding won approval to bring in carpenters and painters for a do-over of their shop interior. When it was finished, the shop supervisor commanded the kind of showplace he'd always wanted. Meanwhile the star in the showplace's firmament continued to turn out flawless gemstones in surprising quantities, also finding time to work on the jade and ivory orders.

One day, Naseby and Glanding both held cups of coffee at the master gemcutters table. "Wellesley," Naseby asked, "what is this about my setting up a training program for other shop craftsmen."

Glanding slowly set his cup on the table. "Where did you hear that?"

"As Pete Weatherwax used to say, a little bird told me."

"Pete Weatherwax, eh? Well you didn't hear it from me." He stared piercingly at Naseby. "Had to be that mealy-mouthed Herrelback, didn't it."

"What about it?"

Glanding sighed. "There's talk. Tolhurst's idea. But he told me to keep it under hat until you developed a little more."

* * *

With semi-official word that he would eventually be asked to put in place a training program for other cutting room staff members, the man known as Nathan Ringling decided to actually develop a training plan *before* being asked. His purpose was ostensibly to expedite future staff training, but actually to excel in demonstrating his own preparedness when authorization actually descended the command chain.

For that purpose, he spent what little extra time he could find for the draft plan, contributing to it both at home and on the job. Obviously any routine time he had, even on the job, was consumed by thoughts of the project. He considered the personalities of his co-workers, with the idea of assigning craft-stage gem faceting to individuals demonstrating specific talents—like Clarence Bergdorff seemingly being especially meticulous; who might develop into an excellent "Brillianteer" who would cut the final forty facets in a "Round Brilliant" gemstone-cut.

Though he planned to retain the role of stone "Marking" and probably most of the "Cleaving", he thought Igor Rajzcic could develop into a trusted expert in "Sawing" the marked stones to approximate the shape of the finished gems.

But whom might he develop to handle the "Girdling"—placing the marked and rough-shaped stones in chucks to rotate on the "Bruting" lathe, rounding the rough stone into a conical shape? Who, in other words, might be considered a developing precision machinist? He decided to set the search for the ideal person aside, to do it himself if he could not come up with a suitable choice.

"Polishing?" Who else but Duncan Domes? Certainly the man was fussbudget enough to be trusted to put as fine a polish to every stone that came his way as any man possibly could.

Naseby paused, pencil in hand, as the thought flashed through his mind: But can any man be as good at polishing as perhaps a woman? Probably lots of women? He shook the idea from his mind as a knock came on his apartment door. When he opened it, Miss Applestrom stood there, shopping bag in hand.

"May I come in, Nathan?"

"Mr. Ringling, Miss Applestrom."

"May I come in, Mr. Ringling?" He stood away from the door.

She went to his kitchen table, saw the myriad sheets of penciled foolscap scattered there and set her bag on the nearby counter. "Have you eaten?" she asked over her shoulder.

"Not yet." He still stood by the door. "I was waiting for someone to join me."

Her patented smile was in place as she turned. "Well my goodness, isn't this your lucky day? Your dinner guest also brought a few odds and ends."

"Not a good idea, Miss Applestrom."

"Is, too, Mr. Ringling." When he made no rejoinder, she rubbed her hands and said, "Do you like bagels? There are some in the sack. Along with some cheese and a bottle of wine. If you have any butter at all, we could make do. Or bacon, or something—anything. A girl likes it much better if a man furnishes something to their homecoming, even if it is just for an evening."

He shook his head and moved to the table, gathering up the scattered sheets and thrusting them into a folder. As he did so, she opened his ice box and said, "Well, well, Mr. Ringling, you have three eggs in here. And you do have butter. Would you like me to crumble some bagel into a pan and scramble your eggs over the top?"

He smiled for the first time. "Of course."

233

"And you have an onion, too. Do you like diced onions in your scrambled eggs?"

He propped knuckles to hips and said, "You're incorrigible. You know that don't you?"

"Only with you. I've not found anyone else who would let me."

Later, he murmured, "Scrambled eggs and red wine go together—I'm surprised."

She smiled, then sobered. "Do you still have the ring?"

"No."

"Why not? What happened to it?"

"I gave it to someone else."

She fell silent, toying with her eggs. At last, she murmured, "I would never have suspected you of having more than one girl on a string."

"Neither would I."

She laughed, a little too high soprano. "But you wasted no time finding another girl to give it to."

"I didn't give it to a girl. I gave it to a boy."

"You WHAT?"

He smiled again. "You remember some weeks ago when we had a crippled soldier into the showroom with a girl on his arm? Obviously they were there to look at our engagement ring selections."

"Y-e-e-s."

"And just as obviously, our selections were all beyond their budget range."

She said, "Do go on."

"Well, when they left, I saw you in tears, so I followed them. It was easy enough to do, for he limped quite badly."

Tears again welled at the thought.

"When I caught them, I handed him the ring telling him

it was compliments of Johnson, Walker, and Tolhurst."

She brushed at her eyes. "That's just like you, Nathan. You are such a fine, generous man."

"Mr. Ringling."

"OH, STOP IT!" He handed her a handkerchief. "My one great regret is that I never took the ring when I had the choice. Nathan—I said Nathan—did you notice."

"Now you stop it."

"I will not. I came over here because I am desperate to have you love me. Now that there's no ring between us to complicate our descent into ecstatic purgatory, I'll find it easier to anticipate forcing you into sin."

He pointed at the wine bottle. "There's still half."

"I don't need to further oil my lust. The mere idea of coming here and forcing myself on you has had me lubricated for three days." When he only shook his head, hanging it so he stared at his feet, she added: "And nights, too."

They made love most of the night. The rest of it, they talked. She left an hour before he did, planning to catch the Clerkenwewll trolley to Southampton Row, then board the High Holburn motor coach back to Hatton Garden in time for Mr. Herrelback's showroom opening (she had not been entrusted with a key, nor was she assigned to stock the empty display cases).

* * *

He was quite tired when he laid the proposed training plan folder on the worktable, switched on the lights, and settled into his chair. He was actually drained. Wellesley Glanding handed him a cup of black coffee and set a dish containing several glittering rough stones before him. He nodded, picked up a large diamond, guessed its weight at perhaps eleven carats, and glanced up in appreciation at the shop supervisor.

235

Glanding said, "I thought you'd like that one. Sir Leonard Rylegate selected that as the rough stone he wishes to present to his wife as a pendant for their forty-fifth wedding anniversary."

"How soon?" Naseby asked.

"Plenty of time: a month and a half. Study the damned thing; see what you can do and let me know."

He dropped the rough diamond back in the dish and picked up his coffee.

"Something wrong, Nathan? You look a little peaked."

"I feel a little peaked, but I'll get better as the day goes along."

"Too much wine?"

"More like not enough."

Glanding laughed as he slid the light screen back into place. "Not likely. Probably had a woman involved with it, eh?"

Naseby blanched at how closely the shop supervisor came to the mark. Then he picked up the diamond and screwed in a jeweler's loupe into his right eye socket. He worked steadily all morning, analyzing and marking the dish of stones. Finally he picked up the diamond once more, made one cleave, screwed in the loupe again and re-analyzed the stone. He heard voices—Glanding showing some visitor or visitors through the new fabricating shop. He was glad Wellesley was so proud of his work place. Everyone should have something in which to be proud. He again peered at the diamond's planes. So far so good. The voices were getting closer.

The screen was pulled back and Wellesley Glanding said, "And this is our secret weapon, sir—the man who will lead our cutting room into the gem faceting future: Nathan Ringling, who, by the way is a fellow Amer ..."

Naseby took out the loupe, turned … and stared up into the face of Charles Gadsden!

Chapter Twenty-Seven

The man known as Nathan Kenneth Ringling froze in paralyzed horror as he watched Charles Gadsden's face wrinkle into a puzzled frown. Thinking quickly, he slapped on his glasses, but the damage was already done. He assumed later that the Yogo Mine Superintendent was momentarily as speechless as the Johnson, Walker, and Tolhurst master gemcutter. But he was obviously puzzled, too. Gadsden must have been momentarily put off by the younger man's center-parted hair, and trim little moustache. Besides, he weighed considerably more than when he was an office assistant and budding butler during his youth at Yogo Village, in America.

On the other hand, Naseby Ringgold had no trouble at all recognizing the mine superintendent who'd stolen his father's sapphires, accused *him* of stealing them from the mine itself, then kicked him and slapped him, finally, when Naseby escaped, turning out the mine's crew to search for him. No! Naseby Ringgold instantly recognized the man he hated most in all the world!

Still, he remained frozen until Charles Gadsden murmured, "Naseby?" Then he bolted, vomiting red wine and scrambled eggs as he fled the fabricating shop. Behind, he heard once more, "Naseby? Is that you?" Just as he slammed the shop door behind, he heard the cry, "Who is that man? What's his name?"

* * *

Brownstone Tolhurst never even bothered to straighten from his slumped and leaning elbow-to-desk posture as Miss Applestrom ushered the office manager, fabricating shop supervisor, and their American sapphire mine superintendent into his office. Gideon Herrelback beelined for one of the two upholstered visitor chairs while Wellesley Glanding waited by the door for the bewildered American mine boss to take the other.

Ernest Walker, the other Johnson, Walker, and Tolhurst, Ltd. managing principal, stood by the office's bay window, staring dolefully outside.

"Should I bring tea now, Mr. Tolhurst?" Miss Applestrom asked.

"Not now. Instead, I'd like for you and Mr. Glanding to bring in chairs from the conference room."

With Glanding at last seated, the new chief usher slid her chair toward Mr. Walker. "No, Miss Applestrom," Tolhurst said. "That chair is for you." Wide of eye, she sank into it.

"All right," the beefy managing director growled. "It's been two weeks since Ringling disappeared. Ernest and I want to know what happened to him? Why? And where he's gone?" He swung his porcine face to stare at the four people ranged before him. "Who wants to begin?"

Almost before the question was out, Gideon Herrelback blurted, "I can tell you that our investigation has disclosed that our new chief usher is still in *flagrante delicto* with the absent absconder."

Face flaming, Desiree Applestrom leaped to her feet to cry: "I don't know what that 'flagrant' whatever means, but ..."

She was cut off by Ernest Walker who waved her back into her seat and said, almost as an afterthought: "Mr. Herrelback, I'm sure Mr. Tolhurst is more interested in the salient, rather than the salacious."

"Undoubtedly, sir. I only meant to assert that Miss Applestrom may have such a relationship with Ringling—or whatever his name really is—that she might be privy to word of him that could be of benefit to Johnson, Wal ..."

Brownstone Tolhurst tiredly waved a hand to cut off his office manager. "First things first. Do we doubt that his real name is Nathan Kenneth Ringling? Apparently Mr. Gadsden believes otherwise. Charles, let's begin with you. You claim to have recognized the man. Go back to the beginning and explain your hypothesis."

"Well, sirs, if I'm right—and I believe I am—the man you know as Nathan Ringling is really an American named Naseby Ringgold, who was the bastard child of a half-black mulatto woman dwelling several miles up Yogo Creek from our sapphire mine. If your man is really who I believe him to be, his father was the original discoverer of the sapphire lode—a fact that I regret I did not know until much too late."

The mine superintendent paused to regroup, visions of the injustice he'd perpetrated on his young servant/clerk intruding into the solemnity of the occasion. "Naseby Ringgold's mother, Millie, was a godsend to our miners during a flu epidemic, arriving of her own free will to help my wife tend to the mine crew while our doctor was incapacitated and I was transporting a shipment of stones to England. Naturally we felt very indebted to Millie Ringgold, and when she died, leaving a young boy all alone at their remote mining claim, my wife and I felt obligated to raise the lad."

Again he paused, prompted at last by Brownstone Tolhurst's, "And...."

"He turned into an excellent office clerk and household servant." Gadsden actually chuckled. "It was rumored around the countryside that Millie Ringgold had been a servant to several American Presidents, but few people believed it. Her son said he'd been trained by her to become a servant, which, in many ways, lent credibility to her assertion." Again he gave an ironic chuckle and said, "She owned two gold mines up Yogo Creek, and had named each after the wives of American Presidents."

"Well, to get on with the story, one evening I caught young Naseby examining a pile of sapphires laying on a table in his room. I ... I jumped to wrong conclusions, assuming he'd stolen them from our traps during the washing process. Despite his crying that they were his, I scooped up the stones and told him to stay in his rooms while I ran downstairs for a pair of handcuffs." The mine superintendent hung his head. "When I came back I discovered he'd jumped from the second story window and disappeared."

Tears actually dripped down Gadsden's face when he said, "Then comes the most tragic portion of my story: I turned out the mine crews to search for the thief. While I was explaining to the crowd of miners what had happened, one of our security staff—a former friend of both Millie Ringgold and Jake Hoover, the mine's discoverer, pushed through the crowd and wanted to know what was going on. I explained how I'd caught Naseby Ringgold in possession of a bunch of our sapphires, and that's when Pete Weatherwax began ..."

Desiree Applestrom's hand flew to her mouth. Wellesley Glanding murmured, "Shit!" And Gideon Herrelback cried out in glee, "Aha! We have him now!"

"I don't understand," Charles Gadsden said.

"He mentioned Pete Weatherwax to me, don't you see? And if I'm not mistaken by Glanding's and Applestrom's reaction, he may have also done so to them."

* * *

Brownstone Tolhurst shifted his massive bulk to sit upright. "Herrelback, let Gadsden finish. What happened then, Mr. Gadsden?

241

"Well, that's when Pete—that's Pete Weatherwax—began cursing me. Some of his words I'd not heard before, and certainly not since. But he did get across that all the stones I'd pocketed from the boy's table were ones given to him by his father when he owned the mine."

"Why didn't you find the boy and explain to him about the mistake."

A half-minute of silence reined, then Charles Gadsden said, "We tried to find him. I even put advertisements in all the surrounding papers. But we never found him."

Then the American mine superintendent added, "Mr. Tolhurst and Mr. Walker, I gravely and wrongly accused that boy of something that has been on my conscience for all these years. I slapped him and kicked him. And I've dreamed of someday getting the chance to apologize for it. I'd do anything—anything!—for that chance. And when it came, I wasn't swift enough to take advantage of the opportunity."

Wellesley Glanding reached over to pat Charles Gadsden on the knee. "You'd have never succeeded, even had you tried, old chap. Not as firmly as I had you by your collar."

* * *

It was true. When both the American mine superintendent and the gemcutter he knew as Nathan Ringling seemed to lose it, Wellesley Glanding's first instinct was to protect his friend and the burgeoning craftsman who was his fabricating shop's signature exhibit. When the gemcutter bolted, vomiting, from his workplace and the shouting mine superintendent made to follow, Glanding grasped Gadsden by the collar, crying, "Easy there! Easy I say!"

And when Gadsden twisted in Glanding's grasp to shout, "Who is that man?" the fabricating shop supervisor released the sapphire miner, but still blocked him from pursuit. "Let's retire to my office, sir, and discuss this." And when Gadsden shook free and tried to dodge around the larger man, Glanding signaled to two of his metal fabricators to hold Gadsden while he went to see if Ringling needed help.

* * *

Brownstone Tolhurst fixed Wellesley Glanding with a piercing gaze. "All right, Glanding, explain in your own words what happened when Gadsden and Ringling/Ringgold met."

The shop supervisor took a deep breath and said, "I was showing Mr. Gadsden through the shop, just as you asked, sir. And when we reached Nathan's station, I rolled the screen back and Mr. Gadsden and Mr. Ringling first saw each other face to face. It was like somebody tossed a stick of dynamite on the table—frankly, sir, I was, to say the least, unprepared for what happened! Nathan bolted and Mr. Gadsden flew into a tizzy of excitement."

"What then?"

"Well, sir, when I looked all over and couldn't find Nathan—or, apparently, Mr. Ringgold, I thought it best to tell you before it got out of hand with gossip and mistaken apprehensions."

With his recap concluded, Glanding took a folder from his lap and handed it across the desk. "Perhaps this will be of some interest, sir. It was something Nathan ... uh, Naseby was working on—a training program for our other shop personnel."

"Yes!" Gideon Herrelback exclaimed. "It was a project I'd told the thief to design."

"Bunk!" Glanding snarled. "You're the one who let the cat out of the bag that Mr. Tolhurst was considering it, before we were ready to suggest it to Nath ... Naseby. He asked me about it after you'd already told him."

Ignoring the shop supervisor's criticism, Herrelback

sailed blithely on: "It was me. I wanted Ringling or Ringgold, or whoever he is, to get a head start on designing a training program for all the others. Too bad he never got the chance to implement the plan before we exposed him for the thief he is."

Tolhurst scribbled something on a sheet of paper, then said, "Herrelback, you've mentioned twice that the man in question is a thief. Explain to us how you've come to that conclusion."

Now the center of attention, Gideon Herrelback took a folder from his own lap and straightened in his chair. "As you suggested, sir," he began, "I contacted my more aggressive investigative contacts among the Bow Street crowd—that's how I learned Miss Applestrom and this thief, Ringgold, were still engaging in an affair."

"Get on with the subject at hand, Herrelback. Had he been back to his flat?"

"Apparently not. But an even more thorough search revealed a ticket for a safe deposit box in a new bank that differs from the one we were aware he was using." Reading from a paper plucked from his folder: "It's the Kings Cross Bank on Farringdon Road, an old and trustworthy one, sir. As you know, they first resisted our efforts to learn the contents of the safe deposit box taken by a man using the pseudonym Norman (none) Richards. That was when I suggested you enlist Scotland Yard, which made the managers of Kings Cross Bank more amenable."

"Get on with it," Brownstone Tolhurst growled.

Taking a packet from his jacket pocket, Gideon Herrelback poured its contents onto the managing director's desk: mostly sapphires, except one diamond and one ruby. The contents also included a piece of jade and one of ivory. Most of the dozen-and-a-half stones were uncut, though two—one sapphire and the diamond—could be rated as finished gems."

Brownstone Tolhurst seemed to sag. "And you're convinced this safe deposit box belonged," he asked, "to the man named … uh … Naseby Ringgold?"

A triumphant Gideon Herrelback nodded. "The safe deposit box ticket in his room is absolutely convincing, sir."

Staring at the packet of jewels scattered on his desk, Brownstone Tolhurst sighed. "And have you already filed a complaint with Scotland Yard?"

"Yes sir! They're pursuing the case."

"And what about the bank down the street?"

"It's clean, sir. Just a savings account with only a few pounds on deposit."

Brownstone Tolhurst sighed again. "Well that cuts it. We had a thief …"

Ernest Walker moved from the window well to Tolhurst's side, sad face drooping even more than usual. "How much value do you place on those stones, Mr. Herrelback?"

Gideon Herrelback spread his hands. "I'm hardly qualified to make a value assessment, sir. Perhaps Mr. Gadsden or Mr. Glanding could help us there."

Gadsden shook his head, but Wellesley Glanding said, "I believe I see where you're coming from, sir. And though I couldn't put a per pound value to the entire lot, I doubt if it exceeds the value of the stones taken from Nathan in America."

"Certainly not," Charles Gadsden murmured.

Walker turned on his heel, pushed the button that swung the bookcase divider between his and Tolhurst's offices, then returned with the jade dragon namestone Naseby had crafted. Setting it carefully down on the desk beside Brownstone Tolhurst ivory namepiece, he turned his sad countenance on the entire group. "Please, gentlemen—and," nodding at Miss

245

Applestrom, "lady, too—have we gone absolutely mad? One needs not be a savant to understand that this man I still prefer to call Nathan Ringling was engaged in his own effort at righting a terrible wrong that was mistakenly perpetrated on him by Johnson, Walker, and Tolhurst, Ltd."

Ernest Walker's countenance began to less and less resemble a bored bloodhound than that of a savage dog nearing his prey. He gestured at the scattered stones. "Obviously there's a few hundred pounds of value in these stones—no more." And he swept up his jade namestone in one hand and the Tolhurst ivory piece in the other. "Cannot you people grasp that the man who created these—who, for God's sake, *could* create these—is worth manifold times more to Johnson, Walker, and Tolhurst, Ltd. than these few paltry stones."

"But the man's a thief!" Herrelback cried.

Walker's face gradually settled back into its most sad and bored bloodhound countenance. "And you, sir, are an idiot." With Gideon Herrleback's shocked look, the firm's principal living partner added, "Now I ask you, which is worst, sir: a blithering idiot who cannot recognize a shining cross in a dismal forest, or an utter and absolute idiot who cannot see an innocent man engaging in an effort to right an egregious wrong done to him years ago?"

When the red-faced Herrelback tried to remonstrate, Walker held up a restraining hand, turning to the firm's managing director. "And you, Brownstone. I cannot understand why you don't grasp the importance of what's at stake here. You were first to see Ringling's value for what it is—pure genius. Yet you let this insufferable (he waved feebly at Herrelback) idiot stampede you with his obvious malicious hatred that he's harbored since Ringling's first day."

Walker threw both namepieces to clatter on Tolhurst's

desk and shuffled back to his window well.

There was a pall of silence in the room until the managing director leaned his immense bulk back in his swivel chair and placed both feet on his desktop. "Thank you, Ernest, for clarifying what's at issue here. You are, as usual, utterly correct."

He shook his head slowly, glaring at the office manager. "Herrelback, withdraw the complaint with Scotland Yard." When the man opened his mouth, Tolhurst snarled, "Shut up! Don't say another word unless it is to suggest some honorable way to bring Nathan Ringling safely back into our fold."

Then the huge man turned his gaze to the lady present. "Miss Applestrom, is there any chance you might know where Nathan Ringling can be found."

She shook her head, biting her lip as tears trickled down both cheeks. "Oh, sir, I wish I did! But you must know this: he did not resume our affair willingly. I did it. I love him so! I went to his apartment the night before he fled and shamelessly threw myself at him. If there's fault there, it's all mine. Not his."

"All right, Miss Applestrom. Thank you."

Staring at his desktop, Brownstone Tolhurst said, "How about you, Mr. Glanding. I believe you had a growing rapport with Ringling. Can you help us in any way?"

When Wellesley Glanding silently shook his head, the big man murmured, "Well, good people, that seems to be settled. The only issue left is:

"*Where is Nathan Ringling?*"

-   end –

Bonus: Chapter 1 of *Sapphires and Swatikas*, Book 3 in the *Sapphires of Yogo Series*, on the next page

Bonus: Sapphire and Swastikas (release date: mid-winter, 2016-17)
by Roland Cheek
Chapter One: Excerpt

SAPPHIRES and SWASTIKAS

Chapter One

"GAS! G-A-A-S!" The sergeant barreled along the trench shouting, "G-A-A-S! Masks, every bloody body! MASKS!" He paused to jerk at the newest recruit, shouting into his ear: "Get your bloody mask on. Didn't they at least teach you that?"

The newest recruit blinked, stared stupidly about. "Teach me what? Has it stopped? There are no guns."

With no more time to spend on a single member of his platoon, the sergeant dashed on down the trench, splashing mud and standing water with each running step. "GAS! GAS!" Down trench, a corporal beat rhythmically on a hanging artillery shell case with his bayonet—a gas-attack warning! Other hollow gongs followed the sprinting sergeant in his dash down the trench.

Already a strange greenish-yellow mist oozed over the side of their trench, following the contour of the ground. Suddenly the recruit is jerked around and his own gas mask thrust in his hands. He stared stupidly, shaking his head, then is gripped by a sudden realization of danger. All others of his visible trench mates have masks covering their faces, corrugated tubes hanging like trunks from a row of elephants at a water hole. He jambed the mask on his mud-encrusted face, knocking his helmet off, then jerked the mask away to swipe at the mud while holding his breath. It was his trench mate who slammed the mask back on his face, slipped the holding straps over his helmet-less head, and wiped around the mask's edges to seal it. The recruit breathes in short puffs, as he's been taught, eyes so wide they filled the windows of his mask. Meanwhile the greenish-yellow mist oozed around him. Unreasoned fear made him leap to climb the trench wall, but he's jerked back down by a mate, joined by another crouching on his other side. They held the recruit against the muddy trench walls until his involuntary jerking subsided, then released him. It all came back to him then, the drill sergeant's instructions:

"Gas moves silent-like. It steals upon you, lads. That's why you mustn't waste time when you knows it." The crusty, crippled old soldier, bushy eyebrows pulled almost together as he slapped the cloth gas helmet adding, "You gets maybe eighteen or twenty seconds to slip this over yer noggin and seal it up around the edges."

He'd listened intently, turning the mask he'd been given around in his hands, trying to quell the rising fear even the thought of a gas attack generated.

"Try it on, lads. Take off yer tin hats." The instructor paused, then sneered. "Don't worry about messin' up yer hair. You might have the slickest topknot in the graveyard, but you'll still be in the graveyard iff'n you don't learn to gets that thing on in a hectic hurry." Again he paused. Then: "As you can see, there's a rubber-covered tube inside. That goes in yer mouth. That's for exhaling. You breathes through yer nose and exhale through yer mouth."

Most of the handful of new recruits had the masks on by

then, so the instructor said, "Okay, now you'll find you can't breathe through yer mouth, right? That's 'cause the exhaust hose is made in a way that keeps outside air from getting in through the exhaust tube.

"Yer mask is good for five hours wearin' time. You'll each be given two masks in waterproof bags; you'll carry both of them while you sleep, shit, march, or eat. To change yer mask during a prolonged attack, you'll take out the new one, hold your breath, pull the old one off, then stick the new one over yer head. Tuck the loose ends under yer collar. Got it?

"Okay, during the gas try to stay high in yer trench w'out sticking yer head over the parapet—got that? Stay high 'cause the gas sinks to the ground. That means the bottom of yer trench is the worst place to be. Climb on the fire step if there's room, long as you don't stick yer head over the top, an' get it shot off—got that?"

* * *

The new recruit "got it" enough to heave himself on the fire step, careful to dip his head below the line of stray bullets. Glancing down, he was horrified to see the greenish mist filling the trench to his knees. The sergeant dashed past roaring through his mask, "Get ready boys, they'll be along any minute! Give 'em billy hell when they do."

He was surprised by the staccato rattling of a machine gun some yards up-trench, then the man next to him fired over the trench parapet. The man elbowed him and said, "Turn around and see what we got comin' for dinner, laddie."

He turned to peer over the berm of dirt serving as a parapet. They came out of no-man's land sprinting forward with mayhem as their purpose. Their respirators with large snouts on the front made them appear surreal. "Your gun, laddie," the man to his left murmured over the bark of his Enfield. "Be nice if

251

you greeted 'em with it." Naseby pushed his own rifle over the top, bayonet first, then peered through the sights, aligning the top of its front blade to nestle at the bottom of the vee. He squeezed the trigger, but it wouldn't squeeze.

"Flip the safety," the man to his left growled as he fired another round, jerked his bolt, then fired again.

Blushing beneath the mask, the recruit flipped the safety, aligned the sights and sque-e-e-ezed. One of the surreal grey-coated invaders, now only fifty yards from their trench, threw up his arms and sprawled across some tangled wire.

"By all that's holy, mate—you're trainable," his trench mate murmured.

He jacked in another shell and aligned its sights once more. This was something he could do. As a boy in the lonely mountain wilds of far-off America, Naseby Ringgold had been accustomed to carrying a rifle ever since he could keep its muzzle from dragging in the dirt. True, it was a small bore .22 and this one he presently sque-e-e-zed was of larger bore, for bringing down larger game. But the principle was the same for both: solid rest for the weapon, careful alignment of sight, squeeze the trigger, target cartwheels or falls or sinks or sprawls.

Behind him, reinforcements were pouring from the communication trenches, crowding to the fire step, adding their firepower to blunting the Hun attack. Apparently the British artillery sited a barrage of curtain fire on the German lines to break up their attack and retard reinforcements. Still they came. They went down in heaps, but more came, overrunning the fallen. Theirs was a mad rush. Naseby's rifle went dry and he fumbled to reload, the mask hindering his efforts to even find his pockets.

"They're coming in down here!" someone yelled from down-trench; the sergeant shouted, "Fix bayonets! Follow me!"

It sounded like sheer pandemonium. But Naseby had his Enfield reloaded and with no time for a situation analysis shot a demonic apparition point blank, almost to leap into the trench. Instead, the apparition fell into it, sprawling into the green mist at the bottom. Another Hun loomed. Naseby's right-hand trench mate held up his bayonet just as the charging soldier leaped. Scratch that one.

Then it was over. The waves of gray-clad nether-worlds fled.

"Don't quit now, laddie," his left-hand trench mate matter-of-factly stated. "Bullets go in the back easy as the front." But Naseby had no more stomach. He leaped down into the trench to pull out the enemy soldier who'd sprawled into the fatal fumes. Dead. So was the one still impaled on his right-hand trench mate's bayonet. He threw up into his mask.

* * *

Naseby Ringgold knew he'd erred by the time he'd crossed Blackfriars Bridge. However, if nothing else during a reclusive childhood, unreasoned flight from unjust accusation, then adaptation in an alien land, he'd learned resilience, fortitude, and accommodation. True, he suspected he'd had the support of influential elements within Johnson, Walker, and Tolhurst, Ltd: Ernest Walker for one, and probably a more or less neutral in Brownstone Tolhurst. Too, he could count on Wellesley Glanding, and certainly Desiree Applestrom. But what of the malevolent charges Charles Gadsden was certain to levee. Could he withstand those?

Never mind that Gadsden, an agent for Johnson, Walker, and Tolhurst, had first stolen Naseby's own gemstones, Tolhurst and Walker—if they somehow learned of his own attempts to right that grievous wrong—would see only that Naseby had stolen from the firm. And hadn't he driven nails into his own

253

coffin by bolting upon the surprise encounter with Charles Gadsden? He even came close to smiling in irony at how, in his panic, he'd abandoned all forms of escape planning he'd concocted throughout his many months while dwelling in fear of exposure.

Had he still carried his carefully copied train and steamship schedules concealed in an inner pocket, would they still be current after so many months since he'd studied them? Besides, wouldn't train and steamship terminals be the first place monitored by pursuers?

His most grievous failure, though, was his present lack of funds. When he'd previously bolted from Gadsden in America, he'd fled with money in his pockets; now he was served only by the few pounds and pence a normal working man carried for his daily needs. The rest of his savings was stashed in accounts held in two different banks, accounts he'd abandoned in his panicked flight from danger.

He resigned himself to making the best of a bad throw of life's dice.

It'd taken the fugitive three days to wend his way through London to Orpington, then three more days to Aylesford and Favorsham. He'd slept, first in an abandoned tenement, then under bridges, in farmers' haystacks, once in a tumbled-down pigsty. By the time his pocket change was exhausted and he was forced to pilfer or beg for food, he'd worked out a rough plan to reach Margate and somehow obtain passage across the Strait to the Continent. Perhaps, if he could then wend his way north to Amsterdam, he could find employment as a gem cutter. These thoughts coursed through Naseby Ringgold's mind as he plodded through Kent on the Shottendane Road, past an army encampment.

He paused to study the rows upon rows of drab tents,

soldiers drilling in nearby fields, trucks and buses and horses moving in and out of the camp, the squad of new recruits shuffling toward him from the train station at Hartsdown Academy. He was hungry. And thirsty. He looked down at his stained and tattered shirt and trousers, then shrugged and approached what he thought was an officer of sorts trailing the squad of forlorn recruits. "Sir," he said to the suspicious sergeant, "may I ask you a question?"

"Ask all ye want, laddie buck, but don't stand in m'way."

"I'd like to enlist. How do I go about it."

The sergeant paused to eye him top to bottom. "You've got to be bloody well daft, mate." Then he took Naseby by the shoulder, spinning him around. "Just fall in wi' the group. Ye'll make just as good cannon fodder as any o' them." When he noted Naseby's hesitation, the sergeant place the sole of his boot against Naseby's butt and shoved. "Get along wi' you. We'll sign ye up later on."

* * *

The battle for Passchendaele (or battles, for there were several) was still raging when Naseby Ringgold, using the fictitious name of Neville Loomis Rungfeld enlisted at Margate in the fall of 1917. After the series of bloody battles, including a single day—October 12—of Allied casualties totaling 13,000 men, the empire was desperate for live bodies to fill the slots of dead soldiers. So desperate were army recruiters that few questions were asked, especially of a healthy young American who'd apparently slipped through that rebellious new-world country's own draft. The new man, who claimed the name Neville Rungfeld (but could provide no reliable documentation) was thrown directly onto the drill grounds for thirteen weeks, then shipped Ramsgate to Calais, arriving in France on the 22nd January. He was just in time for the preludes to the major

255

German offensives in the spring of 1918.

That first prelude came during a German gas attack on the trenches at Arras. He'd been posted to the Third Army under General Byng. It was his good fortune that he was a replacement recruit posted to a veteran division, veteran battalion, veteran company, and a platoon composed of veterans of Vimy Ridge and the battlefields of the Somme.

That Naseby's platoon and company held their position during his first battle demonstrated a key fundamental to the attacking Germans. To the east, a section of line held by a Canadian unit was penetrated by a fast-moving, specially trained force of *Strumstruppen* who were carefully taught to infiltrate then overrun lightly defended targets with speed and dispatch. This newly developing form of warfare dictated that highly trained storm troopers would bounce off strongly defended targets to concentrate their force against ones that seemed either "soft" or to be "softening" during the attack. It was fortunate for that particular Canadian battalion in that particular battle that the German storm troopers who deeply penetrated their lines were merely testing a new battle strategy and were withdrawn after proving that strategy's worth. Those storm troopers withdrawal was to permit staging for a carefully planned major spring offensive; one the German high command expected would win the war.

* * *

"You'll make a trench rat," the blond, ruddy-faced private said as Naseby Ringgold set four tins of tea and a handkerchief filled with biscuits on the plank table.

His company had been relieved the day following the German attack on their Arras trenches, and the outfit had been pulled back via a connecting trench-and-tunnel to a medieval chalk mine. The new recruit—now a bloodied veteran—found the ancient quarry's labyrinth astonishing, with twisting passageways and high ceilings. That this vast warren of electric lights and telephone command posts, complete with a bakery, butcher, machine shop, hospital, and chapel was connected to the forward trenches seemed numbing, bewildering.

On the cavern walls, images of women proliferated, idealized, usually in various stages of undress. The images were, of course, carved by lonesome soldiers with time on their hands. But intermingled with the carvings of women, were others of dogs, churches, farmsteads, the Eiffel Tower, wine glasses, and names of carvers, their regiments and, military icons.

"Not many new recruits can handle an Enfield so well during their first face-off," the private said.

"Wot's this?" the squad's sergeant growled, eyeing the metal cups. "Tea? Bless you mon." The corporal—the one who bayoneted the German who leaped into their trench—smiled. And the private chuckled and held out a hand.

"Everybody calls me "Ringy". Actually I'm Erasmus Ringling, but "Ringy" is better than Erasmus."

Naseby murmured, "I'm Neville Rungfeld," successfully hiding his shock that Private Ringling actually had the same surname he'd utilized as an alias while in London.

The sergeant reached for a steaming mug, blew across the top and said, "I asks wot's this about, private? Gimme an answer."

Naseby said, "I just wanted to thank you men for saving my life—all of you."

"An' you think we did it for you?"

"Yes sir, I do."

"Well take another guess, sonny. We did it for us. Me name's Roxli—*Sergeant Roxli* to you."

"And I'm Drillmeter," the corporal murmured. "What

Ringy means is that for a recruit you didn't do too bad when we started paring apples out there."

Taking a biscuit to hide his embarrassment, the recruit said, "In America, we call these cookies."

"And that's another thing wot puzzles me," the sergeant growled. "How is it that we recruits a guy like you in our outfit when Yanks are pouring in to France in a flood?" Each of his tablemates paused with biscuit in one hand and cup in the other for Naseby's response. He lied:

"I was on a small steamer—Norwegian. It knocked around the Orient for a couple of years and the captain wouldn't let me go from my contract. Docked at Portsmouth in October, and I jumped ship. Enlisting in England seemed like I could get in the war quicker than trying to find passage to my own country, then get shipped back ..." Their silence seemed deafening, so he added, "... crossing the Atlantic twice, you see." He was rambling and he knew it. But he was rattled by their suspension, biscuits still halfway to their mouths, faces blank, tea tins anchored by a fist. "Silly, I suppose...." He let the words dribble to a halt.

They were interrupted by two latecomers to their table, another corporal and a "first class" who seemed totally engaged in their private conversation about what they saw as a near-Hun breakthrough in their own trench sector. Sergeant Roxli's brushy eyebrows closed as he pointedly stared at the newcomers, teeth audibly grinding. They took the hint and moved to another table.

Naseby trailed fingers along one of the walls where the name "Raymond Marsh" had been carved on the chalk walls. Corporal Drillmeter murmured, "Odds are good that's the only mark Raymond Marsh will ever leave to the future. Odds are good Ypres or the first Passchendaele ate him for breakfast."

258

Naseby's fingers fell away, as if burned.

Drillmeter continued: "They mined chalk for making quick lime and sometimes they cut blocks out of the walls to use in buildings. That might be the why for the size of this particular hole." When the new man's widened eyes traveled the cavern's circuit back to the corporal's bemused smile, the non-com added, "There's lots of these old chalk mines around. Before the war, nearby farmers used 'em for storing wine." Pointing, he added, "Down that tunnel, close to where it wanders left, there's a couple of kraut names in pencil. Engineers, we think, back in fifteen, when they held this sector."

"You mean the Germans were ..."

The corporal nodded. "Three times. These shafts have changed hands three times."

The private, Ringy, added, "That's the tunnel where the kraut sappers dynamited, ain't it, Drill?"

Drillmeter nodded, "Not far past where they scribbled their names. That's why we think they were engineers maintaining a listening post." He shook his head, stared into his empty cup and muttered, "Our boys were drilling down to blow them to kingdom come, but they touched their stuff off first. Got twenty-six of the Durham boys, so they say."

Naseby strolled down the lighted tunnel until he found it: *"Gott fur Kaiser! Hanschel Ock."* When he returned he carried a tin pot of tea and a second handkerchief filled with biscuits. His companions all had their Enfields on the table in pieces, cleaning them.

Private Ringling looked up, saw the re-supply tea and biscuits and chuckled. "Make it through Flanders, Rungfeld, and you might make some Bloomsbury Dandy a fair-to-Epping butler."

259

This constitutes the end of chapter 1 of *Sapphires and Swastikas,* book three of *Sapphires of Yogo Series*, due for release autumn, 2016.

Nonfiction

Learning To Talk Bear
Learn About Elk
Dance On the Wild Side
My Best Work Is Done At the Office
Chocolate Legs
Montana's Bob Marshall Wilderness

Fiction

Echoes of Vengeance
Bloody Merchants War
Lincoln County Crucible
Gunnar's Mine
Crisis On the Stinkingwater
The Silver Yoke
The Dogged and the Damned
For Love of Sapphires
Sapphires At War

(more)

Unless you're largely devoid of most outdoor graces, or at least outdoor inclinations, you might appreciate exposure to others of Roland Cheek's work. Perhaps the best single location to find a range of his work will be through his website at:

http://www.rolandcheek.com/

* You can visit his bookstore, view each of his twenty books, read each of their first chapters, and order print copies directly from the author, should you wish.

* There are also links to Roland Cheek's page on Amazon's Kindle store where most of his titles can also be downloaded into electronic reading devices at reduced prices.

* While you're on his website, perhaps you'll want to visit Roland's and Jane's audio/visual library where they take you on the 1930's construction of Ptarmigan Tunnel in Glacier National Park, demonstrate the magic of Jane's campfire lobster (and other culinary delights), and lead you on an expedition to track the ancient Anasazi.

* And finally, there're Roland's blogs:

Campfire Culture is the long-running weekly outdoor's blog, where Roland brings decades of experience throughout much of the mountain West to your reading pleasure. Posted each Saturday. Click here to follow him vicariously through a lifetime of adventure:

http://www.rolandcheek.com/Newcampfireculture/index.html

Then there's his sometimes irreverent, sometimes humorous, sometimes introspective *Mountain Musing* blog, most often posted each Tuesday. This blog has, over time, evolved into picturing Roland's love affair with America's best-loved Wilderness: the Bob Marshall. With over 2,500 photos taken over a forty year period, it's unlikely he'll run out in this lifetime.

http://www.rolandcheek.com/Mtn%20Muse/mtnmuse.html

And finally, it's not too hard to find some of Roland's stuff exposed elsewhere. If you were to google "Roland Cheek," you'll find hundreds of listings where his work may be found.

Roland says, "I'm proud of my craft; proud to be an American; proud to have lived and loved in the Mountain West. Nothing will please me more than to see readers seeking out and browsing through pages where I've spent half my life smearing creative blood."

Thanks for being you!